THE DRUID

ALSO BY JEFF WHEELER

Collections & Nonfiction

Tales from Kingfountain, Muirwood, and Beyond: The Worlds of Jeff Wheeler
Your First Million Words

The Dawning of Muirwood Trilogy

The Druid

The First Argentines Series

Knight's Ransom
Warrior's Ransom
Lady's Ransom
Fate's Ransom

The Grave Kingdom Series

The Killing Fog
The Buried World
The Immortal Words

The Harbinger Series

Storm Glass
Mirror Gate
Iron Garland
Prism Cloud
Broken Veil

The Kingfountain Series

The Poisoner's Enemy (prequel)
The Maid's War (prequel)
The Poisoner's Revenge (prequel)
The Queen's Poisoner
The Thief's Daughter
The King's Traitor
The Hollow Crown
The Silent Shield
The Forsaken Throne

The Legends of Muirwood Trilogy

The Wretched of Muirwood
The Blight of Muirwood
The Scourge of Muirwood

The Covenant of Muirwood Trilogy

The Banished of Muirwood
The Ciphers of Muirwood
The Void of Muirwood

Whispers from Mirrowen Trilogy

Fireblood
Dryad-Born
Poisonwell

Landmoor Series

Landmoor
Silverkin

THE DAWNING OF MUIRWOOD

THE DRUID

JEFF WHEELER

This is a work of fiction. Names, characters, organizations, places, events, and incidents are either products of the author's imagination or are used fictitiously. Any resemblance to actual persons, living or dead, or actual events is purely coincidental.

Published by 47North

ISBN-13: 9781542034753
ISBN-10: 1542034752

Cover design by Kirk DouPonce, DogEared Design

Printed in the United States of America

To Rachelle

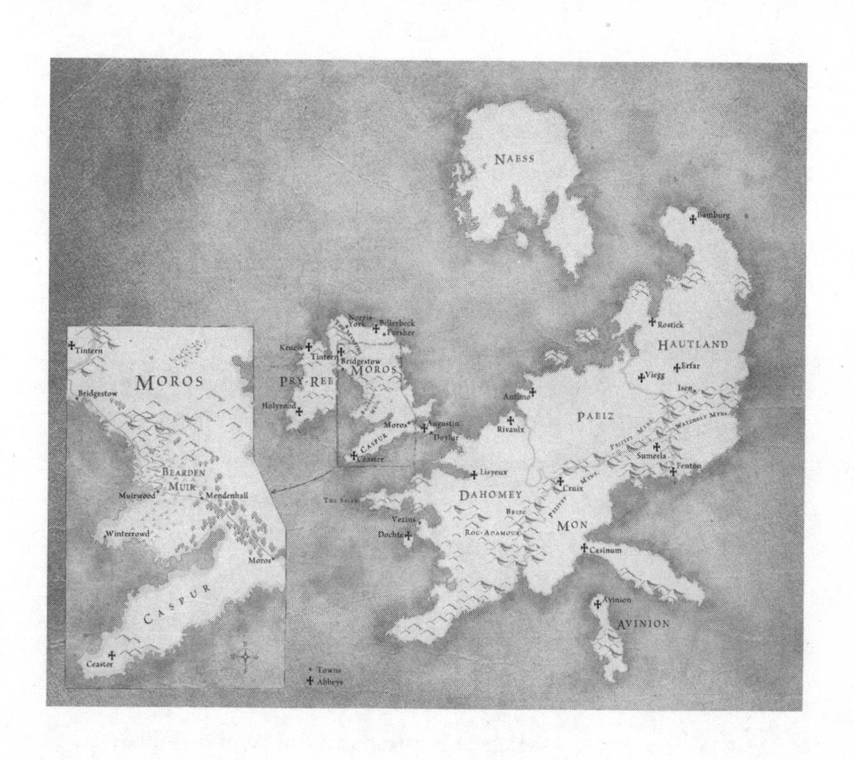

NAESS
Bamburg
Rostick
HAUTLAND
Erfar
Viegg
Isen
Antimo
PAEIZ
Rivaulx
Watchout Mtns.
Sumeela
Fenton
Lisyeux
Cruix
DAHOMEY
MON
Roc-Adamour
Casinum
Avinion
AVINION
Vezins
Dochte
The Spire
Norris-York
Bilierbeck
Pershee
Krucis
Tintern
Bridgestow
PRY-REE
MOROS
Holyrood
Moros
Augustin
Doylur
CASPUR
Ceaster
Tintern
MOROS
Bridgestow
BEARDEN MUIR
Muirwood
Mendenhall
Winterrowd
Moros
CASPUR
Ceaster
Towns
Abbeys

In the tome of Tullius, one of the Twelve, wiser words were never engraved: "One who suspects naught is easily deceived." That message must be internalized by everyone serving in the High Seer's Apocrisarius. Even the meekest wretched, with no family, no known lineage, can be suspect, for who is the least likely to murmur against their station but they? Vigilance is the key. Observation is the lock. Utilize both to reveal the true motives of someone's heart. Find the desire that secretly throbs within every breast, and you know how to master the moment.

Thus the kingdom of Moros fell because of such an observation.

—Mícheál Nostradamus of Avinion Abbey

CHAPTER ONE

A Field of Flax

The sun was nearly down, creating a glorious sunset over the even rows in the field. Brushing the dirt from her hands, Eilean stared at the ridges of earth, spaced apart just so, and imagined what the field would look like when it was blooming with blue flowers. She had dirt under her fingernails, her kirtle needed a good scrubbing, but the smell of rich soil in the recently torn field thrilled her. First the buds would come, then the stalks of flax would grow straight and pale. Everyone in the abbey would come with scythes and sickles to mow them down. After that, the stalks would be bound into sheaves. It was hard work, but the people of Tintern Abbey did their part. Flax was useful in so many ways. Like a wretched.

"I've never seen the sky so orange," said Celyn as she approached Eilean from behind. "What a sunset."

"Aye," replied Eilean. "I wish I could grab it and hold it still. But I don't want to be here after it gets dark."

"No, not outside the Leerings, anyway. Come along. We're both dirty as can be. But at least the field is done."

"Ardys will want us clean as whiskers before we touch anything in the kitchen."

The girls hooked arms and started back to the abbey, which Eilean could see over a row of tall ash trees on the other side of the field. A drover was trying to coax a stubborn mule to pull his wagon back to the abbey, but the beast was having none of it. The smell of the freshly turned earth was thick with the odor of dung. It wasn't an unpleasant smell—just a strong one.

"Now that the field is planted, the maypole'll be set up soon," Celyn declared. "Who shall we dance with, you and I?"

It was just like Celyn to presume they would be asked, let alone that they'd get to pick their partners. "Anyone who asks us, I should think."

"Some of the learners, maybe?"

"Reckon they'd stoop to ask us?" Eilean replied with a chuckle.

"They'd have to stoop to ask me, for I'm so short! But why not, Eilean? Learners have asked wretcheds before."

"Not many have," Eilean replied softly.

Then she saw him, and her heart did a little tumble inside her chest. Aisic stood inside the row of ash trees with three other lads, their heads bent together in deep discussion. Suddenly all she could see was the dirt on her clothes and hands. On Celyn.

"Let's go that way," Eilean suggested in an undertone, tugging her friend's arm to steer around them.

Only she was too late.

"Hoy!" shouted Aisic when he saw them. She felt heat flush her cheeks and rise to the tips of her ears.

"Let's see what they want," Celyn suggested, resisting the pull.

Mortified, Eilean followed along, and they reached the four young men—Aisic, Bryant, Ely, and Llewellyn. They were wretcheds too, of an age with one another, and they'd all been raised together at the abbey.

"We're finished planting in the fields," Celyn said with a smile and look of ease.

"We're not mitching. We finished our work long ago," said Llewellyn—the shortest of the four—while puffing out his chest.

Aisic was regarding Celyn with a smirk. Was it because they were so dirty or because he was pleased the lads had been given a quicker task?

"Have you heard the news?" Ely asked with a twinkle in his eye.

"We were in the field; how could we?" Celyn said with an easy laugh.

"What news?" Eilean asked him.

But it was Aisic who answered. "The High Seer of Avinion is here at the abbey, so she is."

Celyn and Eilean exchanged a surprised look.

"How do you know it is her?" Eilean asked, then regretted it when she saw the flicker of annoyance in Aisic's eyes.

"I'm not thick, Eilean," he scolded. "There are guards outside the Aldermaston's manor. They have bows and these short blades called—"

"Gladiuses," interrupted Ely.

"I know what they're called!" barked Aisic.

"*Shaw*, don't get sulky, Aisic!" countered Ely. He turned to face the girls again. "They say she's speaking to Aldermaston Gilifil now."

One of the most curious things about the mastons was their ability to cross from abbey to abbey without horse or wagon. Even though the island of Avinion was far away, the abbeys were all interconnected through the magic of the Medium. This visit was unprecedented, and excitement tingled inside Eilean. She'd never seen the High Seer before, but the woman had a reputation for being both powerful and impressive. Squeezing Celyn's arm, she signaled she didn't want to stay and talk to the boys any longer.

"I wonder what she's after?" Celyn asked, ignoring the squeeze.

"No one knows. No one's allowed inside," Aisic said. From the look on his face, he too was keenly interested in the visitor.

"Aisic tried talking to the *captain*," Llewellyn said with a laugh.

Aisic glowered at the reminder, and the other boys laughed.

"What's wrong with that?" Celyn asked. She didn't like it when anyone was teased and was quick to rush to their defense.

"He wants to *join* the Apocrisarius," Llewellyn said with a smirk. "Thinks he's high and mighty, he does."

"Shut it, all right?" Aisic said, giving him a shove.

Everyone knew Aisic wanted to be more than just a wretched. He had ambition—a feeling Eilean recognized in herself, although she didn't like to speak of it for fear of being laughed at. If only she'd been higher born, she could have lived in a castle and served a lady. She would have heard about all the goings-on in the realm. Here, there was so rarely news.

"Reckon that's brave," Eilean said, the words spurting out.

Llewellyn's brow furrowed. "Who cares what *you* think?"

"*Shaw*, Llewellyn, don't be rude!" said Ely.

The disdain in Llewellyn's voice stung, and Eilean nearly picked up a clod of earth and threw it at his head. Instead, she yanked her arm away from Celyn's and stormed off.

"Eilean, wait up!" Celyn hurried after her, and it took her a while to catch up because she was so much shorter. "That was very rude," her friend said through gasps of air.

"When one of them is alone, they're reasonable enough," Eilean said, turning back and giving the four of them a hot glare. "But put all four together like that, and they don't have enough brains to make one person."

"They're not so bad," Celyn said. "But Llewellyn shouldn't have said that."

"He acts like he's better than us, but he's just the same."

If only Aisic had stood up for her. He was the biggest of the four of them, and a word from him would have had Llewellyn cringing.

Tintern Abbey began to glow.

"Ooh, I love being outside when the lights come on," Celyn cooed.

At sunset, the eyes of the Leerings set into the stone walls of the abbey brightened. It made the structure visible for leagues in every direction, a bastion of the maston order, a symbol of the strength and mystery of the Medium.

When they reached the kitchen, they hurried inside and walked down the long aisle of tables and benches already crowded with people from the fields, eating and talking boisterously. Everyone helped out, some carrying pitchers, some bowls with loaves, others trays of cheeses, nuts, and gooseberries.

There were Leerings within the kitchen as well, casting warm light on the diners seated at the trestle tables. Even though she and Celyn had labored all day in the field, there would be a lot of cleanup for them after the meal. Eilean didn't resent it, but she was grateful the planting was done.

"Fetch me a drink?" said another boy, Hissop, thrusting a wooden cup at her.

"Fetch it yourself," she said back to him, her own stomach growling.

When they reached the back of the kitchen, the cook, Ardys, was hard at work with her husband, Loren, who was sometimes caught mitching on a stool instead of actually helping. Of course, Ardys was always hard at work. She was the most diminutive person in the abbey but also the most productive.

"The girls are back," Loren said.

Ardys whirled around. "Get cleaned up! Clean as whiskers! The Aldermaston has guests and needs to be checked on."

Eilean hurried to the water Leering first and invoked it. The face carved into the stone bore the appearance of an elegant woman—the kind of lady she wished she could serve. The Leering's eyes glowed blue as water tumbled from its lips. Eilean tugged up the sleeves of her dress and scrubbed her hands quickly. Celyn stood by, awaiting her turn without complaint. Although she likely wished to see the High Seer too, she was allowing Eilean to beat her to it. If Eilean were a better friend, she wouldn't take advantage of such kindness, but her curiosity had gotten the best of her.

After washing, she found a towel to dry her arms and then quickly rubbed her face and behind her ears.

"I'll go!" she volunteered to Ardys.

Ardys looked her over. "Your dress needs washing tonight, but it'll have to do. Take off the apron first. It's a fright."

Eilean did so, and Ardys took it from her. "There is a loaf of pumpkin bread I made this afternoon under that cloth," she said with a wave. "Take it and see if he needs anything for the guests."

"Is one of them the High Seer?"

Ardys nodded. "Aye, lass. Be respectful. Don't ask too many questions. She and her people didn't come all this way to talk to a wretched of Tintern Abbey." She gave Eilean a look of love and patted her cheek. "Go on. And be quick about it!"

Finding the loaf beneath the cloth, Eilean wrapped it up and then went out the back door. The shadows were thicker now, and the purple western sky grew darker by the moment. If not for the chance to see the High Seer, she wouldn't have volunteered to go out of doors at night. Ever since she could remember, she'd had a terror of the dark.

The manor was a short distance from the rear of the kitchen that serviced not just the Aldermaston himself but also the entire population at the abbey. There were twelve scullery girls in all, and Eilean and Celyn, both seventeen, were the oldest.

The chill of night was starting to settle in as well, closing around her like a cloak. As she hurried to the back door, a person stepped out of the shadows, hand on the hilt of a blade.

"Hold there, lass. What's the hurry?"

She couldn't see the man's face, but she recognized his tone of command and halted. He was taller than her, dressed in a hooded cloak and leather armor. And he'd spoken to her in Pry-rian, which she hadn't expected.

"I'm from the kitchen," she said. "The cook sent me to see if the Aldermaston needs anything for his guests."

"What are you carrying?" he asked, pointing at the cloth-wrapped loaf. "Let me see it."

She stepped forward to show him, but he held up his hand. "Stay where you are."

"It's just a loaf of bread." She unwrapped it and held it out. He was still half-concealed in the shadows, and she had the sense he'd positioned himself there on purpose.

His head tilted a little, and then he came closer. With his face exposed, she saw the distrust in his eyes as he looked from her to the bread. He had a handsome, arrogant face, and the makings of a beard that suggested he wasn't too much older than her, but he also had the perfectly disciplined posture and commanding presence of an experienced soldier. She noticed his other hand lingered on the hilt of the blade—a short one, a gladius. A feeling of unease came over her as he continued to stare at her.

He gestured with his fingers for her to hand him the loaf.

She approached him warily, feeling vulnerable and ill at ease, and snatched her hand back after he took the loaf. Then she watched as he lifted it to his nose and smelled it.

"It's pumpkin," Eilean explained.

"I know," he said, lowering it again. "The cook's name is Ardys. She was the cook when I was a learner here for a year." He handed it back to her. "Just making sure you didn't poison it."

She stared at him for a moment, not recognizing his face and so shocked by the accusation that she could not find words, until finally they came tumbling out. "How dare you say such a thing!"

"On your way, girl," he said, waving her to the door, with a look that suggested their conversation was over.

She folded the cloth over the bread again and strode past him, giving him a narrow-eyed glare as she passed, and then yanked on the door handle. It stuck and didn't open. She yanked on it again, flustered now.

"Do you need help?" he asked.

She stamped her foot and tried a third time, and this time, thank the Medium, it yielded. Her heart blazed with anger still, but she did her best to soothe the roiling feelings before she reached the door to the Aldermaston's study. Even outside, she heard voices speaking from within. She knocked timidly.

The door opened, and another cloaked warrior stood blocking the way, hand on the hilt of his gladius.

"I've come with some bread," Eilean said with a little exasperation, "not to murder anyone!"

She heard Aldermaston Gilifil chuckle. "That would be Eilean, one of the kitchen girls. Let her in."

The man still regarded her with suspicion, but he stood aside, giving her a glimpse of Aldermaston Gilifil, whose reddish-gray beard and long locks could be seen beneath the pale gray cassock of his office. He gave her a friendly smile and waved her in.

Standing before him was an older woman in a cassock, with a crown nestled in her hair. There was a sternness and look of discernment in her eyes that made Eilean's outrage shrivel. Even without the raiments of her office, Eilean suspected she would have known this woman was the head of the maston order. What was she doing in Tintern?

"I brought a loaf of bread," Eilean said in a small voice.

"I can see that, child. Set it over there." The woman's tone was that of one accustomed to commanding respect and obedience.

"Surely you can stay for a slice, Your Eminence," the Aldermaston coaxed. "There is much we can still discuss."

"No, I must return to Avinion straightaway. You have your charge, Aldermaston. You will send reports regularly on your progress. Our abbeys will be a bastion of change in the kingdom of Moros. Once the other kings see them rise up from the ashes, they will swiftly bend the knee. This will mark the end of years of war. A time of peace, praise Idumea. And you must persuade your prisoner to disclose the information that we seek."

"Praise Idumea," said the Aldermaston. "Shall I escort you back to the abbey to return to Avinion, Your Eminence?"

"No need. I know the way. And you . . . have much work to do."

"Indeed," said the Aldermaston with a weary sigh. "The prisoner you mentioned. The druid Mordaunt."

"Don't call him *that*," said the High Seer with a curl of her lip. "He's an apostate. If you find where he's hidden it, bring it to Avinion at once."

"Of course. It would be my honor."

"I'm leaving one of my captains of the Apocrisarius to help you," said the High Seer. "There will be more druids lurking in the swamp. They may try to rescue him."

"They will not succeed, High Seer. I assure you. Who is the captain?"

"A Pry-rian, like yourself."

"Captain Hoel?"

She flashed him a smile. "The very one. He volunteered for the assignment because this is where he passed the maston test. He'll accompany you to the Bearden Muir. You'll have to go on foot, I'm afraid. There is no Apse Veil to travel there. Yet."

The Aldermaston nodded, and Eilean's heart thrilled at all she'd heard. Something big was happening. Something that would impact everyone at Tintern Abbey. If she surmised correctly, the High Seer had come to assign Aldermaston Gilifil to build a new abbey in the newly conquered kingdom of Moros.

The guard at the door opened it, and the High Seer left. As the door closed behind her, leaving Eilean and the Aldermaston together alone, she finally set the bread on the table.

"Thank you, Eilean," he said with a fond smile. He looked around the chamber wistfully. "I will be sad to leave this place."

"Has she asked you to found a new abbey, then?" Eilean asked him eagerly.

"She has. In the middle of a forsaken swamp. Tintern is the closest abbey to that spot. This will be the first abbey constructed in the kingdom of Moros."

"What will it be called?"

He smiled at her again. "Muirwood." Then his brow furrowed. "There's only a small castle and keep there now. A dungeon of sorts. And one very dangerous prisoner."

He looked her in the eye.

"I will be bringing many from Tintern with me to help establish the new abbey. I'd like you to be one of them, Eilean."

Some tomes have led to learning and others to madness. Knowledge has always been a double-edged sword, but even though it contains the potential for violent thought, that does not mean it should be abolished. There is a strange cult within the realm of Moros called the druids. Unlike the maston order, they have no written records. All their cultural knowledge is transmitted from druid to druid. How dangerous it is to give so much to so few. These individuals are respected by both king and commoner and often play the judge in disputes between the same. Their garb is typically humble. Some mark their bodies with ink or dye from the woad plant common in their deep forests. All have one thing in common: they wear a talisman around their necks, one that gives them power over the forces of nature. This is a heresy, of course. The King of Moros had such a druid as his advisor. Now he consults with a maston, as he's adopted the faith and is permitting abbeys to be constructed in his realm.

—Mícheál Nostradamus of Avinion Abbey

CHAPTER TWO

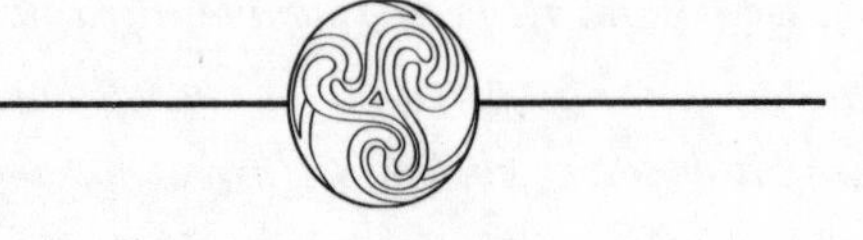

To Be Chosen

Ten days had passed since the High Seer of Avinion's surprise visit to Tintern Abbey. The first wagons sent to the location of the new abbey had returned to be filled with provisions and equipment for the second journey. The Aldermaston had kept busy during that time, meeting with most of the population of the abbey, informing those who had been chosen for the voyage and those who would remain behind.

Although Celyn had been invited to come too, thank the Medium, all three of Aisic's friends had been told they would remain at Tintern to serve the new Aldermaston, who was traveling from Holyrood Abbey and would be arriving any day through the mysterious Apse Veil, just as the High Seer had done. The lads were bitterly disappointed, and while Aisic hadn't yet been informed one way or another, the tension had put him in a dark mood. The four of them sat at their table in the kitchen after the evening meal, conversing in increasingly loud voices as Eilean and Celyn swept the stone floors.

"I'm glad I'm not going," said Llewellyn with a derisive snort. "Think of how much work it will be to build a new abbey?"

"*Shaw*, what about the stones to build it? How are they going to get them to an island?" asked Ely.

"What will they grow in the middle of a bog, anyway?" Bryant scoffed.

An abbey had five years from its founding to become independent, so the Aldermaston would have to develop a plan for making the abbey self-sufficient. That would prove a challenge since Muirwood was situated in the middle of a bog. At Tintern, they had grapes for wine and grew flax for linen. What would their new abbey produce?

But one look at Aisic stopped her imagination in its tracks. While his friends spoke, throwing ideas back and forth, he glowered at the table.

"At least you all know your fate," he muttered angrily. "Gilifool has probably forgotten I even exist."

"Hush! Don't let the cooks hear you call him that!" warned Ely.

Eilean had heard it, and it rankled her that they should use such a contemptuous nickname for the Aldermaston. If she'd possessed more courage, she would have thumped Aisic with the broom for being so disrespectful. But she was sad for him. What if the Aldermaston *had* forgotten about him? She herself had been informed of her fate before anyone else. Since then, Ardys and Loren and, of course, Celyn had been told they were coming. Any Aldermaston worth his salt cared for the welfare and happiness of his cooks, by Cheshu.

"I wish one of those Apocrisarius would stay here at Tintern," said Llewellyn.

The hunter she'd met that first night, Captain Hoel, led that group, despite his young age, and he and his men were a constant source of fascination for the people of Tintern Abbey. Some of the Apocrisarius had escorted the first group of wagons to the new site and back, and another group was preparing to take the next load of supplies. They ate together at the table nearest the kitchen doors, speaking in low voices, and always dispersed quickly. They were unfailingly respectful, but they'd proven sadly reserved when it came to telling stories about their order. Still, Eilean had heard enough to know that the captain's full name was Hoel Evnissyen, although she'd only heard people call him by his first name. People whispered that he was related to the royal family of Pry-Ree. No one seemed to know the nature of the connection.

"They're all going to Muirwood," said Ely. "It's not fair."

"Of course it's fair," Aisic grunted. "They'll be hunting those heretic druids." He clenched his fist and thumped the table. "I would *love* to do that!"

Llewellyn gave his arm a shove. "You'd leave us so easily, would you? Now that's a friend."

Aisic hung his head and muttered something under his breath.

Just then, Ardys circled around from the cooking area, brushing the flour from her hands onto her apron. Eilean stopped sweeping and looked at the cook inquisitively, but the group at the table didn't appear to notice.

"Let's go," Aisic grunted and rose from the bench. "We can talk about Gilifool somewhere else."

He hadn't seen the cook approach, and her face suddenly went stiff with anger.

"Hold there, young Aisic," she said in a scolding tone.

"You idiot," Llewellyn whispered.

Aisic turned in surprise as Ardys stormed up to him. "Now that's gratitude I tell you, calling the Aldermaston names."

"I . . . I didn't," stammered Aisic, his face turning red with shame. Eilean bit her lip, hating to see him shamed in such a way. He could be an arrogant braggart, but his friends were no better, so it was unfair that he should be singled out for a rebuke. Ardys was completely loyal to Aldermaston Gilifil, though, and would tolerate no disrespect toward him.

"I heard you well enough. Sivart Gilifil is a wise and honorable Aldermaston, the best of men. He was the youngest to be made an Aldermaston in Pry-Ree, and with any luck he'll be the High Seer someday! You watch your tongue, young man!"

The cook was much smaller than the shortest of the lads, but they all bore the same cowed expression. No one wanted to be on her bad side.

Aisic muttered an apology under his breath and turned to leave.

"Hold there, young man," Ardys said, still scowling. "As it happens, I came looking for *you*. One of the pages just came through the back of the kitchen. He said the Aldermaston wants to speak with you. Now be smart and get over there quickly. You pay him the respect he deserves, or you'll be eating leek soup for a week."

Aisic blinked in surprise and then nodded vigorously before leaving the kitchen at a run. The other three quickly fled as well, lest they get scolded for being nearby. Eilean went to sweep up the mess she'd gathered into a pile, but Ardys shook her head and took the broom from her hands.

"I'll have Nora do it. The page said the Aldermaston wants to talk to you as well. Get going, girl."

Eilean looked at her in confusion. "But he already told me I was going."

Although Celyn said nothing, she could feel her friend's eyes on her.

"I know that, child," Ardys said. "Go on now! And be quick about it!"

Eilean hurried out of the kitchen. She made it halfway to the Aldermaston's manor before realizing she was still wearing her cooking apron. All the wretched lasses wore kirtles made of flax linen, which was a pale color, like the dun of a sheep. The sleeves had blue lacings—blue from the woad—and they were allowed to decorate the front bodice with embroidery of their own choosing. It was simple fare, not like the colorful garb worn by learners at the abbey. Aprons were helpful in keeping kirtles clean longer, but it felt inappropriate to wear one in front of the Aldermaston. Still, if she went back, Ardys might scold her for being vain.

As she approached the rear of the manor, she peered into the shadows where she knew one of the guards was always hidden. As hard as she looked, she couldn't see anyone there. How did they hide so—

"I'm over here," said Captain Hoel's voice from behind her.

Startled, she spun around, and sure enough, he was right there. He hadn't been hiding in the shadows either.

"Are you trying to scare me half to death?" she asked him with a tremor in her voice.

He quirked his brow.

"The Aldermaston summoned me," she said with an edge in her voice. Her heart was still racing from the surprise.

"I know."

She turned to walk away, annoyed by his ability to needle her, but he stopped her with a question.

"Are you loyal to the Aldermaston?" he asked, his tone enigmatic.

"I am, by Cheshu!" she shot back. "Are you?"

He came closer, his expression visible in the light coming from the abbey. There was a distrusting glint in his eyes, just like there'd been a fortnight previously. "How old are you?"

"What does that matter?"

"Answer me."

She clenched her hands into fists. "I'm seventeen."

"So you have another year left before your servitude is done," he said. "Would you stay with the Aldermaston longer if he asked you to?"

She had no idea why he was asking her such a personal question. Every wretched had to fulfill their debt. Most of them had been taken in as infants, and it was their duty to serve the abbey that had provided them with food and shelter. The work they did taught them important skills, and once their time was served, many of them left to take positions elsewhere.

"If he asked me to stay, I would," she answered, realizing she'd been lost in her thoughts. "He's a good man."

"So I've heard," said Hoel. He stared at her for another moment, his gaze penetrating, then nodded. "On your way."

As she walked to the manor, she looked back and saw him standing there, still watching her with that wary look on his face. Why had he accosted her again? It made no sense.

She opened the door, which thankfully didn't stick, and headed to the Aldermaston's study. This door was solidly shut, and although she could hear Aisic and the Aldermaston speaking, their words were a mystery. She began to pace and wring her hands, her stomach full of bees.

Would Aisic be told to stay behind with his friends? She'd fretted about it for days. Although she knew others might think she was clean off, she'd fancied him for a long time, ever since they'd worked side by side one time during the flax harvest. The sun had been especially hot that day, so much so that some of the other wretcheds had fainted, and he'd complimented her perseverance while others were mitching because of the heat. They'd joked with each other and made a pact to complete their row the fastest. Afterward, she'd craved another morsel of approval from him, but he'd gone back to mostly ignoring her, the way his friends did.

Did she even want Aisic to come? Oh, of course she did, but maybe she shouldn't. Still, a hopeful part of her suggested that he might be kinder, more like the Aisic in the fields that day, if he weren't always in the company of his friends.

The door opened, and suddenly he was there, his face flushed. He looked like he was about to start crying. When he saw her in the corridor, he shut the door behind him and then started to walk toward her, his eyes fixed on the door beyond. He looked so disappointed she knew he'd been rejected too. Her own heart flinched from the sight of his pain.

"I'm sorry, Aisic," she said, amazed that the words made it past her throat.

He stopped, just past her. His head turned slightly but not all the way. "Sorry?"

"Yes. I'm sorry you're not going." She wanted to tell him she'd miss him. She wanted to say something that might make him remember her. But her courage failed, and nothing came past the knot in her throat.

"But I *am* going to Muirwood," he said thickly, "and none of my friends are."

I'll be your friend, she wanted to say. She *longed* to say it. But no words came out.

"I wish I'd never been born," he said with sullen anger and marched to the door.

It hurt to hear him say it. Many wretcheds felt the weight of being so unwanted by either or both parents that they'd been abandoned without name or worldly notice. Many agreed with Aisic and thought it would have been better not to have been born. Not Eilean. She was grateful she'd been brought to the abbey instead of being left to die.

Life was a gift.

Aisic slammed the outer door as he left, and she watched it a moment. He was coming too. And his three friends were not. A little bubble of giddiness tamed the bees in her stomach as she approached the study door and knocked.

"Come in."

The Aldermaston was alone, looking wearied from a long day of speaking to people. He rubbed the bridge of his nose between his thumb and forefinger and gave her a kindly smile.

"I was hoping to speak with you earlier today, but I knew Ardys would need you in the kitchen until after the evening meal." He sighed. "So many preparations to see to before the next journey to the abbey. I won't be making the trip this time, but *you* will."

"I'm looking forward to it, Aldermaston," she said. It hadn't occurred to her that she might be going so soon, but the prospect excited her.

His smile became more uncertain. "We'll see about that. The insect bites cause a lot of itching, and many of our people will be staying in tents because the castle cannot hold you all. But let's put discomforts aside for a moment. The High Seer of Avinion is a powerful woman. It is a great honor that she's given me, Eilean. Founding a new abbey is a challenging task. I've never done it before."

She was still confused why she was there, but she nodded in agreement. "I believe in you, Aldermaston. We all do."

He rose from his chair and put his hands on the desk. There was a tome spread out before him, and the metallic page glimmered in the light cast by the fire Leering. She could see the little scriving marks on part of the page. The remainder was blank, but she could tell it was his personal tome, a record he was keeping of his life. She had seen it on his desk many times.

"Thank you. It's a comfort, truly. I asked you to come see me tonight because the Medium presses heavily on me. Ever since the High Seer's visit, the Medium has whispered to me that you are to be chosen for a special role at Muirwood."

Her stomach flopped. "Aldermaston?" she asked, her voice trembling.

Was he going to ask her to join the Apocrisarius? To train as one of Captain Hoel's people?

A moment later, she realized that was clean off. The captain had treated her with contempt, and her only ability to wield a knife came from cutting vegetables. Her mind was getting away from her.

"My dear, I know you overheard some of my conversation with the High Seer. Let me explain the need that I have. The burden, if you will. The King of Moros is in the process of accepting the maston order in his realm, which is why we've been charged to build abbeys there. He had an . . . advisor. This is difficult to explain, so I beg your indulgence while I try. The kings of Moros used to place their trust in men called druids. They are very different from mastons. Rather barbaric, actually. The king's druid was called Mordaunt. As you might imagine, he rallied the king against us in the war."

Eilean nodded. "I heard you mention his name."

"Ah, good. He's a prisoner on the island. He will remain a prisoner for a long time, lest he try to destroy the first chance at peace we've had in many years. We all wish to see this awful bloodshed end. Permanently. If you heard Mordaunt's name, then you may recall that the High Seer called him an apostate. He . . . used to be part of the maston order, Eilean. It is believed that he took a tome from us—one that should not have been taken—and hid it somewhere in the kingdom of Moros. That is a very large place, mind you. Most of the towns are along the coast, but beyond them there are endless forests and swamps that are largely uninhabited. I'm sure you're beginning to see what I'm getting at."

Eilean looked at him in confusion. "No, Aldermaston. I don't understand."

The look on his face was almost sad. "When we go to Muirwood, I would like you to become Mordaunt's servant, just as you serve Ardys and Loren now."

She blinked, completely caught off guard. "Is it safe?"

"He will not beat you or threaten you. He was the king's advisor, and he submitted to imprisonment as a term of the peace. No, the gravest risk you would undertake would be to fall under his sway. He's highly intelligent." He heaved another sigh. "I've been fretting for days about whom I could trust with such a challenging task. From what I understand, he is not a very agreeable man. He's rude, impatient, and domineering. And he is very, very *clever*. I thought about every person I could entrust with this task. Someone who could see to his needs yet remain loyal and true. I may be fallible—in fact, I often am. But the Medium is not. And that is why I must ask this of you, Eilean."

She was amazed that the Aldermaston trusted her so much. But his request made her sick to her stomach. She was supposed to serve someone who had defected from the maston order to join the druids? She couldn't believe anyone who'd experienced the truth about the Medium would willingly abandon it for an empty superstition. And she was the one who would have to serve him, day and night?

"I can see in your eyes that you're disappointed," said the Aldermaston worriedly.

"N-no, Aldermaston," she said. "I'm just startled."

Was that why Captain Hoel had asked whether she was loyal? Had the Aldermaston revealed the plan to him before he'd shared it with her? Surely that had happened. And Captain Hoel had probably objected. That realization gave her a throb of determination.

"I will do it, of course." She nodded vigorously.

He smiled, the relief evident in his pleased look. "Thank you, Eilean. I knew I could count on you. Bless you, child. This will be a difficult task. And I may need you to serve beyond the next year you are obligated to stay. But if you do, I will help you find a position that shows my true appreciation for the sacrifice you've made. I promise you that."

But she felt strangely excited. Muirwood would provide a new beginning for her, Aisic, and Celyn. A new chance to serve.

A little fear wriggled in her heart at the thought of the task before her. But if the Aldermaston believed in her, she knew she would do her duty well.

"Thank you, Aldermaston. I will do my best."

"I know that, Eilean. I expect no less from you."

Five enemies of peace inhabit us—avarice, ambition, envy, anger, and pride. If these were to be banished, we should enjoy perpetual peace. But in this mortal coil, it is our fate to be burdened by such enemies. Our own thoughts betray us. Our desires. But that is not all. There are also insidious foes known as the Myriad Ones, the Unborn. These are the souls of men and women too wicked to be born. In the Garden of Leerings, they tempted our First Parents with whispers that infiltrated their minds and hearts rather than their ears. Thankfully, the Leerings protect those of us who bolster our minds and hearts from the Myriad Ones' defiling influence.

The Unborn cannot inhabit a human form without permission and instead rave in the feral bodies of swine, wolves, and all creatures that love the dark and loathe the light. The reason the druids are a heresy is that they befriend and use the creatures inhabited by the Myriad Ones. They can command them with their talismans. I've heard reports from the Apocrisarius that when these druids invoke the power available to them, their eyes turn silver and begin to glow.

—Mícheál Nostradamus of Avinion Abbey

CHAPTER THREE

The Myriad Ones

Eilean knelt by the remains of the cooking fire and busily scrubbed the cauldron to remove the burnt remains of the supper she'd made for the travelers. Her own legs were sore after three days of walking. The wagons were surprisingly difficult to keep up with, but she had pressed on, not wanting to be scolded for lagging behind.

She missed the kitchen at Tintern Abbey and already longed for Ardys, Loren, and Celyn. When she'd told them about the special duty the Aldermaston had given her, they'd all gaped in surprise. Ardys had recovered first, pulling Eilean into a cush so tender and loving it brought tears to Eilean's eyes. A cush was more than just an ordinary hug—it spoke of a special bond, like that between parents and children, and Ardys and Loren were the only "parents" she'd ever known. Their pride in her had made her feel a happy glow.

The cook and her husband knew very little about the druids since there had been none in Pry-Ree since the maston order had been established there centuries before. The stories she had heard were little more than tales, some of which she suspected had been designed to frighten children—like the tale of the monster that lived in the mist in the Mynith Mountains. In truth, Eilean wondered the same. Could a druid really transform into a beast and roam the woods as an animal? Surely not—that was against the teachings of the maston order. A superstition.

Four of the Apocrisarius hunters led the journey, and there were about twenty in the company, all on foot except for Wren the laundress, who had twisted her ankle the first day and rode in one of the wagons. Eilean suspected the girl was faking her injury, for she seemed a little too content to ride.

After she finished cleaning the cauldron, Eilean went to the bladder hanging by the edge of the food wagon to get some water to finish cleaning the spoons and knives she'd used to prepare the meal. She'd hoped that Aisic would be sent with her group, but he was still back at Tintern, preparing for the journey he'd be making with the next group. Celyn had made him and the other boys a batch of gooseberry fool to give them a special treat since Aisic would be leaving his friends. Such small kindnesses came easily to Celyn, and Eilean couldn't help but wish she'd thought of it first.

After stowing her things back in the wagon, she added another oak log to the fire to keep the coals going through the night and then settled her blanket beneath the wagon. Ever since she was a child, she'd always slept where she could see the burning eyes of a Leering in the kitchen and always made sure her feet were covered by her blanket. She had a terror that if the lights ever went out, leaving her feet exposed and vulnerable, some monster would bite her toes. Leerings gave her a feeling of safety, even though some of the faces carved into them could be grotesque. They were symbols of the Medium's power, the power to conjure water to wash her hands, to summon fire to cook bread, to keep weevils away from the grain. Now that she was away from the abbey, with no Leerings nearby, she felt more anxious about the journey. Thankfully, their protectors were all mastons.

Captain Hoel approached her diminished fire, walking so quietly she wouldn't have heard him if she hadn't seen him. She turned to look up at him while she finished stretching out her blanket.

"That was a good stew," he said. "All of my men enjoyed it."

"Thank you, Captain. I hope I made enough."

"There was plenty." He squatted down by the fire and nudged the log closer to the center of the flames. Eilean felt a wave of longing for the kitchen. An oven Leering did not give off so much smoke. On their first night Eilean had been half-blinded by it, and after so many days on the road, her kirtle was in need of a washing, not just from the dirt but from the smell of the fire.

"Will we reach the abbey tomorrow?" she asked him.

He made a face. "Depends on the muck. We've already entered the Bearden Muir, though it's not easy to tell. By tomorrow, the insects will start feasting on our blood." He handed her a little wooden tin. "It's a salve to keep the pests away. Rub it on your skin in the morning."

She took it from him and gave him a quizzical look. She hadn't noticed him sharing it with any of the others. But maybe he'd done so discreetly.

"Thank you."

He shrugged and then rose and walked away. Some of the travelers had gathered in a circle to tell stories, but she was weary from the walk. She removed her shoes and nestled beneath her blanket, making sure both her bare feet were covered, and faced the fire. She listened to the snapping noises from the fresh wood, watched the little bursts of sparks, and promptly fell asleep.

Deep into the night, a sound woke her. All was dark, and even her little fire had gone out. She blinked, not sure what she'd heard, and then the keening sound repeated itself. Her heart clenched with fear. She stared at the fire and tried to will it into flames, like she could do with the oven Leerings. But the fire was as quiet as its ashes.

Another burst of sound came. Closer this time.

Eilean pushed up onto her elbows and hurriedly put on her shoes. She rose from beneath the wagon, shivering from fear and the chill night air. Something rustled in the woods. Instantly, her mouth went dry. She looked around the shadows of the camp, everything dark because of the high trees surrounding them. Overhead, she saw the stars but no moon.

A strange, sick feeling started in her navel and rose higher up her chest. The darkness felt real, alive. Worse, something was looking at her. Her teeth began to chatter.

She looked over the wagon into the depths of the woods, unable to see anything in the blackness. Then she saw two glowing points, not from fire but some awful being, lurking in the dark. Fear paralyzed her.

Come.

It wasn't a thought so much as an urge. She backed away and stepped into the ashes of her fire. They were still warm, and the warmth seeped through the thin calfskin of her shoe. Realizing she was standing in the fire, she quickly stepped aside and stamped her foot to keep her shoes from burning. She looked back to the woods and saw nothing but blackness this time.

A cloaked figure approached her, and she recognized the gait of Captain Hoel.

"Go back to sleep. It's just the bugling of elk," he told her in a low voice.

"I saw something in the woods," she said, pointing to where she'd seen the eyes. Her arm trembled.

"Probably an animal," he said. "I'm surprised you could see anything in the dark."

"It looked like two eyes glowing in the dark. Not like a Leering. Smaller and . . . like polished iron."

"Silver?" he asked with sudden interest.

"Yes. Like silver."

Captain Hoel brought his thumb and forefinger to his mouth and let out one quick whistle. The suddenness of it shocked her.

One of the other hunters appeared from the gloom. "What is it, sir?"

Hoel came to stand right next to Eilean. "Point again. Where did you see it?"

"There." Her arm didn't shake so much the second time. She was relieved he hadn't dismissed her claim. Another man might have, and indeed, she'd feared *he* would. In the past he'd treated her as if she were untrustworthy.

"She saw something glowing," Hoel said. "I'm going to investigate. Stand ready."

"Do you want a torch, Captain?"

"No. Better if they can't see me either."

"A druid?"

"Maybe. We're close enough they might have sent one to spy on us."

Sleep had completely abandoned Eilean's eyes, and she watched as Captain Hoel disappeared into the gloom. Worry began to quiver inside her stomach. The other two hunters approached their group after a few moments.

"What's going on?" asked one of the newcomers in a low voice.

"The girl might have seen a druid in the woods. Captain is checking."

Some of the horses began to nicker and stamp.

"Twynho, go settle them," ordered the hunter who had been with her the longest. "Could be wolves."

One of the men nodded and ventured off in that direction.

"Get some sleep, lass. We won't let anything harm you. It is still a way until dawn."

A howling sound came from the darkness, making Eilean gasp in fear. The horses began to shriek in panic, and others in the camp roused.

"What's goin' on?" someone called out.

"Hush the beasts, we're tryin' to sleep!" another cried.

Captain Hoel came back into the camp, his blade drawn. "There was someone nearby. Where's Twynho?"

"He's calming the horses."

"Cimber, you take that side of the camp. Olien, you go that way. Stand vigil the rest of the night. Eilean, can you get that fire going again? We'll need torches."

"Yes, of course," she answered and quickly went to grab more sticks while the hunters spread out to fulfill their assignments. She knelt by the ashes, pushing her hair back so it wouldn't tumble down, and leaned in closer to blow on them. A few winks from embers greeted her efforts. In a few moments, the fire was crackling again as she fed it fresh sticks. Others from the camp gathered around, asking what was wrong, but one of the hunters ordered them to stand aside.

Hoel returned with four torches, and he dribbled oil on the cloth-bound ends before dipping them into the flames she'd built up. He lit two at a time and handed them off to his men before keeping one for himself. Then he ventured deeper into the wood, going the way she'd indicated.

"What's happening, Eilean?" one of the fellow travelers asked her. The blacksmith.

"They think a druid is watching us from the woods," she said.

"*Shaw*, that's not good! They must hate us. But let them hate so long as they fear us too."

His words filled her heart with dread that she was supposed to serve one of their leaders. The druid Mordaunt.

***

When dawn finally came, Eilean cooked up some porridge and added some butter and a drizzle of dark treacle for better flavor. Everyone ate quickly and started to break camp to continue the journey. After she finished her chores and stowed her blanket and things back in the wagon, she noticed Captain Hoel returning from the woods.

She hurried to him. "Did you find the druid?"

He shook his head. "I didn't expect to. I wanted to study the tracks he left. Last night, I think he . . . or *she* . . . tried to lead me to where others would be waiting in an ambush. I turned back and then kept circling the camp to thwart them from trying anything else."

"She?" Eilean asked.

"The footprint was smaller than what I'd expect from a man," he said. "Come—you can see for yourself."

Why would he care to teach her something? While she didn't understand his motives, she was grateful to learn any useful thing. He brought her through the trees and halted her with his arm before she could step in the wrong place. Squatting down again, he pointed to a patch of dirt. The shade of the trees made it difficult to see, but as she looked closer, she saw the distinct outline of the footprint in the dirt, undisturbed.

"Your foot would fit in there," he said. "That's why I can't be sure. Druids can be men or women."

She saw another footprint and pointed to it. "There's another!"

He gave her an amused smile. "I know. The trail leads northeast. After we get to the abbey, I'll send some of my hunters to track the prints. They were unwise to cross us so openly."

She looked at him with curiosity. "I've heard they can transform into animals? Can they turn others into them too?"

"No, that's just a fantasy," he said to her, his brow narrowing in disapproval.

She felt a flush of shame. "I didn't say I believed it. Ardys told me it wasn't true."

"The questions a person asks say a lot about them," he said, looking her in the eye. "But the work they do says even more. You're a hard worker, Eilean."

"I try to be." She wasn't sure how to take his comment. "Do you know what the Aldermaston has asked me to do?"

He nodded and straightened, his look hardening. "He shouldn't have chosen you."

She straightened as well, her feelings wounded again. "You don't think he can trust me?"

"No doubt you've earned his trust these many years at the abbey."

"Then why say what you did? Or are you just being chopsy?"

"Chopsy? I haven't heard that one in a while." Though he didn't say so, she suspected that he judged her for her slang *and* her questions. But he was being a true boor, and she had every right to tell him so. He looked at her for a moment, as if studying an insect, then said, "I have my reasons," and turned and walked away.

She wasn't sure how to feel, but she had the impulse to throw an acorn at his retreating back. Ah, that's what this was: *anger*. Her question may have sounded clean off, but would it have mattered if she'd asked a different one? He'd made it clear from the beginning that he disapproved of her, and he obviously didn't think she should have been chosen for this mission.

She'd prove him wrong.

***

It was easy to see the trail the wagons had left on their last journey, for two ruts had formed through the marshy grass. Thanks to the ointment Captain Hoel had given her, Eilean wasn't troubled by the buzzing mosquitoes and swamp flies, but the air was thick and heavy, and sweat added to the smell of dirt and smoke. Her shoulders were weary from the exhausting march, but they pressed on, not stopping to eat because they were so close to the castle. The oak trees were black with slime and riddled with green and brown varieties of moss. Diseased-looking branches interwove above their heads, blotting out the spring sunlight. As she walked, she daydreamed about the sunny fields of Tintern Abbey and realized she'd traded in her simple existence for a much harsher life.

Murmurs drifted back to her from the head wagon. They'd arrived!

Eilean's shoes were squishy with mud, and her calves and legs and hem were black with the muck. Sweat dripped down her breastbone, her ribs, and even down her back. But at last, after four long days, they'd finally reached the site of the new abbey. She meandered past the other wagons to get her first view.

And gasped in wonder at what she saw.

They'd reached the edge of the woods, which opened to a vast lake. The sky was murky with clouds, but the setting sun illuminated them in layers of pinks and oranges, drawing the eye to the wooded hills in the distance. Or at least it would have if her attention weren't focused on the stone castle on the small scrubby island in the middle of the lake. The building was reflected in the tranquil waters, although there were enough ripples to distort the image. The castle was built in two sections joined together by a narrow wall embedded with a black gatehouse. A few chimneys lined the rooftops, maybe four in all. A small orchard of perhaps twenty trees was situated near the northern wall so that it had ample daylight and little shadow. And many tents clustered around the structure, providing shelter for those who could not find accommodations indoors.

That dazzling sunset. The castle. The lake. It was such a beautiful scene that it made all the trampling in the swamp seem like nothing at all to endure. She was thrilled at the sight of her new home. On the other side of the lake, she saw some shacks had been built, and some lazy smoke drifted up from their chimneys.

"This is Muirwood," said Captain Hoel to everyone who had stopped to gawk at the sight. Now Eilean understood why this place had been chosen for the first abbey of the kingdom of Moros. Looking at it tugged at her heart. A strange feeling came over her. A feeling that this place she'd never visited before was somehow . . . familiar.

"Shaw," she whispered in reverence.

Sameness is the mother of disgust, variety the cure. If you put a man in isolation, in a cell with windows that can see the outside world but bars that prevent him from going there, the monotony becomes worse than shackles. Give him the same guard, over and over, and he will want to wring the man's neck out of boredom, but provide someone new, and suddenly the mood will change.

These are the ways of the Apocrisarius.

This is how secrets are learned.

—Mícheál Nostradamus of Avinion Abbey

CHAPTER FOUR

The Apostate

There was a dock on the eastern part of the island with two wooden ferries for transporting provisions. Because they'd arrived at sunset, they camped at the edge of the lake and didn't venture to the island until the next day. In the morning, all hands were needed to lift the barrels and crates onto the rafts. Once they finished, a few of their party returned to Tintern with the wagons, and the rest of them rode across the lake with the goods. When they reached the other side, workers were waiting to unload the rafts.

"The Aldermaston asked me to introduce you to the prisoner," Captain Hoel told Eilean. "But I have duties to attend to first. Wander the grounds, but don't go into the castle yet."

She nodded, eager to begin exploring. The castle walls were made of old, rough stone, with no Leerings. Smoke belched from the high chimneys. She entered the scant orchard and saw blossoms beginning to bud on the stems. Fruit trees of some kind.

She heard sounds of construction—hammers and saws and the scraping of mortar over stone—and went to investigate. Her eyes took in the sight of wildflowers growing in patches over the turf. After turning the corner of the castle, she saw another structure was being raised. Some heavy timbers had already been raised to form the bones, and blocks of stone were being stacked to fortify the walls. A young man with a beam balanced on his shoulder walked past her.

"What are you building?" she asked out of curiosity.

He turned to answer her question and nearly knocked her head with the beam. "Sorry, lass!" he apologized, speaking the language of Moros but with an accent she couldn't identify. "We're building the Aldermaston's kitchen first."

"Isn't there a kitchen in the castle?" she asked him.

"Aye, a wee one, and it's rather shabby too. Best to put things with fire away from other buildings. Who might you be?"

"Eilean."

"From Tintern by the sound of your voice."

"Yes. We came last night."

Another man shouted for the beam, and the man apologized to her and hurried to obey. Eilean stared at the structure they were building, noticing the thickness of the walls. This was where Ardys, Loren, and Celyn would be working. Not her, though. The absence of Celyn, with whom she'd spent every day since they were both babes, had been a constant ache, but something about exploring this place alone made her feel fresh longing for her friend.

She gazed up at the windows and saw a figure looking down from inside. Was that the druid?

A shiver of fear went down her arms, and she rubbed away gooseflesh.

She visited the small garden and observed the growing shoots. Some turnip tops, carrots, parsley, celery root, and mint. They all had different leaves, and she was accustomed to the varieties from the years she'd spent in the kitchen. She snapped off a little sprig of mint and smelled the sweet aroma of it. Then she walked to the edge of the island and stared at the rippling waters and, on the other side, the hills rising in the distance. It was a clear day, except for a lonely set of clouds in the eastern skies. The swamp they'd traveled through had an eerie beauty to it—the moss and oak trees didn't look so dangerous now. She continued her circuit around the island, seeing frogs and even a turtle along the way. Some otters were playing in the water too, chasing and splashing and tousling each other's fur—the sight so charming it made her grin. All these things distracted her from her nerves, which were prickling more as time passed and Captain Hoel failed to reappear.

After she returned to the orchard, she spied him talking to two of his fellow hunters. The men nodded to him, then made their way to an awaiting ferry to cross back to the other shore. He turned, noticed her standing nearby, and approached her.

"This hardly seems space enough to build a new abbey," she said. "The island is very small."

"It won't be an island much longer," he answered.

She looked at him in confusion.

"They're going to start draining the swamp. This lake will disappear, and there will be much more room to build things."

She turned around, taking in the vastness of the lake, and tried to imagine what it would look like. "How can they do that?"

"What's a lake but a place where too much water comes in and not enough goes out." He pointed to the north. "A river feeds it over there." He turned and pointed to the southwest. "And it leaves in three branches that way. Leerings are being placed to divert the water. Anything left will sink into the mud. New boundaries will be set," he added, pointing to other places along the shore. "The new Leerings will hold the waters back unless the abbey comes under attack. If the situation warrants it, the Aldermaston can release the hold, and the water will come rushing back in to make a lake again."

"*Shaw*, I didn't know Leerings could do all of that," she said.

He gave her a condescending look, which set her teeth on edge. How was she supposed to know these things? "You're going to see things here at Muirwood that will astonish you. Have you ever seen a boulder float in the air?"

"Are you toying with me, Captain Hoel?"

"You will," he said confidently. "Now, it's time we went into the castle. Are you ready?"

She felt uncertain but tried to hide it. He'd already made it quite clear that he thought her ill-suited to her assignment. "I suppose so. I've never met a druid before."

"Follow me."

He took her to the main castle gate. The wooden door stood open, and workers were carrying crates and barrels into the castle. She looked around, feeling small and insignificant amidst so much commotion. Many of the workers had sweat stains on their tunics from their toil.

A group of laughing girls flounced out of the gate, carrying reed baskets filled with dirty clothes. They also wore linen kirtles, but instead of embroidery at the top, each had a dark leather corset. They had blond hair, much more fashionable than Eilean's chestnut brown, and each wore a crown of wildflowers.

"Who's she?" one of them asked as they passed.

"Another wretched, by the looks," said her friend. Then they all laughed.

Eilean felt awkward, but Captain Hoel barely seemed to notice. He forged ahead as she snuck a glance back at the girls. They were probably bringing the clothes out to the lake since there weren't any water Leerings yet, or at least none that she'd seen.

The inner courtyard was small, and it only took them a few moments to reach the castle. As soon as they stepped inside, a grizzled older man approached them.

"Captain Hoel, I presume? You look younger than I expected. I only knew you from the office of rank you wear."

"Yes," he replied stiffly. "Who are you?"

"I'm Critchlow, the steward." He gave Eilean a quick look, but his gaze immediately shifted back to the captain, his expression urgent. "I've heard you sent two additional men away. I can't have that, Captain. We need all the protection we can get. You really should have consulted me first."

"They're my men, and I'm their captain," Hoel replied. "I'm staying myself."

"Oh, thank Idumea!" he said dramatically. "I thought you were abandoning us too. We keep hearing wild animals calling in the night. It's frightful."

"You're in a *castle*," Hoel said with a tone of rebuke.

"It's rather small, compared to what I'm used to. Do you know when Aldermaston Gill-full will arrive?"

"Gilifil," Hoel corrected.

"I'm sorry. I'm not used to Pry-rian speech. I'm from Paeiz. This is the fourth abbey I've helped oversee, but it will be a wonder! I will show you the model I've made of it. The Aldermaston's kitchen will be done before long, and once we've diverted the rivers, we can start digging the fountains while the earth is moist."

"I've another duty to attend to," Hoel said, although Eilean had to wonder if it was partially an excuse to escape Critchlow. He seemed the kind of man who liked to hear himself talk.

"Ah. Very well. And is this the wretched the Aldermaston sent to spy on Mordaunt?"

"I'm not spying on anyone," she said with rising anger. She didn't like his tone.

Captain Hoel gave the steward a withering look. "She's his servant, nothing more. And yes. She's the one the Aldermaston sent."

He gave her a look of sympathy. "I'm sorry, my dear, but he's absolutely horrible. So rude and contemptible. It gets very dark in the castle at night. I can give you an allowance of candles. We have to make do with candles until the Leerings are all carved. I wish I had more lapidaries here, but alas!"

The thought of all that darkness pressing in on her made her shudder, but she was determined not to show weakness.

"Good day, sir," Hoel said and continued on his way.

Critchlow wilted at the sudden dismissal.

Eilean followed the captain and said under her breath, "Now, he's a fine fellow."

"He serves the holy emperor and the order," Hoel said over his shoulder. "They're all rather proud men."

"And you aren't, Captain?" Eilean retorted, only to immediately wish the words hadn't slipped out.

He gave her a look, chuckled to himself, and then brought her to an open doorway leading to a flight of stairs. "This way."

He mounted the steps so quickly she had a hard time keeping up. She was tired from the journey and nervous about this first meeting. At the top of the steps, they reached a landing that led down a corridor with a few doors on each side.

"This is your room," he told her, gesturing to the door just before the end of the hall. He twisted the handle, and the door opened to a small, windowless chamber. A tiny pallet lay on the floor. Fear gripped her stomach. There were no sources of light in the room.

"It doesn't suit you?" he asked with a look that she took as disappointment in her. He'd misinterpreted her reaction. If not for the lack of light, the space would have suited her fine.

The steward had offered her candles, hadn't he? She would have to avail herself of them.

"It'll be fine," she said with an edge in her tone.

"At least it's indoors," he said.

She gripped her hands into fists, but she refused to reveal the true source of her feelings to someone who already seemed to think so little of her. "Can we see Mordaunt, then? I'm assuming his room is at the end of the hall since mine is next to it."

"You're correct. The rest of these rooms have been taken up by other servants sent in advance to prepare for the Aldermaston's arrival. You may be asked to share with another once he comes with the rest of his household. At least until the abbey is built."

"How long will that take?"

He pursed his lips. "Not as long as you might suspect. Once they have all the stones here, it will go quickly. You'll see."

Hoel shut the door and approached the one next to it. There were no guards posted there, so Eilean was surprised when the captain opened it without knocking.

He walked inside as if he were an invited guest, and when she glanced at the interior of the room she nearly gasped. It wasn't a cell at all, but a guest room for a dignitary. In the middle loomed a four-post bed with velvet curtains. Her gaze leaped to the room's occupant next, standing at the window, his back to them.

He was middle-aged by the look of him, thick in the shoulders and heavy at the waist. He wore a simple tunic made of coarse fabric the color of turned earth, belted around the middle, and a pair of weather-beaten shoes. She saw some unruly dark hair beneath the mushroom-shaped hat he wore on the back of his head, and some of the locks above his ears were graying. The sleeves were wide and cuffed, voluminous and heavy—probably wool rather than linen.

He turned, revealing the blue stains of the woad tattoos on his cheeks and neck. His eyes were livid, his expression full of contempt. Her stomach shriveled at the look of intelligence and malice in his eyes. She was instantly afraid of him.

"Who are you?" the man asked. He spoke the tongue of Moros, as did most of the people on the grounds, but with a thick accent that was distinct from what she'd heard. He didn't sound like a native of the defeated kingdom. Then again, neither did she. Still, Pry-Ree and Moros were neighboring kingdoms, and like most of her people, she knew both tongues equally well.

"Captain Hoel Evnissyen. I've brought your servant."

Mordaunt looked at her with disgust. "How kind to treat your prisoner so, Captain. But as I've said before to that fool Critchlow, I need no servant, want no servant, and distrust *your* servant."

"All the same, it is her duty to remain here. Your room isn't very tidy."

"And what do I care about that?"

Eilean noticed the eating table was stacked with dishes, probably made of tin or pewter. They weren't fancy. Crumbs were everywhere. Hoel wasn't exaggerating—the room truly was a mess.

She sensed the presence of a Leering in the room before she saw it. It sat by an old brazier, the carved eyes glowing red. It wasn't a fire Leering. Or water. Something about it made her insides coil. Was this Leering preventing Mordaunt from leaving the castle, perhaps even the room?

Mordaunt glanced at her and made a snicking noise with his lips.

Hoel gave Eilean a worried look, but then he sighed and shrugged. "I've other matters requiring my attention."

"Of course you do, Captain. Prisoners to torture, no doubt." Mordaunt gave the captain a wily smile.

Hoel put a hand on Eilean's shoulder. "See Critchlow if you need anything. The Aldermaston will be here within a fortnight." He ushered her away from Mordaunt and added in a lowered voice, "I know the Aldermaston already offered you this assurance, but the prisoner cannot hurt you."

"Thank you," she whispered to him, and then he left her and shut her inside the room.

Swallowing, she mustered her courage and went first to the table to begin clearing it off. Mordaunt watched her with his dark, intense eyes, but she didn't look at him except for an occasional glance.

"What's your name?" he asked her.

"Eilean," she answered, still not looking at him.

"Ay-Lun?" he said with deliberate exaggeration of the syllables. "Ay-Lun. Where do you hail from, Ay-Lun?"

"Tintern Abbey."

"Ah, Tin-turn. A wretched from Pry-Ree. This is going to be torture. How is your name spelled?" Then he let out a puff of air. "Why am I asking? You're a wretched. They probably never taught you."

"I can read a little," she said, feeling her temper heating up. She didn't look at him as she continued clearing the table.

"Not completely savage? Can you only read and write Pry-rian? The language of Moros is very similar to it, although all of you have a horrible accent. Like someone choking on a fig." He cleared his throat and made some hawking noises.

She collected the uneaten leftovers on one plate—bird bones and carrot tips and some stale pieces of bread, which had turned as hard as stones. Such a waste.

"Can you only speak Pry-rian? Do you write?" he asked again.

"What need have I to write anything?" she answered stiffly. After stacking the plates and cups and flatware, she wiped her hands and looked around the room for something else to tidy.

"What need have I to write anything?" he said, mimicking her tone. "This will be torture. They did it on purpose. They mean to drive me mad. I'm already mad. At least in their eyes. Ay-Lun, my dear, do you know why you are *really* here?"

She steeled herself to meet his fearsome gaze. The stains of woad on his cheek, brow, and throat made her skin crawl. But she faced him still.

"I'm here because the Aldermaston sent me, and Captain Hoel brought me. And that's good enough for me."

He gave her a mocking smile. "Well said, Ay-Lun. Well said." Then he turned around and sighed to himself. "I'm surrounded by *pethets.* Help me."

The power of the Medium is available to all, young and old, wise and foolish, wealthy and impoverished. But just because it is all around us like the air we breathe does not mean it is used by all.

It is not easy to tame one's mind. Very few of us can manage it, even when taught. We doubt ourselves; we doubt the sincerity and motives of others. We cling to childish beliefs even as the evidence around us proves otherwise.

A child thinks it is the center of all. But as they age, they realize others exist, and their needs and whims do not rule the house, let alone the village, let alone the world. The older they get, the more they see this truth borne out in the suffering inherent in this Second Life. Time becomes something they fear, and that fear forges chains in their mind that they cannot break. If only they'd understand that the power that shaped the stars, the brightness of the moon, and the very earth upon which we tread is waiting to reveal to them the deepest secrets of their most enduring convictions, mingled with ardent emotion. A pauper could inherit a palace if only they thought and desired it enough.

Man has no greater enemy than himself.

—Mícheál Nostradamus of Avinion Abbey

CHAPTER FIVE

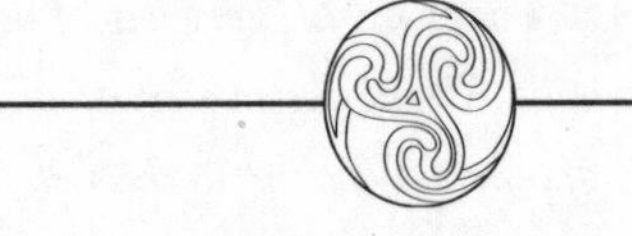

The Medium

It took most of the rest of the day to make Mordaunt's chamber as clean as whiskers. Eilean had to climb up and down the stairs many times, and on one of those trips, she took the druid's sheets and blankets and clothes down to the lake to wash them. The girls she'd noticed earlier, the ones with flower circlets in their hair, gave her disdainful looks, even though they performed the same labor. They came from Holyrood Abbey, she'd learned, in another part of Pry-Ree.

Mordaunt had a voracious appetite, and his requests required her to make several stops in the kitchen. At least his room had a closeted garderobe in the corner so she didn't have to stomach the indignity of handling his chamber pot.

By the end of that first day, she was exhausted, lonely, and wondering if she should have accepted the Aldermaston's special assignment.

Her back steeled at the thought. She could not quit. She refused to let Aldermaston Gilifil down.

Darkness had fallen over the island of Muirwood, and she fetched a candle from Critchlow's stores and carefully took it back upstairs, making what would hopefully be her last trip for the evening.

She went to Mordaunt's room and found him sitting at the meal table, head in his hands. For a moment, she feared he would send her down to the kitchen again.

"Do you need anything else?"

"You say it wrong, girl. Wrong! Any-*thing*. Not any-thun."

"That's what I said," Eilean protested.

"No!" He lifted his head from his hands, looking up at the ceiling rafters as if the wood up there were more intelligent than her. "Try it again. Any-*thing*."

"Can I get you aught, master?" she asked with a sigh, trying out a totally different word.

"I demand passable speech. Bring me passable speech without native slurs, lazy tongues, and indifferent thoughts. Go to your room. I don't need to hear your tiresome accent any longer."

"It's not wicked or tiresome, it's *different*," she said, angered by his mocking tone.

He looked at her with derision, shook his head, and then lowered his forehead back down into his hands.

"Good night, master," she said and retreated from the room and gently shut the door.

She wasn't sure what she'd been expecting from Mordaunt, but he wasn't anything like she'd thought he would be.

Who was this man? The chief advisor of a vanquished king, a mysterious druid, an apostate of the maston order? He'd spent much of the day correcting her speech and showing that he was affronted by the manners of Tintern Abbey. He was very disagreeable, but he did not seem evil.

She opened the door to her little cell and set the candle down on the floor. She stripped out of her kirtle, which was filthy from the journey to Muirwood, and folded it up and set it in the corner. She began to shiver now that she only wore a thin chemise and scurried under the blanket on the thin pallet on the floor. The candle offered plenty of light, but she made sure her toes were safely tucked beneath the blanket anyway. The smell in the room was strange, and the cramped space felt confining, as if she were the prisoner, not Mordaunt.

Despite her exhaustion, Eilean lay awake, her mind unable to settle. She rolled one way, then the other, trying to get comfortable. She was used to hearing Celyn's breathing. Whispers from the other kitchen girls. And the snores of Loren from the curtained bed in the back of the kitchen. Even on the road, there'd been the whispers of the other travelers. It was too quiet here, too bright with the candle, and she was too alone.

Eilean squeezed her eyes shut and tried to empty her head. Captain Hoel hadn't come to check on her since he'd brought her to Mordaunt's room. She wondered where the hunters were sleeping—out of doors or within the castle? Not long afterward, she heard people coming up the steps and voices conversing beyond her door.

"Another exhausting day," she heard, a woman's voice.

"Aye, the work is never done."

"Did you see that new captain today?" asked a totally different voice.

"Ah, Captain Hoel. He's a pretty thing, now isn't he?"

"Those brats from the laundry tried to talk to him, but he just kept walkin' and ignored them all."

"They think they're high and mighty with those flowers in their hair, by Cheshu! But he's nephew to the king. The cheek they have."

"By Cheshu indeed! But can't blame them for trying. His family might be famous, but he's only a captain now. And one of them Aprocrisars."

"You said it wrong!"

Eilean squeezed her eyes shut, listening to the three women talk in the corridor outside her door.

"How am I supposed to know? They're hunting those foul druids. Heathens."

"Let's get to bed. The sooner I fall asleep, the sooner I can dream for something better. That's why he doesn't go by his last name, you know . . ."

Their voices trailed off as they went to their rooms, but their talk, so warm and familiar with each other, made her keenly feel her outsider status. But she assured herself it wouldn't always feel this way. Soon Celyn and the others would come. Aisic would be here too. That thought made her happy.

She must have fallen asleep because she awoke to utter darkness and the smell of smoke. A spasm of terror gripped her heart, and she couldn't remember where she was at first. Sitting up, she clutched her blanket in mortal fear and reached out to where she'd put the candlestick. It was still warm. Her fingers found that there was still a good length of it left, but the fire had gone out.

She couldn't fall asleep again. Everything was as quiet as death, and she couldn't see a thing. The darkness oppressed her. Biting her lip to hold back nervous tears, she pulled her blanket around her shoulders and then lifted the candlestick and rose. Opening the door a crack, she peered into the corridor, which was dark but for the light filtering beneath the door in Mordaunt's room.

The brazier! It was still burning. She could relight her candle and come back to her room. It was the middle of the night, so Mordaunt had to be sleeping. Would he be angry if she woke him accidentally?

Probably. But it would be much faster to use his brazier to light her candle than to find her way downstairs in the dark. And the thought of potentially encountering Captain Hoel or one of his men down there made the decision easier.

She walked quietly to Mordaunt's door and twisted the handle. It groaned a little as she opened it, but it wasn't a screeching sound. The room was dark except for the glow from the brazier and the dimly shining eyes of the Leering in the corner. At night, it looked very different. Despite the grotesque face, there was something comforting in seeing the burning eyes of the Leering. It reminded her of the kitchen at Tintern.

As softly as her bare feet would allow, she went to the iron brazier holding the burning logs, taking note of the chimney that punctured the roof above and allowed the smoke to exit. Eilean lowered herself down by the iron rails of the brazier and slipped the candlestick in between them. When the black wick touched one of the coals, it flickered to life immediately—dimly at first and then more brightly once she'd righted the candle and cupped the flame with her other hand.

And that's when she saw Mordaunt, still at the table, watching her intently.

"Shaw!" she gasped, nearly dropping the candle. "You frightened me!"

"Shaw," he repeated with a mocking smile. "Is that an exclamation, I suppose? Something you say when you're scared?"

"I didn't mean to disturb you," she said. "My candle went out."

"I have eyes, girl. I can see that. It was perfectly rational of you to relight it here."

"Why aren't you asleep?" she asked, seeing he was not in his nightclothes. He sat exactly where she'd left him earlier.

"I cannot sleep," he answered.

"You're not tired?"

"Oh, I'm very tired of being *here*." He chuckled to himself. "But unfortunately, that is not enough to give me rest. And it is too early to send you for breakfast."

She gave him a quizzical look. "Oh." Truthfully, though, she didn't understand at all.

"'He that keepeth watch over Idumea never slumbers or sleeps.' Do you know that saying from the tomes?"

"I've not heard it before," Eilean said.

Mordaunt gave her a weary smile. "I imagine not. But you do know how to write?"

"I do, but only a little."

"I'm happy for you. There will come a day when they stop letting wretcheds read. I pity that future generation."

"Who will stop them? Who do you mean?"

He gave her a probing look. "My dear, you believe me to be an apostate and a heretic. Whatever I tell you, you cannot trust it to be true. Therefore, I will say no more. You have your fire. If it goes out, I have more candles here. Come and get one if you need it. Critchlow's allowance is more than I need."

She was surprised at his words, even more so by his declaration that she couldn't trust him.

"Thank you." She started to retreat toward the door, grateful to have light again.

"It's not the dark you should fear, Eilean," he told her, stopping her in her tracks.

She turned and stared at him, taking in the strange smears of woad on his face. Her heart clenched with dread and worry. Had he seen into her greatest fear? Could he read her mind?

His voice was almost soft as he said, "It's more pitiable being afraid of the light."

***

The next day was as busy as the first, and Eilean spent a good deal of it doing laundry, including her own. Mordaunt treated her the same as he had before, correcting her speech and complaining about everything.

The afternoon was quite humid, and she'd found herself needing some of the salve Captain Hoel had given her to ward away mosquitoes. When she returned to the laundry area, she saw with outrage that her kirtle, the one she'd washed and carefully hung to dry, lay in the mud. As she approached it, she saw the muddy footprints covering the skirt. Giggling filtered through the trees, and she noticed the three wretcheds from Holyrood had hidden nearby to watch her. Under her scrutiny, they grabbed their baskets and swiftly walked away.

Eilean was shocked by what they'd done, but anger soon eclipsed her surprise.

The kirtle that she'd borrowed from Critchlow was too tight on her, and she'd been eager for hers to dry so she could change back into it. She was tempted to chase after the girls and smash their baskets over their flower crowns. But there were three of them and only one of her. Still—such behavior was cruel. Learners sometimes pulled tricks on wretcheds, but it was not the way wretcheds should behave toward each other.

Biting down on her fury, she picked up her soiled kirtle and dunked it into the lake and began washing it again. Her anger hadn't cooled by the time she was done. There were wooden rails with lines for hanging the drying clothes, but she didn't dare leave her kirtle there again. After wringing it out, she dumped it into her basket and started back toward the castle. And who did she find on her way?

Captain Hoel. And the three girls.

"But Captain, it's our duty to serve you and the hunters."

"You must let us wash your clothes as well," said another girl. Devious grins slid onto their faces when they noticed Eilean approaching them.

"No, we take care of ourselves," said Hoel impatiently. "I'd flog any of my men who let you do it."

"That's not fair, Captain!"

"Oh please?" one of them said, giving him an innocent look. "We do all the others' clothes anyway."

Eilean refused to look at any of them, feeling a storm of emotions inside her that she could scarcely interpret let alone express.

"Stop pestering me and my men, or I'll see that you're sent back to Holyrood."

"Don't do that!" said one of the girls, taken aback.

"We're sorry, Captain!"

"Truly. We're sorry!"

Eilean stormed past them, grateful to have heard the threat with her own ears. She couldn't hold back a smile as she continued to the castle.

"Eilean! Wait!"

It was Captain Hoel again. She sighed, hugging the basket more closely. When she turned to look at him, she noticed the three washing girls staring at them with surprise and animosity. They made no secret they were listening to their conversation.

"Yes?" she asked.

He looked at her with concern. "How is the druid treating you?"

"As he treats others, no doubt." She felt embarrassed by the girls' scrutiny, but she refused to give them the satisfaction of showing it.

"Has he threatened you?"

"What?" she asked, surprised. "No!"

A look of relief. "Good. Tell me if he does."

One of the girls stuck her tongue out at Eilean. It was all she could do not to return the insult.

"I have work to do," Eilean said, shaking her head.

Hoel nodded and walked off in another direction. As Eilean approached the castle, she saw Mordaunt in the window, gazing down at her.

She went to her room to hang up her kirtle, but there was nowhere she could hang it. If she left it to dry on her blanket, the blanket would be wet when it was time for bed. There was plenty of space in Mordaunt's room, but she didn't know how he'd feel about her hanging laundry there. And she didn't trust it being outside the castle either.

She went into Mordaunt's room and found him still at the window. He turned and noticed her entering with the basket.

"If I may, I need a place to dry my kirtle."

He pursed his lips and gave her a knowing look. "You mean the one the other girls spoiled with mud?"

Her anger flared again. "Yes," she said tightly, gripping the basket hard.

"We could open the window over there, and you could hang it outside. The breeze will dry it faster."

She was surprised by his generosity. "But everyone will see it," she said.

"Ah, and you're in enough trouble with those *pethets* as it is," he answered. "Hang it over the bedpost, then. No one outside will see it hanging there."

"But you will," she said. "I don't want to disturb you."

"It won't. Clothes need to dry. Even mine. And I already told you I rarely use the bed."

"Thank you, sir," she said, walking to the bedside and quickly tossing her kirtle up onto the frame. "At Tintern, another wretched would never have done something like what they done. The cows."

"'Like what they done?' That isn't proper speech. Like they did. That is how you say it. And they aren't cows any more than you are."

She looked at him again, frustration seething within her. "I don't always speak as I ought, but what does it matter?"

"Proper speech matters a great deal, child. Do you think you could serve as a lady's maid if you spoke like a wretched?"

"Reckon not," she whispered, and he flinched.

"A word like 'reckon' gives you away. Stop using it."

He'd cut right to her secret hope with those words. She blinked in surprise and felt a tremor of fear inside her. But with that fear came another strange inkling—if she did manage to become a lady's maid, something unthinkable given her status as a wretched, it wouldn't be enough. "How can I stop saying things everyone says?" she asked incredulously, shocked by the thought as much as his words.

He came toward her. "I am trying to help you, *Ay-Lun*."

"Why?" she asked in challenge.

"Open your imagination, girl. I'm intolerably bored. Besides, if I help you, I stand to benefit. I would no longer have to endure your egregious speech or indecorous colloquialisms. 'Egregious' means *outstandingly bad*. I'm used to serving in the courts of great kings. Your . . . indecorous manner of speaking reminds me of how far I've fallen. 'Indecorous' means *improper*. Not in keeping with good taste. Uncivilized. But I could teach you how to be treated with respect by those petty creatures who defiled your dress. To make *them* do favors and kindnesses to *you*."

Eilean looked at him askance. "They never would."

He arched his eyebrows. "How little you know of the world. Every creature is part of a hierarchy." He flattened his palm and held it low. "Those who are held in contempt." He moved his hand upward. "And those who are given honors. Even the brainless chickens in a barnyard peck at one another to gain status. How far one rises depends on how one speaks and to whom." He made a little hand gesture as he said the words, the flat of his hand rising and pivoting in higher and higher increments. “Those waifs are testing you to see where you fall within the hierarchy of wretcheds. Show them you are already above them.”

Eilean gaped. “How do I do that?” It was the strangest speech she’d ever heard. No one had ever spoken to her in such a way.

“Talk to Captain Hoel.”

“He would tell me how to best the other girls?”

“No! Don’t be ridiculous. All you need to do is to ensure they see you talking to him. Ask him questions and get answers. And they will know that you are already superior to them. Then . . . they will treat you differently.” He gave her a cunning smile.

“What would I ask him?”

Mordaunt chuckled and gestured with his hand and a shrug. “Ask him if this island is safe. Ask him what its weaknesses are. A man like him would relish answering such a question.”

Eilean felt her stomach tighten. Mordaunt was trying to use her already to find out about the weaknesses of Muirwood. Maybe he thought she was the kind of foolish girl who would do his bidding in exchange for a pretty promise.

“I don’t know,” she said uneasily.

“How can you know I spoke the truth if you don’t try it? You will see for yourself. Everything will start to change for you.”

A certain order must be followed in the raising of an abbey. Strong footings are put in, dug deeply into the earth. Then stones are cut at a quarry, each one designed to nest properly with another when sealed with mortar. The maston builders are dedicated to this craft. They carve onto the bottom of each stone a small sigil allowing the stones to be hoisted into the air through the power of the Medium. These sigils are not faces carved into expressions of human emotions. They are directions of obedience. The stones obey the simple commands of the builders. Once in place, they become immovable and fixed.

This knowledge was passed down from an emperor-maston in a previous age. He who built a city of glory, the fame of all the world. And then the city, the entire island, lifted from its foundations and disappeared into a brilliant cloud to rejoin the Essaios of Idumea. They called the city Safehome, the City of Peace. It is the template for which we all strive today.

—Mícheál Nostradamus of Avinion Abbey

CHAPTER SIX

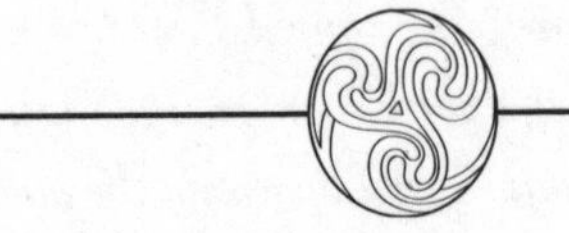

Talisman

Eilean often pondered Mordaunt's advice in the days that followed, but she did not act on it. Her loyalty was to Aldermaston Gilifil, and she doubted he would want her to become the druid's pawn. But the druid's words affected her nonetheless, for she watched with her own eyes as wretcheds from different abbeys vied with each other and formed the very hierarchy he'd warned her about. She overheard the smith scolding the new boys—and one girl—saying they'd learned smithing wrong because they held the hammer differently from him. And the gardener insisting there was only one rational way to prune an orchard. Because of those simple differences, they treated each other differently. The only person to scold Eilean regularly was Mordaunt himself because of her Pry-rian accent. But that didn't make her accent wrong. Only different.

She watched in amazement as the Aldermaston's kitchen went up with remarkable speed. Within a few days, the stone walls had been reared. It had shocked her, at first, seeing the cut stone lifting without the touch of any human hands. But she'd witnessed evidence of the Medium's power throughout her life at Tintern Abbey. Aldermaston Gilifil had once said they should be no less in awe of the Medium's might than they were a tiny seed of flax, which could grow into a stalk, produce a flower, and then become the very clothes that they wore. The Medium was generous in its gifts to the world.

The kitchen was an intriguing design. It had a large square base with rounded corners and rounded supports on each wall. Each face bore a window, positioned too high to be peered into from the ground, and the roof had eight sides, all angled sharply to prevent snow from accumulating on the shake shingles. The facets of the roof converged into a stone cupola that looked like a bell tower, topped with a singular point. She'd overheard one of the builders say that the point was meant to draw the eye to the clouds, in anticipation of the return of Safehome. She didn't understand what that meant, nor did she feel comfortable asking since she'd been listening in.

The exterior complete, the workers had gone inside to finish it, and the master builders had already moved their tools of trade to another part of the grounds. Each day at twilight, Eilean would go inside the kitchen and walk around to see the work that had been done.

She'd heard that the Aldermaston himself was coming soon, that he was traveling with the next group from Tintern to officiate over the ceremony of the laying of the cornerstones of the abbey.

Evening fell on the fourth day. Eilean needed to fetch Mordaunt his supper, but she wanted to visit the new—although still not operational—kitchen again beforehand. The workers had all gone by the time she opened the wooden door. There was no light, save the dim glow from the small arched windows, so she left the door ajar. As she walked through it, running her hand over the cooking tables, sweeping sawdust from them, she imagined Ardys and Loren hanging pans and pots from the iron hooks. There were two enormous ovens in the far corners, easily large enough for a person to step inside, and on a whim she approached one of them and did just that, looking up at the dark flue and listening to the wind whistling through it from outside. Leerings had already been carved into the stone, and the familiar faces heartened her.

The kitchen went darker, and she heard the door close.

Eilean stepped out of the oven, wondering if someone had shut the door as they passed outside. But a feeling of warning in her chest told her that she wasn't alone.

"You're the lass who serves in the castle." The voice came with a very strange and unfamiliar accent.

She searched the bleakness for the source. A shadow darker than the others stood out. A sickly feeling wrenched in her stomach. Then two silver eyes glowed to life near the door, and the intruder—a druid, it had to be—began walking toward her.

Fear knifed into her belly, turning her legs to water and making her want to cry. She braced herself against the stone of the oven wall, feeling the terror blacken her mind.

As he approached, glaring at her with those silver eyers, she saw his dun-colored tunic, frayed and dirty. Her own limbs were locked in place.

When he reached her, he grabbed her arm and squeezed it hard. "You'll take me to him, lass. If you know what's good for you. Take me there now."

Her throat clenched as panicked thoughts collided in her mind. How had he made it to the island undetected by the hunters? Was this the same man she'd seen in the woods during her journey there? She tried to wrest her arm free of his hold, but he was stronger than her, and his glowing eyes revealed a menacing frown. She also saw a bit of twine around his bare neck and the upper edge of a bronze amulet worn beneath his tunic. He smelled of mud and smoke.

She tried to speak but felt a sob come out instead.

"Take me to the druid. Take me to my master!" He squeezed her arm even harder.

Eilean looked away from his terrible glowing eyes. And then her eyes caught on the Leering inside the oven. She stared at the face, the stone pristinely carved and unblemished by soot, and felt a little pulse of peace in her heart.

She met its eyes and invoked its power.

Flames burst from the Leering and swarmed the oven in licking tongues. A blast of heat came with it, and the orange glare brightened and reflected off the smooth stone walls.

"Gorm!" the intruder shouted in alarm.

She wrenched her arm free and ran for the rear doors of the kitchen, the closest exit.

"No!" barked her assailant.

She wrenched at the handle as he grabbed her from behind. He locked his hands and hoisted her off her feet and away from the door. They fought each other, breathing fast and hard, Eilean struggling to escape just as intently as he was attempting to restrain her. He threw her on the ground and pinned her there, clamping his palm against her mouth, but she clawed his face with her nails. He snarled in pain and let go, turning his face away. Another wave of insidious feelings flooded her, but the fire was still burning in the oven, and the flames gave her courage.

Eilean brought her knee up, and suddenly he toppled to the side with a groan of pain. She scrambled to her feet and rushed to the door, managing to yank it open without being accosted this time. Once she was outside, her chest heaving with the rush of emotions, she cried out for help and ran toward the castle.

She hadn't yet made it to the door when one of the abbey hunters reached her, his cloak flapping, his hand on his gladius. Not Hoel, but another man she recognized—Twynho, one of the hunters who had remained behind instead of going back to Tintern. Relief unfurled in her chest. She clutched his tunic with one hand and pointed back to the kitchen.

"In there!"

"What's wrong?" he asked.

"The . . . d-druid! He's in there!"

Twynho put his finger and thumb to his lips and blew out a shrill whistle. Turning toward her, he said, "Wait by the castle door. You're safe now." Then he unsheathed the gladius and started moving.

As Twynho reached the door she'd left, she saw a dark shape emerge from the other side of the building.

"He's fleeing!" she shouted, pointing.

She heard a bowstring twang, and the running figure dropped and began to shriek in pain.

Eilean covered her mouth in surprise but then started to run toward the fallen man. Twynho had heard her warning and come out of the kitchen. They reached the druid at the same time, but not before Captain Hoel did. He held his bow at the ready, another arrow nocked and aimed at the wounded druid, who'd taken an arrow in his leg.

"Turn him over," Hoel said to his companion, still aiming his bow at the man's chest. At such close range, a direct hit would be a given.

Twynho gripped part of the man's tunic and yanked him over onto his back. In the fading light, Eilean saw little more than the man's beard and unkempt hair. The druid bared his teeth in fury, and his eyes went silver again.

"Take the talisman!" Hoel ordered, drawing the bow back. Eilean covered her mouth again, worried she was about to watch a killing.

Twynho dropped to his knee and rifled through the man's tunic, but he wasn't quick enough. A blast of fear struck Eilean, so powerful it made her wet herself. She couldn't stop the rush or do anything other than feel the hot wetness run down her leg.

The hunter fished the medallion from the tunic and yanked it hard, but it didn't break. It did, however, jerk the druid's head back hard enough to daze him. Twynho brought the tip of his gladius up and sliced through the twine. Once it was severed, he tugged the medallion away and held it dangling from his grip.

The glow in the druid's eyes vanished, and he fell back down, groaning in agony. The unnatural fear vanished with it, and the stink of Eilean's clothes rose to her nostrils. She was humiliated.

Twynho handed the medallion to Captain Hoel, who took it with a wrinkled nose and held it away from him. Another hunter came running up to the scene, his bow at the ready.

"Everything all right, Captain?" asked the newcomer.

Eilean backed away, shame burning her cheeks.

"Bring him to the dungeon below the castle," Hoel ordered. "Then fetch a healer and tend to his injury."

"He's a druid, by Cheshu, isn't he?" said the newcomer.

"His tunic is still damp," said Twynho, pressing his palm against the prisoner's chest. He glanced up at Hoel. "He swam here."

"A change of clothes for him too, then," said Hoel. "Don't want him to catch his death. Wait, Eilean."

She had turned and was about to hurry away, but his words stalled her. Her mortification grew as he approached her from behind.

"Did he speak to you?"

Can we not talk about this tomorrow? she nearly said. "Yes."

"What did he say?"

"He wanted me to take him to Mordaunt."

"Where did he find you?"

"The kitchen."

"His face was scratched. Did you do that?"

The memory of the attack rattled inside her, bringing her back to that moment next to the ovens. "Yes. Can I go?"

"Did he use the charm against you? The talisman?" She turned her head and saw him still holding it in his hand. The pattern looked like a three-petaled flower woven around a circle.

"He did." She felt the shame thicken as he studied her. All she could feel was her wet clothes.

"How did you escape?"

"I was by the oven. I summoned the fire Leering."

He blinked and then chuckled. "You can activate a Leering?"

"I'm not the only wretched who can," she said. The Aldermaston had always urged her to keep the extent of her ability to herself, for fear of making the other wretcheds jealous, yet part of her wanted to needle the captain, and she found herself adding, "And why shouldn't we if we can?"

"Why indeed," he answered. "It's not a surprise he attacked tonight. The Aldermaston should arrive tomorrow with the next company."

"I'm grateful to hear it. I should go . . . get . . . Mordaunt his supper." The words tumbled out awkwardly.

He gazed at her, his expression inscrutable at first, then she saw the pity in his eyes. That look told her he knew exactly why she was in a hurry to get away, and her cheeks burned ever hotter. He turned and went back to his men, who were hoisting the druid between them and preparing to carry him to the castle.

She looked up at the upper room of the castle and saw Mordaunt standing at the window, curtain parted, gazing down at them.

In every era since the First Parents partook of the fruit of the tree of knowledge, there have been those who have deliberately spurned the teachings of the maston order. They know the sayings of the tomes by heart, and they recite them to justify their own misguided delusions. These apostates are the most dangerous enemies of the maston order. While the High Seer seeks to unify the kingdoms, factions of apostates aim to break them apart. One Aldermaston in Hautland—Utheros—wrote his blasphemies on shingles of wood and nailed them to his abbey door for all to see. Some of the princes of Hautland condemn him. Some claim he should be elevated to the high seership. The apostates seek only to create schisms, to sow distrust. It is the purpose of the Apocrisarius, which I lead, to hunt down apostates and bring the Medium's justice on them in a trial of fire and faith.

—Mícheál Nostradamus of Avinion Abbey

CHAPTER SEVEN

Words of Power

"You're late, and the food is cold."

Eilean was indeed late in bringing Mordaunt his dinner, for she'd washed her dress to purge the stink from it. And yes, the food was cold for both of those reasons, but she was too jittery from her experience that night to excuse herself. Having delivered his food, she lifted the now empty tray and prepared to leave without saying a single word to him.

He stopped her.

"Wait, child. Don't go."

She clutched the tray to her chest, trying to blink back tears. "I'm not a child."

"Compared to me, everyone is. If you prefer, I will call you sister. Isn't that the way? Sit down. It's dark anyway, and you have nowhere to go but that miserable cell. You are the prisoner more deserving of pity."

"I'm no prisoner," Eilean said, turning around with a flash of anger in her eyes.

His dark eyes flashed as well. "I'm *not* a prisoner," he corrected.

She wanted to smash the tray on his head but resisted, deciding she would hear him out—although she wasn't sure if she should sit on the floor by the fire or join him at the table. He'd never invited her before.

"Sit," he prodded, nodding toward the chair, and again she had the strange suspicion that he could somehow read her thoughts.

Eilean obeyed and let out a sigh as she lowered herself into the chair. He picked up the knife and began to carve into the cold meat pie. He chewed it noisily, and the smell of onions, garlic, and crushed dill wafted to her, making her own stomach growl in protest. She hadn't fetched any food for herself because she'd been so frantic. But now that her muscles were starting to ease, she felt the prodding of hunger. With his strong hands, the druid wrenched the bread in half and set one part in front of her.

"I saw a commotion outside," he said after chewing some of the bread's fluffy innards. "A man was captured?"

"He was a druid," Eilean said, looking at him coldly. The shame of wetting herself still stung.

"That's hardly a surprise, you know. When the Aldermaston comes and other safeguards are put up to protect the abbey, it will be impossible for someone like that to enter the grounds."

"I should hope so, by Cheshu."

"By Cheshu," he snorted. "Another Pry-rian term no doubt."

"He attacked me," Eilean said, her feelings finally bursting out. Her voice was shaking.

Mordaunt turned serious. "I'm sorry, Eilean." He sawed another piece of the pie and ate it. "Was he trying to get to me?"

She nodded and wiped a stray tear that had fallen down her cheek, her eyes gazing into the flames dancing within the brazier. "His eyes glowed silver." She looked at him. "Can yours do that?"

He met her gaze. "No."

"Because you don't have your talisman?" she said, feeling like shouting but restraining herself.

"Druids use their talismans to commune with ancient spirit creatures, who in turn use their magic to benefit them. The help is freely offered and freely accepted. No compulsion. But there are other druids . . ." His voice trailed off, but it had grown harder, as if he were warning her. "They use their talismans to commune with the Unborn. You know of the Myriad Ones, do you not?"

"Yes," she answered, stifling a shudder. "We're taught to fear them. I . . . I do."

"As you should. They would seek to take over your body, *if they could*, to make you a puppet for their evil thoughts. You faced one of the dark druids. I'm glad you were unharmed."

"He called you *master*," she said, giving him an arch look. She couldn't pretend, not tonight.

Mordaunt set down his knife and fork. "That does not make it so. The dark druids wanted to capture me as well," he said, "but the mastons got to me first. I'm not a dark druid, Eilean. I fight against them."

She tilted her head. "How can I believe anything you say?"

He chuckled with contempt. "You can't. You shouldn't. But I'm sorry you were attacked. The Myriad Ones cannot enter this castle, so they had to rely on a man, a person, to do their bidding. How did you escape him?"

She'd already told Captain Hoel, so it hardly mattered if she told Mordaunt. "He followed me into the kitchen, the new one they built, and I summoned fire into the oven. That startled him."

"It's unusual for a wretched to be able to command a Leering," he told her.

"Not in Pry-Ree," she shot back.

"Interesting." He made a *hmph* sound, then said, "You said you know how to read, Eilean. Let me draw a word and see if you can name it."

He rose from the chair, his meal half-eaten, and went to the brazier. He took a smaller log from the stack in the woodpile, dipped the end into the soot and ashes, and ground it in. The log caught fire, but he drew it out and blew out the flame. He held the smoking tip out, showing it to her, and then crouched on the floor and began to trace some symbols with the soot.

Eilean rose from her chair to watch him. She didn't recognize any of the characters, which more closely resembled squares and triangles than the alphabet she knew.

"What language is that?" she asked him. He'd drawn maybe four different letters, or perhaps fewer since she wasn't entirely sure where one ended and the next began.

"The language is Idumean," he said, turning his head and looking up at her as she gazed down at the symbols. Each one was about as large as his hand. The smell of the soot was strong.

He wagged the stick at her.

"What does it say," she asked.

"Gheb-ool," he said. As he spoke the word, she felt a chill go down her arms, making the hair stand on end. It felt like the Medium did when the Leerings were working, but the feeling faded quickly, like a spasm in her heart that slowly unclenched.

"Did you feel something?" he asked her.

She was worried but also intrigued. "Yes."

A smile lifted the corners of his mouth. "The word means *border*, a boundary. Say it."

"Border."

His eyebrows knitted. "No, say the word I taught you."

"Gebool," she answered. Nothing happened.

He shook his head. "Say it *properly*. Precisely. With the proper respect and emotion. This word will provide you with protection. Defense. A boundary no one can cross to touch you. *Gheb-ool.*" When he said it again, she felt the same tingling down her arms.

She swallowed and repeated the word. *"Gheb-ool."* This time, she felt a zing all the way down to her toes.

Mordaunt nodded. "Excellent. You felt it, didn't you? You felt when you did it properly."

Excitement and fear mingled inside her. "I did."

He took the stick and drew another series of markings, different from the first. *"Kozkah,"* he said, his voice as rich and powerful as if he were addressing a king. She felt another pulse from the Medium. "That Idumean word means *strength*. Force. Even violence. A king must maintain his power through violence. Such is the world. He cannot show weakness, only strength. *Kozkah.* Say it. Mean it."

Her mouth went dry. Was it wrong to learn from the druid? Would it corrupt her?

It didn't *feel* wrong. Perhaps this was even what the Aldermaston intended.

"Kozkah," she said, getting it right the first time. A sensation of strength swelled in her, rising like the sun, but it faded again just as quickly.

"Put them together. 'Strong border.' Say them together, just as they are written here."

Eilean felt confident she could. *"Kozkah gheb-ool,"* she said. It was as if she'd shoved Mordaunt away. He tumbled backward from her, dropping the stick in the process, and his eyes widened with surprise. Then he started to laugh.

"You are no *pethet*," he said with triumph as he slowly made it back to his feet. "Well done. Well said. The language of Idumea contains words of power."

She felt the tingling sensation fade, and a weariness came over her. Exhaustion so powerful she began to sway where she stood.

"To the chair, come on," he said, coming forward and helping her to sit down. Then he seated himself across from her, clasping his hands together. "If someone tries to attack you again, just remember those words. Use them with reverence. If you toy with them, the Medium will warn you. If you persist, it will forsake you. Use them only in grave situations. Like tonight."

"Thank you," she said, amazed at what she'd done. What her words had accomplished.

"I'm no longer hungry," he said, pushing the plate toward her. "You eat the rest." He rose from the table and smeared the words he'd written with his shoe until they were nothing more than a stain.

Eilean ate the rest of her bread and devoured his dinner, even though there was too much onion in it. She missed Ardys's cooking very much. Her pumpkin bread was particularly delicious, and Eilean wanted to share it with Mordaunt to repay him for his kindness. But perhaps she was being naïve—he surely had his own reasons for showing her kindness. Well, if the druid thought he could turn her against the Aldermaston, he would be disappointed.

The weariness was growing worse. She crossed her arms and let her head rest on them.

And promptly fell asleep.

***

Fingers poked her in the back and then shook her shoulder. "Wake, child. The Aldermaston has arrived."

Eilean lifted her head, blinking at the sunlight streaming in through the window curtains. She'd slept all night at the table. She still wore the clinging dress she'd changed into, still sat in front of the tray and empty dish. A few bread crumbs littered the table. Mordaunt stepped away from her and returned to the window, flicking aside the curtain to gaze down below.

She noticed her gown had been hung up to dry by the brazier, and panic seized her. Hurrying to her feet, she rose from the table.

"How did you leave the room to get my dress?" she asked him, wondering why the Leering hadn't stopped him.

Still facing away from her, looking out the window, he said, "The Leering prevents me from leaving the castle, not the room. Do you remember the words I taught you last night?"

Kozkah gheb-ool. She didn't say them aloud, but she still felt the tingling sensation shoot down her arms.

"Yes."

"The Leering gains its power from those very words, although not even the lapidaries who made it understood what they were doing. It has made a strong boundary." He turned and looked at her. "Even if the dark druid had come here, even if he'd tried to drag me out by force, the Leering would have stopped me from going and stopped him from taking me. I cannot leave this place without the Aldermaston's permission. When they've set the other boundary Leerings, ask him if he will extend my prison. I would like to walk the grounds if I may. With his permission."

He had been cooped up in the castle for who knew how long. Yes, she imagined he was sick of his room and the castle walls.

"I'll ask him," she said. "But I donna think he'll agree." The improper word slipped out too soon, which tended to happen when she was upset.

"I don't think," he corrected. More gently this time.

She licked her lips, collected her gown, which was dry now, and took the tray with her on her way out.

Back in her room, she quickly changed and then hurried downstairs. The castle was in an uproar of excitement about Aldermaston Gilifil's arrival. She deposited the tray in the interior kitchen and found the steward, Critchlow, pacing with eagerness.

"Is he here?" she asked him, smiling brightly.

He nodded. "He's with Captain Hoel right now, but he'll be out soon. The others have arrived as well. This is a banner day, I tell you. A banner one!"

Eilean went out the back door of the castle and saw the kitchen door had already been thrown open. A few young men, including Aisic, were carrying crates into it.

"Aisic!" she called.

When he turned and saw her, a grin lit his face, which was pockmarked from mosquito bites. He looked tired and weary, but it was the first time she'd gotten a genuine smile from him since that day she'd worked the harvest with him. Like he was happy to see her. Something lit up inside her. She followed him into the kitchen and nearly started sobbing when she saw Ardys standing on a chair hanging pots from the iron racks.

"Eilean!" shrieked her friend Celyn, stepping out from behind some crates. The two embraced and started crying as they cushed each other. Their reunion lightened something Eilean hadn't realized was heavy. "I've missed you so!"

"You're here, you're finally here! I was so lonely," Eilean said, pulling back slightly. She lifted a hand to one of the welts on her friend's face. "I see the bugs took a liking to you."

"*Shaw*, they wouldn't leave me be."

Ardys climbed down from the chair and came and embraced them both. "Look at this fine place they made for us! It's clean as whiskers! Let's work hard and keep it that way."

After cushing Ardys and Loren together, Eilean turned and saw that Aisic had left again. But he reappeared before long with another crate, his arm muscles bulging from the weight of it in a way that drew her attention.

"Where do you want this one?" he called out to Ardys.

"On that table, over there," Ardys answered.

"I'll help," Eilean volunteered and went to grab the other end of the crate.

"I've got it," Aisic said, rebuffing her. He grimaced and heaved it over to the table. When it settled, she heard the thud of iron and realized it had a cauldron—or two—in it. She left the kitchen to help the others bring in more supplies but hadn't made it more than a few steps before Twynho called her name and waved for her to come to him. "The Aldermaston wants to see you," he said.

Eilean had wanted to prove to Aisic she could carry heavy things too—the same way she'd labored by his side in the fields that day—but it would have to wait. She followed Twynho to the castle, glancing back once to watch Aisic walking with the others.

When they reached the Aldermaston's study, the door stood open, Critchlow standing within the frame. He noticed her approach.

"Ah, she's here. I'll wait until you have need of me, Aldermaston. There is so much to discuss with the building."

"Of course," said the Aldermaston patiently. "Come in, Eilean. Thank you, Twynho. You may go."

She stepped inside, and the hunter shut the door behind her. The Aldermaston stood in front of some leather-bound chests. A tome had been set down on one of them, suggesting that he'd been reading it recently. Perhaps before Critchlow's enthusiastic visit.

In the Aldermaston's presence, her worries and concerns began to ebb.

"I'm interested in meeting the druid of the castle," he said, gazing at her. "I'd like to get your opinion of him first."

"He is as rude as we were told to expect. You weren't wrong. But he taught me, just last night, two words of power from the Idumean language."

The Aldermaston's eyebrows shot up. "Truly? Which ones? Can you write them?"

She shook her head. "I've never seen that kind of writing before, Aldermaston, but I recall the words. 'Strength' and 'boundary.' I sensed the Medium as I heard them and as I said them. It felt . . . natural."

He rubbed his reddish beard with the gray streaks in it. "Has he taught you anything else?"

She nodded quickly and began to relate his explanation for why the various wretcheds were chopsy with one another, always arguing and trying to prove themselves. She spoke hastily and tripped over her words at times, but she shared everything with him, even Mordaunt's suggestion that she talk to Captain Hoel to make the other girls jealous of her.

"I didn't act on his advice," she confessed. "I felt it would be . . . disloyal. To you."

The Aldermaston nodded in sympathy. "Do you trust me, Eilean? Do you trust the Medium?"

"I do, Aldermaston. I truly do."

He walked toward her. "Then listen carefully. I want you to give the impression you are on his side. Show some pity on him. Show appreciation for what he's taught you. This may give us an opportunity to recover the tome he stole. Don't ask about it, for that will make him suspicious. If you show you are a quick learner, which I know from experience you are, he may confide in you. Share it with me, always. Earn his trust. You are doing the Medium's will. I can feel it. Can't you?"

Excitement lit within her. She *did* feel that way. "I'm worried, Aldermaston, that he can tell my thoughts. Sometimes I've thought things, and then he's spoken about something very similar. I don't think I can fool him."

He shook his head. "You're not fooling anyone, Eilean. I want you to be sincerely interested. If I'm reading you correctly, you already are interested. Remember, he's an apostate from the maston order who became a druid by choice. I highly doubt he can discern your thoughts, but he knows how you've been raised. He's highly intelligent, and he is intentionally making you doubt yourself. He's manipulating you. As long as you're aware of the intention, he cannot succeed. If you begin to doubt anything, come speak to me. If he asks you to do something you feel is wrong, come speak to me. We are partners in this, Eilean. I suspect the Medium chose you because you are the one who will bring him back to the true light."

His words filled her with purpose and determination. "I won't fail you, Aldermaston."

He touched her cheek tenderly. "I know it, Eilean."

"He did ask for permission to leave the castle. When you set the boundary Leerings, he'd like to be able to walk the grounds."

The Aldermaston pursed his lips. "Not yet. But maybe soon. If he teaches you more."

Do you suppose there is any living man so unreasonable that if he found himself stricken with a dangerous ailment, he would not anxiously desire the blessing of health? The Medium can provide Gifts of Healing through a maston ritual, but it only happens in conjunction with the Medium's will. Not every illness should be healed. Not every injury either. There are many lessons to be learned in suffering. We would never learn to be brave if all evils were removed by the asking.

—Mícheál Nostradamus of Avinion Abbey

CHAPTER EIGHT

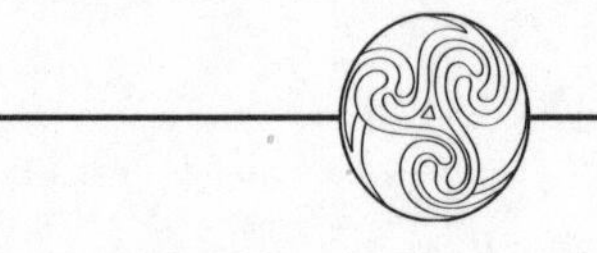

The Sweating Sickness

The world had changed around Eilean in the fortnight following Aldermaston Gilifil's arrival at Muirwood. She'd watched in awe as boundary Leerings diminished the lake surrounding the island, exposing the marshy land beneath. The wet earth was then tilled and sown with flax seeds in a meadow, even though it was later in the season than usual. A series of boulders had been revealed beneath the water, along with a vein of stone that could be used in the construction of the abbey itself, and work crews began quarrying the building materials. A huge pit was already underway, in preparation for the placing of the cornerstones.

Eilean had accepted the Aldermaston's assignment with eagerness, and each day brought new lessons and stories from Mordaunt. He was an apt teacher and she an eager learner, and she began to change her manner of speech in keeping with his corrections.

She saw Aisic every day, although there wasn't often an opportunity to speak to him. He was part of the pit crew, digging away at the earth to create a foundation for the abbey. The cracking and crashing of stone rang through the air, interspersed with metallic clangs from the blacksmith's forge as tools worn down and broken from the constant work were repaired.

At the end of the fortnight, after another day of hard toil by the workers, she went to the Aldermaston's kitchen to see her friends and get the evening meal for Mordaunt. She'd passed the pit and seen Aisic laboring in the depths, but her heart had sunk when he didn't look up.

Inside the kitchen, which had transformed now, she paused in the doorway and gazed at the neatly organized barrels and sacks and sausages hanging from hooks, thinking of the druid's attack. It felt so long ago now, with the scent of baking bread wafting through the air. She approached Ardys and Loren, who were finishing up a massive meat pie, both of them dusted with flour, but there was no sign of Celyn.

Although they couldn't spend as much time together now as when they'd both worked in the kitchens, they made a point of seeing each other several times a day. They'd toured the grounds together, counted what she had learned were apple trees in the orchards, and watched the progress of the abbey. But she hadn't seemed herself yesterday, and Eilean had urged her to get to bed early.

"I don't see Celyn about," Eilean said. "Where is she?"

A worried look came to Ardys's face. "I sent her to the healer earlier this afternoon. She took a sudden turn. She's not feeling well."

Eilean's stomach twisted in concern. "I'll go check on her," she said. Although she'd come down to fetch Mordaunt's supper, it was obvious it wouldn't be ready for some time.

"Thank you. I was going to visit myself, but we have to finish this pie. We're already behind."

Loren gave Eilean a nod to go, and she left the kitchen. She hadn't adjusted to the changed terrain. It felt as if the lake should still be there, but all that was left of it was a pond for the laundry girls, fed by a water Leering. A small roof had been installed to shade the wretcheds from the heat of the sun.

Eilean passed the pit again on her way to the healer's tent. Noise from the bottom attracted her attention, and she noticed some of the laundry girls had gathered at the edge. Then came the sound of a fist smacking flesh. Hurrying to the edge of the pit, she saw two young men holding Aisic by the arms while a third punched him in the stomach. A streak of crimson spurted from his nose already, revealing he'd been the victim of the earlier blow.

Her stomach fell as she watched the fight. Three on one wasn't a fair number. She looked around for one of the master builders, but none were around—they'd probably left work for the day.

Aisic pulled himself up and kicked at his attacker, but the blow missed, and it earned him another fist to the face. His head jerked back and he slumped, his legs no longer supporting his weight.

"Stop it!" Eilean yelled down at them.

Her warning alerted the laundry girls to her presence, and they started to snicker at her. The boys holding Aisic's arms let go, and he flopped to the ground, moaning slightly. The boy who'd punched him kicked his shoulder, and then the three of them clambered up the ladder to where Eilean stood. Their tunics were filthy from the dirt and mud they'd worked in all day.

The ringleader, or the one who looked to be in charge, gave her a disdainful look as he and his companions walked by. The laundry girls hustled up to them.

"He was the brawest wretched from Tintern," one of the girls said in a respectful tone.

"The bigger the tree, the harder the crash when it falls," answered the ringleader with a chopsy grin. He spoke the common speech of Moros, but with an accent she couldn't pinpoint. Was it from Paeiz? She'd been learning about different accents from Mordaunt.

She gave the ringleader a withering look and hurried down the ladder. Aisic was still groaning when she reached him. He was on his knees now, dirt smeared into the blood on his face and the sweat on his neck. He looked like he'd been dragged across the bottom of the pit.

She didn't know what to do or say, but she grabbed his arm to help him stand.

He looked dazed still, but when he twisted his neck and saw her, an expression of shame came to his eyes.

"I'm going to the healer," she told him. "Let me help you."

He jerked his arm away from her. "No!" he barked. He made it to his feet on his own power, swiped his bloody nose against his sleeve, and looked at the smear. From the way he held his other arm, cinched close to his side, she suspected his ribs pained him too.

She winced. "You're hurt."

"I'll be fine," he sniped.

"It was three against one," she said, feeling awkward but determined to show him that she cared. "That wasn't fair."

"When is life fair?" he shot back. "Just . . . leave me be."

He went to the ladder and climbed out of the pit, leaving her at the bottom. She felt awful for him, but his rejection still stung. She'd have tended him, wiped blood from his face, gotten him a drink. Anything. But he'd refused. He didn't want *her* help.

Unsure what to make of her conflicting feelings, she waited until he was off the ladder before she climbed up herself. When she reached the top, she noticed Captain Hoel standing at the edge, watching her, a bemused look on his face.

Anger kindled inside her, hot and unexpected. He wasn't that far away, so she walked up to him, feeling her cheeks burn.

"Did you see the fight in the pit?" she asked him.

"It wasn't much of one, but yes."

That made her even more furious. "Why didn't you stop it?"

His brow wrinkled a little. "I wouldn't dream of it."

"Why not?"

"That is the way of boys becoming men," he answered. "The same kind of squabbling happens everywhere, whether they're knights, farmers, or rat catchers. It's a competition of sorts. A ranking."

"So it happens among hunters as well?" Eilean demanded, trying to keep from shouting at him. He had a lofty way of speaking given he was only barely older than them. Besides, his answer didn't make it right. Three against one!

"Of course," he said. "Though there are *other* ways of earning respect."

"You should have broken up the fight. It wasn't fair."

His eyes crinkled. "Or *maybe* the lad from Tintern should have watched his tongue," he said, lifting his eyebrows in a way that suggested there'd been more to the fight than Eilean had known.

It felt like a cool breath had been blown on her fire. "I didn't see what started it."

He gave her a measured look, one she couldn't hope to read, and then started away.

"Captain Hoel," she called.

He stopped and looked at her inquisitively.

"He wanted to join you and your hunters."

"I know that, Eilean."

Her brow creased. "Why didn't you accept him? Because he's a wretched?"

"Cimber was a wretched too. That makes no difference to me."

Cimber was one of the hunters who'd escorted Eilean's group to Muirwood. She'd had no idea he'd been raised a wretched.

"So why didn't you choose him?"

"He's ambitious but not patient. And patience is vital to what we do. Much of the work is drudgery. Boys like him only see the arrows and blades. You'd be a far better hunter than he."

Something in his voice, a thread of iron, assured her that he wasn't mocking her. He was serious. And, out of nowhere, she found herself wondering if Captain Hoel had asked the Aldermaston for permission to train her. She wanted to ask but didn't have the courage to do so. Because why would Hoel have wanted to train *her*?

"What happened to the druid you caught?" she asked, wanting to change the subject, worried she'd come across as being clean off. "What's to become of him?"

She'd wondered these last weeks but hadn't asked.

"He's still in the dungeon for now," Hoel answered. "Trying to decide whether he wants to be useful or endure a trial by fire without a talisman." His lips quirked into a smirk. "I think the worry is starting to break him. Then he can lead us to the others."

"Would you really kill him, Captain? Or is it just a threat?"

The smirk faded. "I don't make threats, Eilean. Only promises."

Then he turned and walked away, his cloak ruffling in the breeze. She felt a shudder course through her, and was struck by the sense that he was a very dangerous man. When she turned the other way to go to the healer's tent, she saw one of the laundry girls standing in the distance, watching her. She'd been watching as Eilean talked with Hoel. Then she remembered Mordaunt's advice—he'd encouraged her to do exactly as she'd done, telling her it would change her status among the wretcheds.

Must everything be a competition, though? A game of reputation?

She remembered Celyn again and hurried toward the healer's massive tent. When she arrived, she was surprised to find many people inside, lying on hay-stuffed pallets, two to a bed.

A young wretched approached her, dressed in a gray-brown gown with a pale blue apron and matching headscarf. "Are you hurt?"

"No, I want to see Celyn," Eilean answered.

"She's very sick," the girl said, her words making Eilean's heart lurch. "Come this way." They came around one of the side partitions, and Eilean bit back a gasp when she found Celyn shivering and sweating beneath a wool blanket.

"What's wrong with her?" she asked in horror.

"She's got the sweating sickness. Several came down with it crossing the Bearden Muir."

Eilean had never heard of the sweating sickness before. It wasn't something that happened typically at Tintern Abbey. She looked at her friend in concern, taking in her clammy skin and her pale lips. "But she's been here for a fortnight."

"Aye, but the sweating sickness usually doesn't start until after a fortnight."

"How long will she be sick?"

"It could be a while," said the girl with a sympathetic frown. "Some never get better."

"Eilean?" whispered a weary voice from the blanket.

Eilean dropped to her knees and put a hand on Celyn's chest. Her heart quailed as she took in her friend's violent shudders beneath the blanket. "Ardys and Loren are worried about you."

Celyn's teeth were rattling. "I'm . . . not much . . . help right now."

"You'll get better, I promise," she said. "I'll ask the Aldermaston to give you a Gift of Healing."

"T-thank you, Eilean. I'm so c-cold."

Eilean touched her forehead and found it wet with sweat and burning. "I'm sorry you're sick. Yesterday you seemed off, but this came on so suddenly."

"Yes. I didn't feel well this morning, but in the afternoon I was s-sweeping, and suddenly I felt so tired . . . Everything makes me tired."

"You're going to get better," Eilean said firmly. "You have to. I won't accept anything less."

"You're a good friend," Celyn said, trying to smile, but her look of suffering quickly returned.

Glancing up at the other girl, Eilean asked, "What can you give her?"

"Valerianum to help her sleep. That's about all. She's not the only one who has it. But if you know the Aldermaston, maybe he can come and bless all of them?"

"I'll talk to him," she said with determination.

The other girl walked away, and Eilean stayed with Celyn awhile and sought to distract her by telling her of the fight she'd seen inside the pit.

"P-poor Aisic," Celyn said. "They bloodied him up bad?"

"He refused to come here. Wouldn't even let me help him."

"You're kind for trying." Celyn shuddered again, the force of it sending another chill through Eilean. In her head, she heard the other wretched saying *some never recover*, the words repeating again and again.

"I wish there was something more I could do for you."

"Just be with me. That's enough."

It was getting darker, and she knew Mordaunt would be wanting his meal. But she wouldn't rush her visit. Celyn was hurting.

Still, she didn't tell her friend about her conversation with Captain Hoel. Or the strange thought that had come to her mind.

It couldn't have been a whisper from the Medium.

Some people live in a dream world, and others face reality, and then there are still others who turn one into the other. One of these was the Emperor-Maston of Hyksos. He ruled a coastal kingdom, a trading nation, that grew in power and fame—and corruption. The wealth of his people filled them with pride, and they turned their backs on the poor, the widowed, and the wretched. Dignitaries came from Paeiz, Mon, and Avinion to curry favor with this mighty emperor, yet he was too tortured by the suffering of his people to treat with them. Though he led by example, it didn't change the hearts of his people. Some of his advisors mocked him, calling him foolish and naïve and saying men and women are greedy by nature and will prey on one another. They said he lived in a dream world where all was fair and just and no one ever starved. But it did *change. The people in the city, eventually even those advisors, became one in thought, one in emotion, one in wealth—Safehome. And then the island rose into the sky and fled this world to join a better one—Idumea. What changed this emperor-maston and allowed him to harness the Medium in ways that had never been considered? Those who know the story could tell you. It started with a woman. A harbinger.*

—Mícheál Nostradamus of Avinion Abbey

CHAPTER NINE

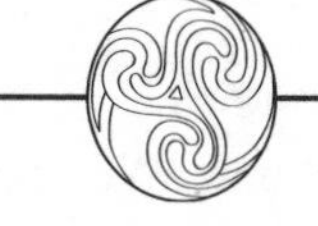

A King's Desire

"You are late again, sister. Is not diligence one of the virtues of the Medium? Were you distracted in your duties?"

Eilean couldn't tell whether Mordaunt was chiding her. She set the tray of food down on the table in front of him, but he didn't even look at it. His gaze was fixed on her. Although she didn't like being late, she was more worried about Celyn's sickness than she was about pleasing the druid.

"My friend is doing bad," she answered, then began tidying the room. Mordaunt seemed to delight in moving things around while she was gone, presumably so he could then watch her right them. A blanket tossed on the floor. Two weather-beaten shoes across the room from each other. The stack of wood by the brazier knocked over.

"You torture me with your speech at times. Is she evil or is she unwell?"

"She's very sick," Eilean said while folding the blanket.

"Describe what ails her. A sour stomach? Was she injured?"

"She's got a fever and chills. Even under the blanket she was shaken something awful."

"Shak*ing*," he corrected.

Eilean set the blanket down at the foot of the bed and started to sort the wood, feeding some logs into the coals at the bottom of the brazier. "The healer said she fell sick while crossing the Bearden Muir. But she was fine when she got here."

"It's the sweating sickness, then."

"I've not heard of it until now. Will she get better?"

"Most do," Mordaunt said with unconcern. "She will be weak for a while, a fortnight perhaps. But I won't lie to you—the sweating sickness is not to be taken lightly. I've seen it kill before."

His words made her stomach clench with dread. "I'm going to talk to the Aldermaston," she said. "I promised I would. She needs a Gift of Healing."

Mordaunt's eyes narrowed slightly. "He won't do it, sister."

Eilean stared at him in surprise. "*Shaw*, why do you say that? He's not unfeeling."

He closed his eyes and shuddered. That bit of slang particularly bothered him. Then he shrugged and picked up his fork. "Maybe you're right, Eilean."

His words had disturbed her. Aldermaston Gilifil was a kindhearted man—he cared about the wretcheds. The room brightened noticeably once the logs caught fire, but Eilean lit a candle anyway and brought it to the table.

"Who was the young man you tended in the pit?" Mordaunt asked, sawing off a piece of roasted pheasant with his knife.

So he *had* seen that. He was always watching from the windows.

"He's from Tintern. I . . . I knew him there."

"Not very popular, it seems."

"None of his friends were chosen to come here," she said defensively. "Three other men punched and kicked him. The awful brutes."

"I told you that would happen." He set down the fork after thoroughly chewing the last piece of meat, then wiped his mouth on the linen napkin. It was strange seeing him eat so politely with the fading woad tattoos on his face and neck. Sometimes she didn't even notice them, but tonight they seemed to glare at her. She'd always been taught that only a savage would mark his face so.

"But why? They all have to work together, so why beat on one another like that? Just because he's new?"

"They did it exactly because he's new." The druid gave her a cunning smile. "I've told you, even the barnyard chickens peck at one another. They'll even kill one of their own."

She put her hands on her hips. "But why?"

"Why does the sun rise from those hills and then set over these?" he asked, stretching his arm one way and then the other. "Why do the apple trees blossom before bearing fruit? Even *kings* act this way. Look no further than King Aengus of Moros, whom I once served as advisor. Even *he* acted this way until a stronger bird, the High Seer of Avinion, came strutting and pecking and showed him *she* was the more powerful foe. And he submitted instead of getting his eyes pecked out."

His voice gained intensity with each word, flooded with a feeling she couldn't identify. What was it—resentment? Anger?

"Is that the only choice, then?" she asked. "Submit or be maimed?"

"You are intrigued?"

She was. She'd always been fascinated by the nobility. Visitors were rare at Tintern—they usually only came when dropping off their sons and daughters to learn at the abbey. No one of note had come to Muirwood since her arrival as there would be no learners until the abbey was built.

"I would like to learn . . . if you're willing to teach me."

"Sit, then," he offered, gesturing with his palm to the chair opposite him.

There was still more work to be done, but she obeyed him.

"Long ago, a high king used to rule these shores. Aengus and his neighbors were constantly competing to claim that title. King Aengus spent many years at war, fighting for placement. Some challenged his authority. Some his strength. Each challenge made him stronger and brought him more respect. More men bent the knee. Think on that, Eilean. It takes a lot to get one man to willingly promise obedience to another."

"How did he convince them?"

"By showing a measure of mercy and ruthlessness. His lack of consistency altered the game of chance, you see. If he'd always shown mercy, they would have perceived him as weak. Too harsh, and he'd be a tyrant whom everyone would work together to depose. Most kings who win their great seats cannot pass their power down to their children."

Eilean wrinkled her brow. "Why is that?"

He steepled his fingers. "There was a king long ago, in a faraway land. He had a rival who was his equal in power and ambition. The kingdom was divided between them, and neither could defeat the other." His eyes glittered as if the memory was close to him, one of his own, not just a tale he was telling.

She leaned forward. "What happened?"

"They knew they'd destroy each other if the rivalry continued. If two wolves are equal in strength, they may destroy each other. And so the two kings decided to make a truce—they would divide the land between them equally. A feast was proclaimed to celebrate, and both kings came to attend."

Eilean stared at him with interest. In her mind, she could imagine such a feast—the roaring fire with animals roasting on spits. The clink of goblets and lilting music of bards playing lutes and pipes. The bright pops of color from the courtiers' outfits.

"But one king had what the other had not. A beautiful wife. Amidst the revelry, the king commanded his wife to dance before the hall. He did it deliberately, flaunting her beauty in his enemy's face. She was part of the connivance."

She wrinkled her brow. "I don't know that word."

"'Connivance' means *trickery*. His enemy was so fired up with lust that the truce ended before it began. He tried to take what belonged to the other man. Betrayal ruins trust. It leads to drawn blades and, finally, howls of murder. You see, the unmarried king had a Wizr, one who had great power."

Eilean tilted her head. "What is a *wiser*?"

"It is not a word you hear in these lands. It would be considered heresy. A Wizr is one who knows the words of power. The ancient tongue of Idumea."

She stared at him.

His eyes seemed to lose their focus on her. He looked to the table, his shoulders starting to slump. "Desire is a powerful motivator, child. As you know from being raised at an abbey, that which we conceive in thought and marry to desire becomes *real*. Unfortunately, most lack the will to persist. They quit too soon. But for those who do not, the Medium provides the harvest. Even if it isn't good for us. The lesson is there for us to learn, but if the point must be made again and again and the subject is particularly stubborn, the Medium might cut them off, like it did with your Aldermaston."

"What happened to the kings?"

"While they were warring against each other, the lusty king commanded his Wizr to put a spell on him. One that would make him *look* and *sound* like his enemy."

"Shaw!" Eilean gasped.

Mordaunt chuckled. *"Mareh,"* he whispered. She watched as his features changed, his hair becoming a reddish gray and a beard sprouting on his face. In an instant, he looked like Aldermaston Gilifil. But it lasted only as long as a breath.

She stared at him open-mouthed, feeling the Medium tingle down her arms as she gaped at him.

"One word was all it took. The Wizr warned him not to use it. He prophesied the disaster that would come. But the lusty king stole his enemy's wife for one night. And on that night, her husband, who had been preparing for battle, was killed in an ambush." Sadness filled his tone. "She conceived that night. And her kingdom was about to be destroyed, so she sought the favor of her enemy, the man she hated. He did not tell her that the child in her womb was his." Gently, he pushed the plate away.

Eilean felt a strange pulse of excitement. Although he hadn't said so, she felt sure that Mordaunt was the Wizr in the tale.

"He married her?"

"Aye, lass. He did, and she loathed him. And when her son was born, he told her the truth of it, that the babe was his all along. The truth always comes out, usually when it is the least convenient. She hired a kishion to kill her husband and her child."

Eilean gaped once more. "A kishion? Those are murderers!"

He shrugged. "But the Wizr stole the child before it could be slaughtered. And hid it in a castle pigpen as a wretched of sorts." He smiled at her. "Do you not find that strange?"

Her heart churned with feelings. "What kingdom was this?" she asked him.

He chuckled softly. "That's another story. For another time."

"Is the child still a wretched? Does he know his father was a king?"

"Another time, sister. It's getting late, and you've not had your supper yet."

Her mind whirling with the tale, she gazed at him, firm in the belief that it wasn't just a story. "Tell me more," she pleaded.

"You've an unhealthy fascination in such tales, child." His look was approving, though.

"I've always wanted to be a lady's maid," she confessed. "So I could hear my fill of stories. At Tintern, we heard so little about the world around us. Here . . . much more."

"You could *be* a lady, Eilean. If you could but control that tongue of yours."

"Now you are having me on," she said with a burst of laughter. "Me? A wretched?"

"Stranger things have happened. There was once an urchin who lived on the streets of Antimo in Paeiz. When she was a desperate, hungry young woman, she stole from a nobleman. His servants caught her, and instead of flogging her, he carved a likeness of her into a Leering. Everyone demanded to know whom he had used for the sculpture, but he would not say the truth, only that she was a lady. They insisted he produce the evidence, but he said she was away. He bought her new clothing and taught her to speak like an upper-class woman, and when she 'returned' from abroad, she convinced everyone she was of noble birth. She became a duchess, I tell you." He grinned and laughed heartily. "It is more honorable, my dear, to be *raised* to a throne than to be born to one. Fortune bestows the one, merit obtains the other."

She was about to say *"shaw"* again, but caught herself before it left her tongue. His words had fired her imagination. One could be raised to a throne? Even someone like her?

Surely that couldn't be true?

"It's a true story, I assure you," he said. "I met the sculptor who did the trick. Sadly, he fell in love with the very woman he'd elevated, and his feelings were not returned." His look began to darken again, another memory that tormented him.

"I should go see the Aldermaston before he goes to bed," Eilean said.

"After you ask him to heal your friend, ask him again if he will let me wander the grounds. Seeing the fruit swelling in the apple orchard from afar is acute torture. I should be grateful for even a small jaunt about the castle."

"I will, but I can't promise anything. The last time I asked, he forbade it," she said.

Mordaunt sighed. "I am patient."

She wasn't sure how much of that statement was true. After rising from the table, she stacked his dirty plates on the tray and brought them downstairs. The castle was quiet and dim, and she realized she'd been up talking to the druid for a while. She found Critchlow walking down the hall with a candle in hand.

"Master Critchlow!" she called.

"Yes? Oh, it's you. What is it, Eilean? Why aren't you abed?"

"Is the Aldermaston awake?"

"I just left him a moment ago. He was reading from a tome. But it's late. Save it for the morning."

"It's important," she told him.

"Very well. Good night."

"Good night, Master Critchlow."

She went to the Aldermaston's study and set the tray down outside before knocking softly on the door.

"Enter."

She stepped inside and found the chamber bright from an activated light Leering. Aldermaston Gilifil sat at his desk, forehead wrinkled with concentration and a golden tome spread open before him. His eyes left the page and found her in the doorway.

"What is it, Eilean?"

She shut the door behind her. "I learned another word of power tonight. But that's not why I've come."

His eyes brightened. "Really? Why did you come, then?"

"Celyn has the sweating sickness."

He blinked at her. "I know. Loren told me when he brought my supper. Poor girl."

Eilean was surprised he didn't look more concerned. "She needs a Gift of Healing from the Medium, Aldermaston. You could give her one."

His brow wrinkled more. "I'm sure she'll get better. She's young and strong."

"She's very sick. I saw her in the healer's tent. I'm worried about her."

She saw a little flicker of impatience in his eyes. "I'm sure she'll get better, Eilean. Trust in the Medium's will." He turned back to the tome.

A pit of disappointment opened in her stomach. She'd thought he would at least send another maston to see to Celyn. It hadn't occurred to her that he might say no.

"Sorry for disturbing you, Aldermaston," she said, backing up to the door.

"She'll feel better in the morning. You'll see. Good night, Eilean."

"What if she doesn't?"

He lifted his head again, his eyes narrowing with anger. "Good night."

She left and shut the door behind her, feeling sick to her stomach. Tormented by all the thoughts chasing through her mind at the same time. What if Celyn died?

She stooped and picked up the tray, one thought echoing through her head again and again.

Mordaunt had been right.

A wise Aldermaston once said, "To know nothing is the happiest life." Knowledge is always a sword with two edges. It cuts away falsehood but reveals hypocrisy. Too much truth can lead to heresy. Such we are experiencing in Hautland with an Aldermaston who defied the High Seer of Avinion by hanging shingles decrying the established order. He has agreed to face trial at the abbey of Viegg. If he does not recant his deeds, he will be branded a heretic and excommunicated. He has agreed to come to the abbey on the condition that he will not face a trial of flame. His intention is to answer for his actions by citing the words of the tomes.

He will be condemned.

It did not have to be this way. He could have had a happy life if he had just remained silent.

—Mícheál Nostradamus of Avinion Abbey

CHAPTER TEN

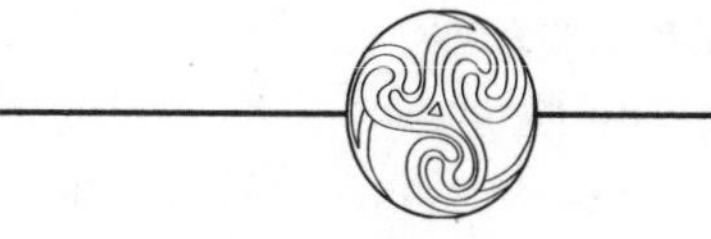

The Power of a Smile

Celyn grew sicker and weaker each day, and Eilean became increasingly anxious that her childhood friend and companion might die. The Aldermaston had, in the end, relented and sent one of the mastons to give her a Gift of Healing. But it hadn't lessened her suffering, and Eilean resented that the Aldermaston hadn't cared enough to bless her himself.

Celyn had been moved back to the kitchen so that Ardys, Loren, and the other helpers could attend her. That gave Eilean opportunities each day to visit her friend, to hold her hand and whisper promises that she would get better. Promises that felt like lies on her tongue. She could see the anxious looks that Ardys and Loren gave each other. Although neither had said so, she could tell they shared her fears.

As Eilean left the kitchen with a tray propped on her hip, one of the laundry girls approached her.

"How is your friend?" asked the other girl, reaching up to adjust her flower crown. This was one of the same girls who'd laughed at Eilean, but to her surprise, there was no mockery in her voice now, only sincere interest.

"Not well," she answered, feeling the press of it. Celyn had seemed worse today. She always seemed worse.

The other girl sighed. "I'm sad to hear it. She was always kind to us."

Celyn was that way to everyone.

"She's awake if you want to see her."

"That's good to hear. I was hoping to. Thank you, Eilean."

"What's your name?"

"Rhiannon." She offered a smile and then walked past Eilean to enter the kitchen.

The encounter was so surprising that Eilean was still thinking on it as she entered the castle and climbed the stairs leading to Mordaunt's room. She arrived before the sun set, which was getting later every day with summer coming nigh. But she'd also made it a point to hurry her tasks so that she could learn more from the captive druid.

When she arrived, she set the tray on the table. Mordaunt didn't praise her timeliness. He only rebuked her when she was late.

"Your supper," she said, calling to him at the window.

"They planted apple trees behind the kitchen today," he said. "Did you see? A new orchard."

"I've not been behind the kitchen that often," she answered, arranging the dishes, the cup, the bread and knife.

He turned from the view. "They dug up some of the smaller trees growing by the castle and moved them to fresh pits they recently dug. The gardeners did the work, of course. It was the wrong time of year to plant, though. Should have happened earlier in the spring. Many of the saplings will die."

The remark troubled her, although she couldn't say why. Then a thought struck her, unbidden. Was he talking about Celyn, being dug up from Tintern and replanted in Muirwood?

"You know more about trees than I do," she confessed.

He came to the table and looked at the food, sniffing the steam wafting up from the bowl. "I suppose I do. Do you know what 'druid' means, Eilean?"

"I couldn't tell you."

"It comes from one of the barbarian tongues. Two halves that make a whole—the words *'deru'* and *'weid.'*" He said both in a strange accent. "It means *oak-knower* or *oak-seer*. There are certain trees that possess magics most do not know about. The mastons think druids are sorcerers, that their magic is a heresy, but they only say this because they do not understand."

He sat down and began to eat the soup rapidly, making little sounds of pleasure as he did.

Eilean tidied the chamber again, wondering why he spent so much time each day throwing things into disorder. Perhaps it was a test of her ability to find what he had set amiss. Or maybe he simply did it out of pique. Either way, she wished there were a word of power that could make the room as clean as whiskers for her.

By the sound of the spoon rattling in his empty dish, she could tell he was done, and so she approached again. "Did you like the soup?"

"The Aldermaston's cook is one of the finest I've encountered. I always look forward to her meals."

"In the autumn, she makes a creamy fish soup and bakes pumpkin bread," Eilean said. "The bread is one of my favorites."

"Alas, I may not be around long enough to taste it," he said with a sigh.

She gave him an inquiring look. "Why do you say that?"

"It's only a matter of time before they send me to Avinion for trial. I've enjoyed your company, Eilean. Your service to me. I shall be grieved when they take me away."

His words put a knot of worry in her stomach. "Reck—you *think* it will be soon?"

"It's hard to say. It depends on how impatient your Aldermaston becomes. He's not a patient man when he wants something." His mouth quirked into a small smile. "Like knowledge that does not belong to him."

"You're wrong on that count, master," Eilean said, the knot in her stomach tightening. "He's very patient."

"You mistake patience for cunning. They are two different words. I am patient. He is cunning. They claim I stole what was rightfully mine. A tome of knowledge. That is what your Aldermaston wants from me."

That knot cinched tighter still. She didn't like anyone to speak ill of the Aldermaston—he was a good man, a wonderful leader. But she was also starting to see admirable qualities in Mordaunt.

"I see by the furrows in your brow that you disagree. Let me just suggest, lest I risk offending you further, that I am a little older and wiser than you. I have known many kings, mastons, and Aldermastons, as well as the plain and simple folk of the world. I know his kind."

She frowned. "And what do you mean by 'his kind'?" she snapped.

He gazed up at her, still sitting in his chair with an air of satisfaction. "He cannot use the Medium, sister. Because it too sees into his heart and finds him lacking. Have you ever seen him brighten a Leering? Or summon water?"

She stared at him, incredulous.

"You have not because he cannot. He surrounds himself with capable and devout men and women who do those things for him, out of courtesy, because he knows he cannot achieve them himself."

"You're lying," she accused.

"To what aim, my dear? I've known dozens of this sort. Men, *especially* men, who feign righteousness to others, yet are driven to reckless behavior by their own ambition. I told you that he would not heal your friend. He sent another to do it because he could not. The Medium abhors pride and hypocrisy above all."

His words filled her with righteous anger on the Aldermaston's behalf. "He's a good man."

"He *pretends* to be one. I knew I might not be here much longer, so I wanted to open your eyes to the truth. I've taken his measure. I know his sort. If anyone challenges him, he becomes angry, defiant, and . . . unfortunately . . . cruel. You've not experienced this firsthand because you worked in the kitchen. He needs you to be one of his followers who helps maintain the illusion."

It was like he'd unleashed fire ants inside her mind. She shook her head, troubled to her core. "He warned me about you," she said.

"Of course he did. I'm not asking you to believe me, Eilean. Test my words. See for yourself."

"How can I? He told me the Medium bid him choose me for this assignment."

Mordaunt rubbed his forehead. "Naturally. Because you are loyal to him, you believed him. You have strength in the Medium, unusual for one in your situation. The fact is, you have more power in the Medium than he does. I can see it clearly, child. He's using you for his own ends. Tell me, has he advised you to keep the extent of your ability hidden from others?"

"*Shaw*, and you're not tricksy yourself?"

"Stop speaking like a wretched," he snapped. "You could be so much more!"

She began to gather up his dishes, filled with an overpowering desire to leave. Maybe Mordaunt's plan was to trick her into defying the Aldermaston, into helping him escape Muirwood before the

Apocrisarius took him to Avinion. Maybe he deserved to go there to face the consequences of his deeds.

"You're upset," he said.

"I'll not listen to you," she said, taking the tray. "He's a good man."

"How he treats *you* is not how he treats *others*. Open your eyes, Eilean. Before it's too late."

She hurried from the room and slammed the door, her heart racing in her chest and her mind a beehive of stinging thoughts. As she walked back down the steps, trying to banish the worried feelings growing inside her like weeds, she nearly bumped into Critchlow and quickly apologized.

She went outside, grateful the fading light helped hide her burning cheeks. The Aldermaston *was* a good man. She'd grown up around him at Tintern, listening to him and seeking his approval. She *knew* him. But there, buried in her memories, were instances when he'd lost his temper. When his eyes had flashed with anger and disapproval at something she'd done. Every time he'd looked at her thus, it had made her flinch and worry and seek to please him. Or at least not provoke his anger again.

She was being wrenched in two. Those memories, long since buried, made her wonder if Mordaunt truly was trying to help her. But no! He was a druid, an enemy of the maston order. A prisoner. This was why Aldermaston Gilifil had trusted *her*.

She walked around the kitchen to the rear, intending to enter it from behind, and noticed that saplings had indeed been planted in small rows.

Balancing the tray with one arm, she opened the door and entered the rear of the building. It was noisy and crowded, full of workers come to get a meal after a hard day of labor. One of the younger scullions came and took the tray of dishes from her. Eilean rarely ate with the other wretcheds now because her schedule was so different from theirs, and she felt a prick of self-consciousness.

Worse, the lack of Celyn was like a wound. She should be scuttling around, smiling at people, making everything brighter and better, but instead she was lying in Ardys and Loren's rooms at the back of the kitchen, struggling to breathe.

"Eilean! Over here!"

It was Rhiannon, waving to her from one of the benches. Two of the other laundry girls sat with her, across from a couple of the strong boys who'd hurt Aisic.

And then she saw Aisic, sitting against the wall by a barrel, holding an empty bowl in his hand, looking miserable and weary. And excluded.

Eilean got herself a bowl of soup and two small rolls, and then walked toward the laundry girls' table.

"Come sit with us," Rhiannon said.

Eilean smiled but shook her head. "I'm going to sit with Aisic. He's a friend of mine from Tintern."

Mustering her courage, she left the others and approached his table, dropping down into the chair next to him. She said nothing but handed him one of the two rolls she'd gotten and then dunked hers into the soup. Warmth seemed to radiate from him, touching her hip, her side.

"Thank you," he mumbled. Staring at the roll, he took a bite from it.

Celyn was always bringing things to people without being asked. In the past, Eilean had always been too afraid.

Eilean said nothing, just ate her soup and let the expectant silence between them shift her thoughts from the beestings Mordaunt had inflicted on her mind. Back at Tintern, she'd always been too embarrassed to talk to Aisic. It felt like it had been a long time ago.

"I'm sorry Celyn's so ill," Aisic said, the roll only half-eaten. He seemed to be savoring it.

"So am I," she answered, staring down at her meal.

He turned his head to look at her. "I hope she gets better. Truly."

She glanced at him, feeling a shy smile start. "Thank you. You miss Llewellyn, Ely, and Bryant, don't you?"

He nodded with a sullen smile. "I wish just *one* of them had come." He looked down. "What is Mordaunt like? Everyone keeps asking about him. No one else gets to see him up close, but he's always watching from the windows."

She wasn't sure how to answer his question. "He's rude, but he's very knowledgeable, and he has been many places. I enjoy his stories actually." Her stomach knotted again. "Most of them."

He nodded encouragingly, but her shyness prevented her from telling any of them.

"Are you glad you're here?" she asked. "Or do you wish you were back at Tintern?"

"I had no choice," he said with a grunt of disaffection. "When Gilifool told me I was coming, I begged to join the hunters. That's what I really wanted." He shook his head. "The scolding he gave me was for aspiring above my station. I've never seen him so angry." He chuckled. "And when I left his study, you were there. Remember?"

She swallowed, the sickening feeling twisting her stomach again. "Yes."

"Sorry I was a git to you, but I was shaken up." He paused, then added, "He's never yelled at you or Celyn."

Her hunger ebbed with his confession. She felt sick to her stomach and could almost see Mordaunt giving her a smug look from his window.

"No, not since I was little."

"Everyone talks about how wise and strong he is. Especially these poor sots from the other abbeys. *Shaw*, it feels good to be able to talk to someone. How come you're never here for supper?"

"I have to take Mordaunt—"

"That's right. I forgot. I'm so tired every day. It's minging hard work, by Cheshu. We're digging a tunnel from the abbey to the castle. Isn't that strange?"

"What for?" she asked him.

He shrugged. "I've no idea. Maybe it's related to the maston test?"

She turned and looked at him, and it dawned on her that she was finally seeing him as a person, not as someone she'd idolized. And it felt good. It felt very good.

And yet . . . his words had confirmed part of what Mordaunt had told her. Again he was right. She and the kitchen helpers had been treated very differently from others at the abbey.

Aisic took another bite from the roll. Then he gave her a sideways look. "Do you want to see the tunnel?" he asked with a mischievous smile.

It would be dark outside. The tunnel even darker. Fear gripped her heart and squeezed.

"No."

His brow furrowed, and he shrugged. "Oh. All right."

She'd disappointed him. The moment was being ruined.

"I'm terrified of the dark," she said to him.

His expression flickered with something—did she dare hope it was relief?—and he nodded. "I didn't know. Maybe tomorrow afternoon? Before it gets dark?"

"Yes," she said, feeling something wonderful swell inside her.

"I'll see you then." His smile felt like a promise, and it kindled an answering warmth within her.

Was he finally interested in her?

And why, if that was so, didn't that warmth feel quite the way it used to?

Man's mind is far more susceptible to falsehood than to truth. I must agree with the wise Ovidius, one of the original Twelve, who wrote in his oft-quoted tome, 'We are slow to believe that which, if believed, would hurt our feelings.' Such is the predicament that Aldermaston Utheros of Hautland faces. He cannot conceive that he is wrong, that his mind has been led to error, and his defiance of the High Seer will soon result in excommunication. No one wants to be wrong.

—Mícheál Nostradamus of Avinion Abbey

CHAPTER ELEVEN

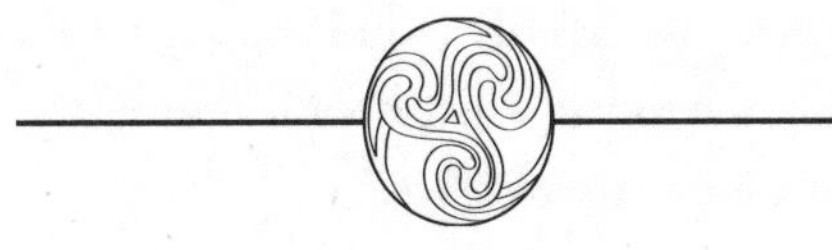

Into the Dark

From the window in Mordaunt's room, Eilean saw the late afternoon sun bathe the castle grounds with a warm glow. From the same window, she'd watched in fascination as the cornerstones of the abbey were laid by the master builders. These hulking pieces had floated down into the pit, guided by the Leerings carved into them and directed by the mastons who oversaw the work. She was excited to see the building site up close, and even more so that Aisic would be the one to show it to her. Anticipation and the thrill of eagerness had dominated her thoughts that day, helping her overcome her misgivings about Aldermaston Gilifil and Mordaunt.

"You keep staring out the window, little sister. The cornerstones are laid. That is all."

She turned and gave Mordaunt a challenging look. "You stare out the windows all day long."

"Don't get saucy. You have the freedom to come and go as you wish. I cannot venture out of the castle at all."

"Then why do you torture yourself by looking outside?"

"Such insolence! Maybe you are a *pethet* after all."

She stepped away from the window, ignoring his chiding tone. She was used to his moods now, could tell when he was serious and when he was teasing.

"What is a *pethet*?" she asked. "You keep saying that word. What language does that come from? What does it mean?"

"I thought you were eager to leave?"

"What makes you say that?"

"You've been unusually excited today. I've seen you smile without cause several times, and you keep staring out the window. Surely the burying of stone blocks hasn't brought on this change in mood?"

She felt her cheeks begin to flush, but it didn't escape her attention that he was trying to draw her away from her question again. "What does *pethet* mean? I'm not fetching your supper until you tell me."

His eyebrows lifted in surprise. "Never make a threat you cannot fulfill. What if I held out for days or even weeks? Would you still deny me nourishment?"

"Stop being difficult. Just tell me."

"Difficult? I deny the accusation. But since it's obvious you won't be thwarted, I will satisfy your request. On the continent, in the Peliyey Mountains, there are several abbeys that are especially secluded. Cruix Abbey stands between the kingdoms of Mon and Paeiz. People of many different backgrounds study there. You can hear nearly all the tongues of the civilized lands. Even that horrible native tongue of yours, Pry-rian."

"It's not horrible. But go on."

"The word *'pethet'* is Sumeelan. That's another dialect you find in those mountains. There isn't a word in your language for it, but the closest is 'hypocrite.' It's a term of contempt for one whose actions bely their thoughts. The Aldermaston of Cruix Abbey uses that word for learners who are pretentious, double-minded, and blind to their own folly."

She wrinkled her brow. "Do you truly think *I'm* a *pethet*, master?"

He gave her a cynical look. "You're pining, girl. It's as plain to see as the apples growing on the trees down below. You don't want to be here with me. You want to throw yourself like a fool at the feet of some castaway. Be gone, then. You can *pretend* to fetch my supper now."

Instantly, she felt shame and then a hot burst of outrage.

"I'm not mitching. I work hard. You only care about yourself," she said, flinging the words at him.

"Mitching is it now?" He snorted. "Oh, I care about a great many things that I'm powerless to do anything about. I've offered to teach you the secrets of the universe, and you prefer to waste your potential with a filthy drudge."

The flush in her cheeks made her entire face hot. She clenched her hands into fists, her words boiling out in a rush.

"Maybe you haven't noticed, but I'm lonely and worried because my best friend keeps getting worse!"

Eilean knew she would start shouting at him if she stayed a moment longer, so she rushed out of the room, slamming the door behind her, and hurried down the stairs so fast she nearly tripped on her skirts. As she stormed down the hall, she heard a pair of familiar voices. Critchlow and the Aldermaston.

"The cornerstone blessing was well said, Aldermaston Gilifil. Your wisdom and prudence will be cherished for generations to come."

"Thank you, Critchlow. This is to be the first abbey built in the kingdom of Moros. I hope it will endure for a long time."

"Oh, it shall, I assure you! The emperor himself will want to visit for the dedication blessing. Imagine that, the emperor himself!"

"It would be an honor to finally meet him."

"He is rather busy, you know. Dealing with that heretic Utheros has been taxing, to be sure."

"Has he been excommunicated yet?"

"No, the trial at Viegg is still underway. But there can only be one possible outcome. Utheros will be condemned. And once he is, the High Seer's attention will return to your prisoner."

Eilean didn't know what they were talking about, but the two men walked into sight, coming from the direction of the rear door she planned to use to get to the kitchen. They took no notice of her in passing.

"Progress has been slow," the Aldermaston said. "He's a crafty fellow. I hope the High Seer doesn't lose patience with me."

"She is a very patient woman, I assure you, Aldermaston. That is one of the key virtues of the Medium. I hear Captain Hoel has managed to break the druid he captured?"

"Indeed. The hunters are going into the Bearden Muir to find more of them. We'll root them out, one by one."

"I can't abide their ghastly tattoos," Critchlow said, his voice quavering with dread. "They're positively barbaric."

"The kingdom will be made anew," the Aldermaston said forcefully. "The superstitions of the druids will be revealed, at last, as nothing less than the deceptions caused by the Myriad Ones."

"Of course. Now if you'll allow me a private audience, I should like to discuss a matter of sensitivity with you."

"Yes, come inside my office."

Eilean had paused before exiting the building, listening to the conversation until Critchlow and Aldermaston Gilifil were gone. Who was this renegade Aldermaston they were talking about? She'd never heard of an Utheros before. Did Mordaunt know who he was? The thought of asking him, after having stormed out of his room earlier, made her sick inside. But she was still angry at how he'd belittled Aisic and implied that she wasn't consistent in her mind and actions.

As she hurried toward the kitchen to check on Celyn for the third time that day, she heard Aisic's voice call to her.

"Eilean!"

She saw him wave and approach. He'd been waiting in front of the kitchen—he had been waiting for *her.* Just that thought made her stomach clench with delight.

"There is plenty of light down in the pit," he said, hooking his thumbs in his belt. "Do you still want to see the tunnel?"

"I do," she agreed, smiling at him.

"Come on, then!" he offered and started in that direction. She caught up and walked alongside him. Her elbow brushed against his on accident, and it sent a prickle of pleasant awareness through her. As they walked, she didn't look up at the windows of Mordaunt's room, but she felt the druid was standing there—watching her, judging her—and it dampened her joy.

When they reached the ladder, Aisic went down first and waited at the bottom for her to join him. He gazed up at her as she came down, and she had the thought that he was looking up her skirts. She shoved it out of her head immediately, giving a disapproving warning to herself not to fancy such things.

When she reached the base, she saw the nearest cornerstone, which was taller than her. She could feel the Leering carved into it and sensed, as she often did, its purpose. She knew that was a rare ability for a wretched. Mordaunt was right—the Aldermaston had cautioned her not to speak about it around the others, and she'd listened to him.

Questions swirled through her, but she tamped them down by focusing on the Leering. It had been designed to levitate the stone so it could be safely transported to its present position. She imagined how many horses it would have taken to drag it over. The earth at the bottom of the pit was compacted, and several other stones had already been positioned now that the cornerstones had been laid and blessed. Did blessing the stones require power in the Medium? Was this evidence that the Aldermaston could use its power? Or was the blessing merely ceremonial?

"This way," Aisic said, and she followed him. The laborers were all gone, although she saw some of the master builders—all mastons—walking around the pit and talking to each other about the coming day's work.

At the side of the pit closest to the castle, there was indeed a tunnel. A little taller than Aisic, it was situated about halfway up the side of the pit. Stones had been set around the edges for bracing, and she reached up to test the height. She could touch them, and the stone felt rough against her hand. Aisic went into the darkness first, and Eilean felt a throb of worry and concern when he immediately disappeared. But she was brave enough to go in after him, especially since the light from outside still beamed through the opening. The sun wouldn't set for a while, thank the Medium.

Earthy smells greeted her nose, and she could also smell the not-unpleasant scent of Aisic, who was still sweaty from his labors. His shoulders were broader now than they'd been at Tintern, proof that the builders had been working them hard and there was little mitching.

At first she was blinded because of the dark, but her eyes became used to it. The thrill of being here with Aisic, of sharing something with him, helped her overcome her hesitance.

She ran her hand along the dirt wall, feeling pieces of it trickle down as she brushed against it. Then she bumped into Aisic, who'd stopped suddenly.

"It'll get darker if we keep going. Maybe this wasn't such a good idea. Are you scared?"

She sensed a Leering farther down the passage.

"There are Leerings down here?" she asked him.

"Yes, but the builders don't keep them shining during the night."

Eilean reached out with her mind and invoked it, and light spilled down the length of the tunnel.

It revealed his face, caught in a surprised expression. "Did *you* do that?"

"They're just Leerings," Eilean said. Now that there was plenty of light, she could see the Leerings had been spaced at even intervals down the tunnel.

"I didn't know you could use them," he said, sounding impressed. "Have you always been able to?"

"For as long as I can remember living in the kitchen," she said. "How far back does it go? Does it reach the castle yet?"

He grinned. "They're digging from the other side as well. I'm not part of that crew. But they hope the tunnels will join soon. If we're off by even a little, the tunnels won't meet up at all. Come on."

They started walking again, he in front. It was a little frightening having nothing but earth above and around her. Stone braces had been installed at intervals, however, and it was that stone that the Leerings were carved into.

"Has it ever collapsed?" she asked him.

"A few times, but it mostly just rains dirt on you. The laundry girls have to work hard to clean our clothes."

The thought of a cave-in made her stomach clench with dread. But the light beaming from the Leerings up ahead made her more hopeful. At last, they reached the end, where pickaxes, shovels, and buckets had been left. She touched the dead end of the wall, feeling the hardness of the earth and roughness of stones. It was brutal work.

"How far do you *think* we've come? How close to the castle?" It was so hard not to use "reckon" all the time! She'd never noticed that before.

"We measure by the length of our strides," he said. "Reckon we're about halfway there right now. Some of the builders say that the Aldermaston may want us to do another tunnel as well."

"Where to?" she asked.

"Leading toward the quarry," he said. "Which is getting pretty deep. Have you seen it?"

A trickle of dirt landed on her head, and she started and held up her arm.

"That happens a lot down here," he said with a chuckle as she brushed the dirt from her hair. "They'll be putting another brace in soon."

The darkness at the edges of the tunnel was beginning to get to her, but it was a delight to be down here with Aisic. It was the first time they'd really been alone together. The soft glow from the Leerings was bright enough for her to see the smudges of dirt on his throat, the stains on his clothes. The curves and ridges of his face.

"Who's down there?" shouted a voice from the mouth of the tunnel.

She flinched with dread.

"One of the masters," Aisic said. He glanced toward the entrance with a defiant expression. "Let's go back."

"Will we get in trouble?" she asked.

"Don't worry."

He offered her his hand, and she took it. It was calloused, dirty, and she thrilled in his strong grip. They walked back toward the entrance, hand in hand, and despite the possibility they might get in trouble, she felt wonderful.

"Come on now, hurry up!" barked the commanding voice.

But Aisic was in no hurry. He glanced at her, giving her a crooked smile as they slowly made their way, and then the tramp of boots filled the close space as the fellow came toward them. He was older, clad in a dirty tunic and shirt, with a trimmed beard the color of walnuts.

"Oh, it's you," he said to Aisic. Then he gave him a scolding look. "What you bring the lass down here for?"

"Wanted to show her what we'd been doing," Aisic said.

"How'd you get the Leerings going?" demanded the builder.

"She did it," Aisic said proudly.

She flushed.

The builder's eyes narrowed. "Who are you?"

"Shaw," said Aisic with a disgusted tone. "Don't you recognize her? She's the Aldermaston's wretched. The one who lives in the castle. We're both from Tintern."

"What were you doing down there?" the man asked again with suspicion.

"Just looking, I said," Aisic answered, exasperated. "She wanted to see the tunnel. I took her. That's all."

"Get on, then," said the man. "I don't think the Aldermaston wants folk peeking around down here. These tunnels are supposed to be secret."

"What are they for?" Eilean asked, intensely curious.

"None of your business if the Aldermaston hasn't already told ye," he said gruffly. She felt a throb of the Medium, and the Leerings went dark. "Light them again."

Eilean did.

"I told you it was her," Aisic said as they all glowed to life.

The builder looked at her in surprise. "Just being sure, lad. Just being sure. There are folk who can make Leerings work with charms they wear around their necks. But their eyes glow silver when they do. Just making sure we don't have a druid on our hands."

"There are female druids?" Aisic asked.

"Of course there are. Don't be an idiot. Now get on out of here. Don't bring her back." He marched past them, moving farther into the tunnel, perhaps to ensure their visit had been as innocent as they claimed.

When they reached the entrance, Aisic squeezed her hand. "Turn the lights off!" he whispered with a grin.

Eilean did, and they heard a shout of anger from behind as they took off running back to the ladder leading out of the pit. The cavern was in full shadow by now. Aisic motioned for her to go first, but something warned her against it—again, she thought about the vulnerable position she'd be in. How he'd be able to look up her skirt.

"You first," she said, stepping aside.

Disappointment flickered in his eyes, but he shrugged and clambered up the ladder. She followed, and he offered her a boost when she reached the top.

The sun was peeking over the hills to the west, coloring the clouds a dozen brilliant shades of pink and orange and deep yellow.

"Have you seen the starlings in the morning?" he asked as they walked toward the kitchen.

"The little birds?"

"They come every morning," he said. "Thousands of them. You'd think they're clouds or something, but they're swarms of birds. Reckon they roost in the pasture at night. Then they all take flight in the morning. They're picking at the growing flax, driving the farmers mad."

"I've noticed the fields aren't growing very fast," she said. "I didn't know it was because of the birds."

"This isn't the right kind of earth for flax. I've heard others talk on it. They'll need to find another crop. That's why they planted those apple shoots over yon. They know apples'll grow in this minging soil."

She imagined Mordaunt listening to their conversation and groaning at the way they spoke.

"It'll be sad if the flax crop doesn't grow."

"Aye. Those blue flowers that bloom? Nothing prettier in all the world."

Hearing him say that made her feel like she was sitting in front of the hearth on a cool day. She loved the smell of flax, loved walking the field and running her hands over the flowers. A pang of missing Tintern gripped her chest.

"I miss the abbey sometimes," she admitted.

"Aye, me too," he said. He took her hand again and gave it a squeeze.

They'd reached the doors of the kitchen, and he moved to open the door for her.

The sound of weeping cut through the quiet. Even though it was suppertime, the kitchen was empty except for a few people. Eilean's heart dropped like a stone. Loren stood in front of them, cushing Ardys tenderly, and both had tears in their eyes.

Aisic and Eilean entered, their shoes crunching the new floor rushes that had been installed.

Oh no. The emptiness of the kitchen, the tears streaming down Ardys's and Loren's faces—it could only mean one thing.

Eilean broke away from Aisic and rushed to the back of the kitchen.

Where she found Celyn stiff and cold and pale.

By excommunicating Utheros as a heretic and burning his tome, we may rid a shelf in the study of him, but we will not rid men's minds of him.

—Mícheál Nostradamus of Avinion Abbey

CHAPTER TWELVE

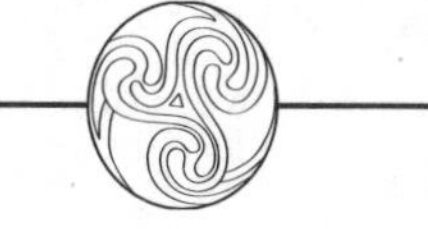

The Power of the Medium

Eilean's devastation crushed all feeling within her. At last, her tears were all wrung out, her sobs relented, and a sense that nothing would ever be normal again settled over her like a shroud. Ardys and Loren tried their best to comfort her and themselves. If she'd lost a sister, they'd lost a daughter, or as good as. They'd never had any children of their own.

"The Aldermaston will be missing his supper," Ardys said after wiping her red-rimmed eyes and stifling a weary sigh.

"I will bring it to him," Eilean offered. It used to be her duty. She could do it again if it would help.

"I'll set out some bread and honey for the workers," Loren said. "No doubt there are hunger pangs to be comforted. Everyone at the abbey loved our dear girl." He sniffled and kissed Ardys's head.

Eilean assembled a tray with a simple meal. The soup was burnt, so she fetched cheese, a slice of cold sausage, and a thick heel of bread.

The Aldermaston liked fruit tarts as well, and she found one from the previous day and added it to the tray. A similar offering was prepared for Mordaunt, but Eilean would bring it to him after she delivered the Aldermaston's dinner.

As she carried the tray out of the kitchen, it occurred to her that she hadn't seen Aisic since the awful news was first delivered. He must have quietly slipped away. Disappointment roiled through her. He'd known Celyn as well. But he'd offered no comfort. He'd said nothing at all. Still . . . when were men ever able to speak of their more delicate feelings? If they even had any.

It was dark when she stepped outside. As she approached the castle, she spied one of the hunters in the shadow.

"Sorry to hear the news, Eilean," Twynho said. She recognized his voice, even in the dark. He went before her and opened the door.

"Thank you, Twynho," she said, grateful for his kindness. She wondered if Captain Hoel already knew. He probably did. He seemed to know everything.

She maneuvered down the corridor, around another servant, and knocked on the Aldermaston's door.

"Come in."

She turned the handle and entered, finding the Aldermaston at his desk, the light from the Leering shining brightly, a golden tome spread out before him, his finger pressed to the shining metal page. His brow was furrowed, his red beard a little grayer than she remembered it.

He glanced up from the tome. "Eilean?" he said in surprise as she set the tray down next to the tome.

"Do you know about Celyn, Aldermaston?" she asked, her voice low.

"Critchlow told me. It's a terrible thing when the Medium takes one so young." He sighed, leaning back in his chair and crossing his hands over his stomach. "This second life is so brief."

Eilean swallowed, feeling resentment against him spark in the ashes of her emotions. "Why didn't you give her your blessing, Aldermaston?"

His brow furrowed, and she saw a glint of anger in his eyes. "She received a Gifting, Eilean. But even the strongest Gifting cannot forestall the Medium's will."

"But you're the Aldermaston. You're the strongest in the Medium, aren't you?"

She'd broached his defenses. It was clear from the frown that twisted his mouth and the sudden blaze of anger in his eyes.

He rose from the chair, planting his palms on the desk, his knuckles suddenly straining as if he wanted to seize her and shake her.

"Guard your tongue, Eilean," he said in a scolding tone, his voice throbbing with fury. "I grieve for Celyn's loss. My heart is sickened by it. But you speak against the Medium, not just against me. That is a dangerous road you walk down, child. Do not let grief twist your judgment. I will give you lenience just this once, because of your grief, but don't you dare speak to me like that again."

The look on his face terrified her. She'd thought she was beyond feeling, but the rage and intensity in his eyes, the unspoken threat that he could dismiss her from his service and send her into the world with nothing felt like a blow.

"I'm sorry, Aldermaston," she mumbled, her voice seizing up. Feelings of darkness, abandonment, and terror wriggled in her chest.

"Go," he ordered curtly, nodding to the door with a look that showed he was disgusted by her.

Eilean fled the chamber and then the castle, racing back to the kitchen where she'd once felt safe. She was sobbing again by the time she got there, unable to say what had happened—not daring to for fear of being scolded by Ardys and Loren. They imagined it was grief alone that made her weep, and held and comforted her. But it brought no solace.

She felt very small within the shadow of a world that now seemed cruel and uncaring. If only they'd never left Tintern. Celyn wouldn't have gotten sick. Eilean wouldn't have experienced the Aldermaston's dark temper. They would all be healthy, and a little boredom would be more than worth it for the safety of those fields of flax.

There was another thought she could not shake.

If she hadn't gone to the tunnel with Aisic, she would have been there before Celyn had died. She couldn't forgive herself for that.

Regret was possibly the worst of the feelings torturing her.

***

Celyn's body was wrapped in linen and laid on a table in a vacant room in the castle. It was the custom of the maston order to burn the bodies of the dead with a fire Leering to prevent sickness from spreading to others. The bones were then collected into a stone ossuary, which would be buried in a cemetery blessed by an Aldermaston. Because Muirwood was new, there was not yet a cemetery, but a location had been selected by the path leading to the quarry, beyond the new apple orchard.

The ossuary sat on the floor beside Celyn's body. It had been crafted by one of the builders, and although it was well made, it made Eilean sick to her stomach.

When Eilean touched the body's arm, it felt cold, devoid of life. As the order taught, Celyn's spirit had returned to Idumea. What was left behind, her body, would rest in the ground until all the dead were revived again, to live forever in another world.

Eilean had always believed that truth. But now, seeing the stillness of death, she wondered if it were true. Grief and sorrow consumed her. She performed her functions without spirit, without happiness. It felt awful that her friend was no more. The world was a darker place without her smiles, without her kindness.

She heard the door open and turned to find Critchlow standing in the doorway.

"Ah, it's you . . . again. Eilean, I'm going to lock the door tonight. It isn't seemly to spend so much time with the bones of the dead. Say your last farewell. Tomorrow morning her body will be gone."

Eilean had cried so many times in the last two days that there were no tears left now. She felt she was made of wood. But she reached out again, touching Celyn's still arm one last time, then bent and kissed the crown of her head.

"Good-bye, Celyn," she whispered.

After she left, she heard Critchlow lock the door. The steward muttered something, but she was too lost inside herself to hear it. She walked up the stairs to see to Mordaunt.

Surprisingly, he wasn't at the window. He was sitting at the table, his eyes looking down as if he were discouraged.

Without speaking, she began to tidy the room, but there wasn't much to do. When she saw the Leering in the corner, the one that bound Mordaunt to the castle, she felt the irrational urge to take a hammer to it—to smash off its face. The surge of anger only lasted a moment, however, before it bled into despair.

"You've stayed in the kitchen the last few nights," Mordaunt said.

"I'm needed there," she answered. He knew about her loss, and to her relief, he seemed sympathetic. There had been no jokes, only kindness and understanding in his eyes.

"You're needed here."

"So you can scold me for not talking the way you want me to?"

She regretted the words as soon as they were uttered, but what was one more regret added to the heap? She rubbed her forehead and grabbed the broom, even though the floor wasn't dusty. It was something to do.

"I see you need more time to mourn. You may go."

Gripping the broom in her hands, she squeezed it hard, but all the energy seemed to leave her. She set it back against the wall, nodded to him, and left. She couldn't bear to go to the kitchen, so she walked the grounds of the abbey. She watched the stone blocks float in a tidy row from the quarry to the foundation pit. Listened to the clamor of shovels and picks and grunting of men hard at work.

How strange that the world should go on as it had before, when everything within her felt so different.

She found herself at the little apple grove at the base of the castle. A gardener approached her with a wheelbarrow half full of fruit.

"Are the apples ripe?" she asked.

"They don't look it, for their coloring is strange. But I've never tasted better. Here . . . have one." He gestured to the wheelbarrow. "I'm taking these to Ardys later."

She stopped and stooped over the collection of apples, red with golden streaks. Some had blotches in them, as if they had a blight, but when she lifted one, the peel felt smooth and firm in her hand. She wasn't hungry—she hadn't been hungry for days—but when she held the apple close to her mouth, it had a pleasant floral smell. She took a bite, and the crunch and flavor made her start with surprise.

"See! See!" chortled the gardener. "I've never tasted an apple like this. It's not a common breed. But the taste! Reckon it'll make excellent cider too."

Eilean bit into it again, enjoying the tang that added depth to the sweetness. "Ardys will love them," she said, feeling the beginning of a smile. It didn't last. Celyn would have loved them too. And she'd never be able to taste one.

"Muirwood apples," said the gardener. "I'm only picking the ripe ones. They'll be done producing before the second crop comes in the fall. Those tend to be smaller fruit. You grew grapes in Tintern, lass. Isn't that right?"

"Yes. But I don't think the land here is good for them."

"No, I'd expect not. I come from Holyrood Abbey. You're the Aldermaston's girl, aren't you?"

It didn't feel like a compliment now. Still, she didn't wish to be rude, so she nodded to him before smiling in farewell and walking away. She enjoyed the rest of the apple as she continued her stroll, then admired the seeds in the core and found herself considering the fact that each one had the potential to grow into another tree.

The rest of the day was a blur of aimless walking. She went to the flax fields, where the plants looked limp and listless, then circled back to the orchard. And again. And again. She kept darting glances at the castle window, but Mordaunt was never there when she looked. Finally, she heaved a sigh and headed back toward the kitchen. By the sun, it was time to go get supper. The apple had helped revive her hunger, and the thought of some bread sounded good.

To her surprise, all three laundry girls came racing toward her as she made her approach. Rhiannon was in the front, her eyes bright with excitement.

"We've been looking all over for you, Eilean! Have you heard?"

"Heard what?" she asked, shocked.

One of the other girls started to speak, but Rhiannon shushed her. "Quiet, Liz! Celyn! It's about Celyn! The Aldermaston raised her from the dead!"

Eilean stared at them without comprehension. If this was a joke, it was the cruelest sort.

Rhiannon grabbed her by the arm. "She's back in the kitchen! I swear it by Idumea's hand! She's been asking for you!"

Eilean wanted to believe it, but the news was beyond astonishing. She ran with the other girls back to the Aldermaston's kitchen. A crowd had gathered outside, even though it was still early for supper. She pushed her way through, then gasped at what she saw inside.

Celyn was there with Ardys and Loren, and everyone was weeping with joy. Her friend looked tired, as if she'd been asleep for days, but she was *alive*. When she saw Eilean, a grin lit up her face, and the two friends ran to each other and embraced.

She kept hearing murmurs from the others about the Aldermaston and his strength with the Medium. The Gift of Raising the Dead was the rarest of blessings, but it was spoken of in the tomes. The original Twelve had all possessed that Gift and could perform it according to the Medium's will.

Eilean cushed her friend tightly and kissed her, so relieved she was speechless.

"What . . . what happened?" she exclaimed.

Celyn shook her head. "I don't know. I awoke on a table, wrapped up in a linen sheet. My face was uncovered, but the rest of my body was tightly bound. I had to struggle to get loose. The door was locked, so I kept pounding on it. Finally it was opened by Critchlow—scared, as you can imagine! But when he saw me, he flew to the Aldermaston and said a miracle had happened."

"It *is* a miracle," Eilean breathed, feeling terrible at how unjustly she'd accused the Aldermaston. His anger had been deserved.

Others wanted to see the miracle for themselves. Because of the crush of people moving into the kitchen, Eilean left out the rear door and dropped to her knees. Her shoulders trembled as she thought a silent prayer of gratitude to the Medium for bringing her friend back to life. If she hadn't seen Celyn with her own eyes, she would have doubted it was possible. Her friend had truly been dead. But the Medium had the power to connect things the human world had torn asunder—even a departed soul to its fallen body.

She was so grateful, she hurried to the castle to apologize to the Aldermaston. He wasn't in his study. Nor was he in the great hall. She found him in the chamber with the ossuary, standing by the empty table, his hand grazing the linen cloth that had recently wrapped the body.

"Aldermaston," she breathed with reverence.

He turned, and she saw the struggle on his face. The incomprehension, the look of bafflement. And she knew, immediately and instinctively, that he wasn't the one who had raised Celyn.

She knew who had.

A good portion of speaking will consist in knowing how to lie. This may, on its face, seem ludicrous, but understand that one of the oaths an Aldermaston takes bars him or her from deliberately speaking a falsehood. No Aldermaston is perfectly honest, and all fall short of the ideal, but it is the reputation of honesty that grants the position so much esteem and trust. These trusted persons persuade so many to follow them by the office that they hold, and thus great care must be taken by them to guard their speech meticulously, lest an overt falsehood be uttered and discovered.

A lie is best inlaid with a veneer of truth. Thus may a heretic Aldermaston deceive even the most astute. And why the members of the Apocrisarius are trained to detect even the smallest inconsistency.

—Mícheál Nostradamus of Avinion Abbey

CHAPTER THIRTEEN

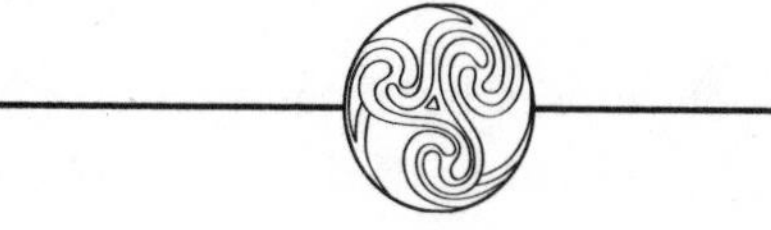

Confusion

As Eilean carried the tray up the steps, which seemed to have multiplied since her last visit, she felt her arms trembling, her stomach twisting, her throat tightening. She reached the top landing all too soon and paused at the door, steeling her courage. Then she turned the handle and opened it.

Mordaunt, standing at the window, turned to look at her a moment before glancing away.

She carefully entered and placed his tray on the table, wishing she had brought him a feast instead of the same humble meal she'd brought the Aldermaston. She was confused and frightened, but those feeling were both overpowered by her determination to test if her insight had been correct.

Without saying a word, Mordaunt came to the table and sat down. He looked fatigued, as if he'd been climbing the stairs up and down all day. She'd never seen such exhaustion in his eyes. He took a drink first and then laid waste to the supper, eating it in large mouthfuls.

The silence between them grew heavy, like a wet cloth covering a bowl of rising dough. Eilean looked for something to do in the room, something to tidy, but there was nothing. All was in its proper place. That too was unusual. Intuition itched between her shoulder blades.

"You used to set everything amiss so I'd spend more time in here," she accused.

A grunt was her only answer, but it confirmed the thought.

Instead of leaving, she went to the window and gazed out at the dimming light. Only a sliver of brightness in the western sky could be seen, and it would be gone in moments. Another sunset. But the day that was ending was unlike any she'd known before. Her best friend had been raised from the dead. The weeks of agonizing despair and worry, which had ended so awfully, had been transformed, leaving only joy and new hope.

"Thank you," Eilean said, turning around and facing Mordaunt.

"For making messes?" he said gruffly, pausing in the annoying chewing of his meal.

She approached the table and sat down in front of him. She looked him in the eyes. "Thank you for Celyn. Everyone thinks it was the Aldermaston. But I *know* it was you."

His brow wrinkled. The woad of his tattoos had faded so much she didn't really notice them anymore. There was a sharp intelligence in his eyes.

"What can you mean, child? Haven't I been here in my room all day?"

"I wouldn't know. Were you here all day?"

He gave an approving smile. "I did go down and visit your friend."

"Did any of the servants see you?" she asked.

"No. There is a particular word of power that renders the speaker invisible."

"And another that unlocks doors?"

"Of course. Even a lock must obey the proper command. A key forces it to. But locks respond to words just as easily as bits of folded iron." He rested his forearms on the table. "And there is a word, a sacred word, that wakens the dead."

She felt a shiver go down her back. "I thought only the Medium had such power."

"It *is* the power of the Medium, Eilean. That is the only power I know. A Leering," he said, extending his arm and gesturing to the one that kept him imprisoned, "is powered by an unspoken word carved into permanence. That's what anchors the power and prevents it from being drained by the user. But there is only one source of magical power. The Medium."

She studied him closely. "You've told me that the Aldermaston cannot use the Medium."

"He cannot."

"How do you know this? How can I trust what you say?"

He leaned closer. "How can you doubt what the Medium has already told you?"

"All my life, I've believed Aldermaston Gilifil was a good man."

"There are many parts of him that are good," Mordaunt said simply. "But his knowledge, his reputation, his standing has filled him with pride. That blocks the Medium. The magic can sense our innermost thoughts, Eilean. It whispers to us constantly to do better, to be better. When we resist, when we choke those whispers with pride, it stops speaking to us. Not because our pride silenced it. Because we have proven we will not listen."

She let out a deep breath. "You're not a heretic?"

"What? Does that mean everyone else has been deceived to believe that I am? Well . . . there are a few who aren't *pethets*, who will not accept something just because the High Seer says so."

She squeezed her hands into fists and lowered her head. "What should I believe? I don't want to be deceived. By you or anyone."

"No one wants to be deceived, Eilean, and men and women are very capable of persuading with their speech. You cannot trust my words until you learn for yourself whether I speak the truth. I doubt the Aldermaston has outright lied to you. But he lies without speaking by letting the world believe he is who they think him to be. You must learn this for yourself."

She bit her lip. "I'm grateful for what you did. Celyn is dear to everyone who knows her. She is the most kindhearted person I know."

"I know, little sister. And because *you* loved her, I petitioned the Medium to bring her back. I did it for you, Eilean. Not to prove anything. Not to deceive you. But because you were *hurting*, and I had compassion for you. If the Medium had rejected my petition, then I would not have spoken the word of power that brings *breath* back to the dead." He smiled at her. "There is so much the Medium can do. It connects things. It brings water from one place to another. It brings heat and fire from beneath the foundations of the world, where it is abundant, and spews it out up here."

She looked at him with fear and wonder. "What else?"

"In the tomes of one of the Twelve, you will find these words engraved. *Which of you can think and add one cubitum unto his stature?* Do you not see the power of thoughts? I've seen the Medium transform a man and make him grow. It can alter the visage as well, making one person so closely resemble another that a wife might be deceived into thinking another man is her husband. That power can be used for good or ill depending on a person's thoughts." His nostrils flared. "Pride is poisonous, but not ambition. You can be more than what you are,

Eilean. You are not like the laundry girls I see from the window, whose thoughts are as fleeting as flax in the wind, blowing whichever direction it pushes. Not like spinners and weavers who fancy naught beyond the kirtles they make. Your thoughts are like the roots of an oak tree when they take hold. You have potential they do not."

She was no one, a wretched. But he suggested she could be more.

"Ambition is not evil. Fire can bake a loaf of bread or destroy a mound of hay. The difference is in how it is tended. Let me train you, Eilean. Let me train you in the Medium."

She wanted it. His words had awakened a sort of hunger inside her. But she didn't trust it. She didn't trust *him*.

She rose from the table. "I don't know."

"You must decide, of course. No one should compel you to do anything against your will. But I see such promise in you."

"But what if it is the Aldermaston who is right?" she asked. "What if you are trying to trick me?"

"You cannot ask him, for you know what he will say," Mordaunt answered. "If he is the one lying, in deed if not in word, then he's unlikely to stop. No, little sister. There is but one way to know, and that is to ask the Medium."

"And how do I do that?" she said, almost laughing. "It isn't a person. Do I go to a Leering and whisper to it?"

Mordaunt chuckled. "The power of the Medium can be felt strongly within the walls of an abbey. But that is not the only place. If you would know, then leave the abbey grounds. Go beyond the borders protected by the Leerings."

She gasped and stared at him in shock. "That is where the Myriad Ones are!" Although they'd slept beyond those very borders on their way to the castle, they'd been protected by mastons who had the ability to cast the Myriad Ones out.

"Their influence is stronger at night," he said, undaunted, "with the absence of light, than it is during the day. Go at dawn when the sun is first rising. That is when their power begins to wane. Go find yourself a grove of trees. Oak trees would be preferable, but any will do."

"Why oak?"

"For reasons I will not explain to you unless you decide I can be trusted. Go with an open heart. Banish your doubts and fears. If the Medium senses you are sincere, that you truly wish to know the truth and act as its ambassador, then it will be more likely to respond to your petition. It may not. You should not try to force the Medium to answer you. Rather, open yourself to it. Express your willingness to heed it. Then cast your thoughts like a fisherman casts his nets. You may only catch one fish. You may catch a net full. But you will know for yourself. It may take several days. It may take longer. The Medium rewards diligence."

"But if I leave the borders, won't the Myriad Ones try and harm me?"

He looked at her seriously. "Yes. They might. They will be drawn to your thoughts. But remember the words of power I taught you. Those will repel them."

She rubbed her arms. "I don't know."

"You *know* what to do if you want to learn the truth. You must decide how much you want answers. What fears you are willing to face." He sighed deeply, then tilted his head, studying her. "You think I may have fooled you, but I have not. The Myriad Ones cannot bring someone back from the dead. There's a certain snake in Dahomey whose venom gives one the appearance of death, and enemies of the Medium have used its poison to deceive others into believing they are strong with the Medium. But that is trickery, and such snakes do not live here in the kingdom of Moros. It was not venom that injured your friend. She died because she was bitten by a tiny insect that carried a plague. I've been sick with it myself, long ago. That is the truth. It was the Medium that brought her back. Find out for yourself, Eilean."

"But why must I leave the grounds?"

"If you stay here, you will be reminded of things made by man. Even the apple trees in the orchard have been cultivated, trimmed, and shaped. Walk away. Go into the Bearden Muir and see the wild beauty that exists so close to us. Watch the butterflies and swarms of starlings. Listen to the wind and the drone of the bees. Remove yourself from the presence of mankind. Then fall on your knees and feel the wetness seep into your skirts. Empty your mind of everything. Do this, little sister, and you will know what it means to listen to the Medium. Then you will know whose words you can trust. Then you will know, as I do, that you are precious to the Medium."

She felt a tug of longing in her heart. The thought of heeding his advice, of going outside the boundaries, felt *right*. It caused a pleasant feeling, a welcoming one.

What if he was the deceiver?

A throb of doubt caused the good feelings to withdraw.

"Believe, Eilean," Mordaunt said to her with an earnest look. "Put your trust in the power that leads you to do good, like your friend always has. To be just and fair, even if you are mistreated. To walk humbly always. To discern the hearts of others. That is the Medium."

"I'll try," she answered. She left him but paused at the door after opening it. "Thank you. I just wanted to say it again."

"Don't thank me," he answered. "Thank the Medium yourself."

Tomes have led some to learning and others to madness. The words themselves can be taken different ways, and many will make excuses for themselves because of what they read. Such is the case of the heretic Utheros. As was said of one of the Twelve long ago, too much learning made him mad.

—Mícheál Nostradamus of Avinion Abbey

CHAPTER FOURTEEN

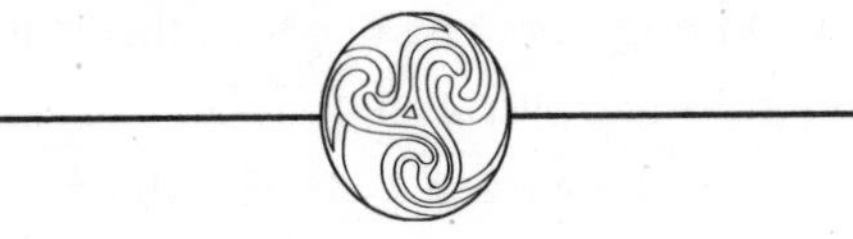

Starlings

The sun had not yet risen in the eastern hills when Eilean walked away from the castle the next morning, moving past the trees of the new apple orchard, the fishpond, and then beyond. The long grasses whisked against her skirts, and her shoes were wet, but it was early summer, and the air had no bite to it. She folded her arms as she walked, trying to tame the growing fear as she approached the boundary of the Leerings.

Each stride took her farther away from the familiarity of the castle.

Was she making a mistake? She didn't think so. Everything she had learned growing up at Tintern made her believe the magic of the Medium was sentient—that it could be coaxed to come closer if treated with determination and meekness. Pride was anathema to it, but she didn't feel proud. She felt . . . humbled.

The first ray of sunlight peeked over the hilltop. The clouds in the sky were thin and trailing, stretching across the canopy of the heavens.

Farther on, she began to hear the croaking of frogs and whistle of cicadas. Still she walked, going farther than she had in her previous explorations.

A strange sight caught her eyes, and she stopped. It wasn't a cloud but a flock of tiny birds, which lifted off the wetlands and began to swarm. She'd forgotten what Aisic had told her about the starlings coming to life in the morning. She watched in fascination as the birds, thick as gnats, plunged and rose, spiraling one way, then another. It was the most majestic thing she had ever seen.

The starlings made a sound as well, like the murmuring of tiny streams that grew louder and softer depending on the direction of their flight. After a while, the birds settled into the reeds again, but they took off moments later, flying overhead, and she knelt down, delighted and a little frightened. Craning her neck, she gazed up, feeling a silly smile on her mouth as she watched them race in one direction before suddenly shooting off in another.

The warmth of the sun on her cheek was pleasant. Smelling the earth, the reeds, the tang of the turf brought her a rare tranquility.

Mordaunt had been right. Getting away from the noises of the construction of the abbey made her feel more connected to the land, to nature itself. The starlings flew away, leaving her in the damp, still on her knees.

She rose and kept walking, moving toward a Leering she sensed in the distance. A pillar of stone came into view, a small face carved at the top. A waymarker—the kind of Leering that announced the grounds of the abbey. When she reached it, she touched it and felt its purpose: to keep out the Myriad Ones and hold the waters at bay. Two words of power echoed in her mind, as if whispered by the stone, and she recognized one of them. *Gheb-ool.* Mordaunt had told her it meant boundary. She couldn't make out the other, but it was part of the magic, part of the protection. It surprised her that she understood it instinctively. Were her powers with the Medium growing?

With her hand still resting on the rough stone, she stared into the marshland before her. Crooked trees thick with mossy limbs. Twisted oak trees. She'd reached the border of the former lake. Biting her lip, she wondered if she dared to venture farther. It would be so easy to go back. To give up.

But if she did that, her question would remain unanswered. Whom should she trust? Aldermaston Gilifil or the druid Mordaunt? Or maybe neither? Maybe the truth lay somewhere in between the extremes they represented. She had to know. She *wanted* to know.

Eilean stepped past the boundary and began walking toward the trees. When she passed the first few without incident, she felt relieved, but fear set in as she moved deeper into the Bearden Muir.

Stinging nettles snagged her dress and stabbed at her legs, and the snap of a twig made her whirl, her heart suddenly in her throat. Had one of the hunters followed her? She gazed into the thicket of trees but saw no one.

Fear crept up her spine, and her courage began to wilt. But she'd come this far. She wouldn't turn back without finishing her errand. Slowly, she knelt down next to an oak on a patch of turf clotted with mud.

Another cracking sound. She turned at the waist, trying to discern the source of the sound, but saw nothing. A cloud blotted away the sun, and fear bit at her like the nettles.

Still, Eilean bowed her head, opening herself up to the Medium. Inviting it to come to her.

More cracking sounds filled her ears, and birds took flight in a sudden panic. She felt the malevolent presence of the Myriad Ones, the same feeling she'd had crossing the Bearden Muir on her journey to Muirwood. In a moment, they'd converge on her, and the terror was real and powerful.

It wouldn't stop her. She wouldn't let it.

Eilean lifted her head and said the words of power aloud. *"Kozkah gheb-ool."*

A thrum of power jolted down her limbs at the command. Nothing around her visibly changed, but she felt the blast of energy come away from her, like a heavy rock dropped in a pond, making ripples. The invisible beings were thrust back. None of them could come near her. In her mind, she heard a screeching sound, a wail of angry protest. She clamped her hands over her ears, but the shriek didn't stop.

A shudder shook her all the way to her knees. Swaying against the blast, she kept hold of a single thought—a plea for help—as she sagged forward and caught herself with one hand. A thorn stabbed her, but still she stayed strong. She squeezed her eyes shut and maintained the barrier against that awful sound.

Her enemies wanted her, but they were powerless.

And then, at last, they turned away and left her alone.

Eilean found herself gasping for breath. The feeling of dread, of malevolence, was gone, and the sun had once again emerged. Overhead, a squirrel began to chitter at her. She lifted her face to the warm light and gasped. It wasn't from the sun. She was still in the midst of the trees' shadows.

A strange, otherworldly shaft of light had pierced the Bearden Muir and enveloped her. It filled her with peace and comfort and a feeling of safety she hadn't experienced since she was back at Tintern. Tears began to stream down her cheeks as the warmth of the Medium's light suffused her.

Precious.

It was whispered in her mind, not so much a word as a feeling. *She* was precious. She was loved. She had unlimited potential and was cared for with the deepest tenderness. She didn't understand what she was experiencing, but it made her weep. There were no Leerings there. This was a pure connection between her and the Medium, and she bowed her head and savored it.

"What do you want me to do?" she whispered, her voice trembling.

Be patient.

That was the closest way of understanding the thought in her mind. She needed to be patient, and the Medium would reveal its will to her in its own time.

"But which of them is right?" she asked. In her mind, she thought of the faces of Mordaunt and Gilifil.

Be patient.

In that moment she knew—the answer wasn't coming at that time. She could ask again and again, but the Medium would only tell her when it was ready. But it had answered her. A feeling of love swelled in her heart, so powerful it would have been impossible to utter another word. Bowing her head, she submitted to the Medium. She would do anything it asked of her.

She felt a throb of gratitude not her own.

Was the Medium *thanking* her? A shiver went through her.

The feeling of pure love expanded, growing larger and more powerful until Eilean grew dizzy from it. And that was all she felt until the world went dark.

***

She awoke to the feeling of a hand pressing against her neck. Her eyelids were so heavy she couldn't open them.

"Is she dead?" The voice came from far away. She recognized it as Twynho.

"I feel her pulse." It was Captain Hoel. "Eilean?"

She felt a hand snake around the back of her neck, and someone slowly lifted her.

"There's blood on her hand," Twynho said.

"I think it's from that nettle. She might have passed out from the pain. Bring your flask."

She tried to open her eyes, to move, but her body was as exhausted as if she'd been forced to run past her endurance.

"Unnghh." It was the only sound she could make.

"Eilean? Can you hear me?"

Someone lifted her hand, and then water splashed on it. She barely felt it. A rag was swiped over her palm, catching on some broken bits of thorn, but it didn't hurt as much as it should have.

"There's a few thorns still in there," Twynho said. "I'll get them out."

That meant it was the captain holding her.

"Careful. Don't hurt her," he said, the words making his chest rumble.

She felt her head loll against him. After another failed attempt to open her eyes, she just rested there, taking in his familiar scent. Twynho began to pluck the bits of thorn from her hand.

"There. Think I got them all."

"Eilean, can you hear me?" Captain Hoel asked.

She tried to speak again, but it came out as a groan.

"I don't see any other blood," Hoel said. She felt his hand against her throat, then he searched for injuries on her head, his fingers moving through her hair. "No bumps or knots."

"Probably fainted," Twynho said. "Let's get her to the healer to inspect more closely."

"Aye. I don't think she'd want us disrobing her here in the marsh."

Hoel scooped Eilean beneath her knees and lifted. She felt powerless to move, and the sudden motion made her dizzy. It almost felt like he was cushing her.

"You're not carrying her back to the abbey grounds like *that*, Captain? It's a bit far."

"No. You're going to help get her up on my shoulder."

The two hunters rearranged her, and Eilean found herself hanging over Hoel's back. Her left arm was flung around his neck, her wrist held securely in his hand, and his strong arms trapped her legs to his chest. She felt like a sack of flour but was completely incapable of moving let alone objecting.

The two hunters began to hike back toward the abbey. Once they were clear of the trees, she felt the sun again, and her eyes finally opened. She was bouncing heavily against the captain's back, and it mortified her that she was so weak he had to carry her. Her stomach growled with hunger. How long had she been gone? It was difficult to tell, bouncing as she was.

"Cap-tain," she said, her voice frail.

"She's awake," Twynho said.

Hoel stopped and dropped down on one knee. Twynho helped remove her from his back and prop her up, and her vision swam and she nearly collapsed.

"Easy, there." She felt Hoel's hand against her cheek. "What were you doing out here, lass? Did someone hurt you?"

She blinked, trying to speak, but her voice was too hoarse. Hoel lifted his own flask, which was strapped to him with a strand of leather, and uncorked it and pressed it to her mouth. She took a few sips, but the taste of leather made her wrinkle her nose.

"I saw the starlings," she said.

"The what?" asked Twynho in bafflement.

"The starlings. The birds," Hoel said. "Why did you go alone, Eilean?"

She didn't want to tell him her true reasons. "Someone told me about them. A friend. I wanted to see them."

"Why did you go beyond the waymarkers?" he asked, worry in his voice. "That's dangerous, Eilean."

"It was foolish, yes," she agreed. She looked up into his eyes and felt part of her stomach twist. Hunger. Yes, she was very hungry.

Hoel wiped his mouth, his brow furrowing. "Do you think you can stand?"

"I don't want you carrying me the rest of the way," she said. He rose first and offered her his hand. She took it, noting it was warm and calloused and strong, and then promptly swayed and fell against him, which made her cheeks burn.

"I'm sorry," she mumbled, pushing against him.

"Don't try to walk yet. Just get your balance."

She took in a shaky breath, and her legs felt stronger. The light-headed feeling was terrible, but after a few more breaths, she felt more like herself.

His set a steadying hand on her shoulder. "I can carry you back."

Twynho gave them a knowing grin that put a frown on her face. What, exactly, had Hoel told him? Were they laughing at her? "I can manage. You go on ahead."

"I don't think so, lass," Twynho said with a chuckle.

"Are you hungry?"

"No," Eilean answered, too quickly, for her stomach gurgled.

Hoel opened a pouch at his waist and then withdrew some bright red berries. "Found these earlier," he said. "Try one. They're a little bitter."

She bit into one and found it surprisingly tangy. She had a few more but refused the rest when he offered them.

"You're not as pale now," Twynho said, folding his arms. "Shall we go back?"

"Reckon I can manage," she said. She started walking, slowly at first, to test her strength. The weariness was still overpowering, but she kept at it through sheer stubbornness. As she walked, she thought of the experience she'd had in the grove of oak trees. The powerful feeling of love. A surge of emotion washed through her, and suddenly she was crying again.

"Are you in pain?" Hoel asked in a worried voice.

She felt ashamed of her tears, but she couldn't find the words to describe what was happening to her. So she shook her head no and kept walking, wiping her eyes on her sleeve. "How long was it before you found me?" she asked, stifling a sniffle.

Twynho gave Hoel a meaningful look, which the captain returned with a glare of warning.

"You weren't gone long," Hoel said. "Are you sure you're well?"

"Yes, but not well enough to talk right now," she said forcefully.

There were more meaningful looks between the two, and she felt her cheeks burning.

"Ah, we're almost there," Twynho said, pointing ahead.

As they reached the edge of the new apple orchard, Hoel steered her toward the healer's tent.

"I don't need to go there," Eilean insisted. She wanted to go to the kitchen, and so he escorted her there. Twynho went off another way.

Hoel stopped her at the door, his hand on her shoulder again. His voice was pitched low, and his expression was serious. "Why did you go into the Bearden Muir? Did Mordaunt tell you to?"

He had, actually. But not for any reason Hoel could guess. Rather than answer directly, she decided to lead him another way.

"I went because I wanted to ask the Medium something."

That was true enough. She'd say no more.

"And did you get your answer?"

She felt that surge of love again and just nodded, unable to speak.

Perhaps he'd been hoping for more of an answer, or maybe he just didn't believe her, because his brow furrowed again. "I'll check on you later. Some more food will do you good, I think. Your hand will heal quickly."

"You don't need to check on me, Captain."

"I know I don't need to. But I will."

He looked over Eilean's shoulder, then dropped his hand and pushed the door open for her before turning and leaving.

As Eilean reached for the door, she noticed Rhiannon and the other laundry girls watching her from behind, their eyes glittering with jealousy.

How fortune brings to earth the oversure. Aldermaston Utheros has been stripped of his rank and authority. His safe conduct will last for three days. After that, he will be a hunted man, a heretic, an apostate. He refused to bend the knee and so will face the trial of fire when he is captured. He believed his cause was just. But despite his convictions, he owes loyalty to the head of the order. And that loyalty was not repaid.

I return now to Avinion to learn what has happened recently in the wilds of Moros. Communication with that secret abbey has been difficult. But once it is built and we can use the Apse Veil to travel there and back, we will gain more timely reports.

—Mícheál Nostradamus of Avinion Abbey

CHAPTER FIFTEEN

Excommunication

Several days had passed since Eilean's encounter with the Medium. She felt a different person, more calm within herself, more observant of what was going on around her. She'd been touched by power beyond understanding, and the effects had lasted for several days before she'd begun to feel normal again.

It had not escaped her notice that her friend Celyn had had a similar experience. Since her return from death, she was quieter, more thoughtful, and even more helpful inside the kitchen than she'd been before. Ardys and Loren had both commented on the change, and Celyn had shrugged off their comments and insisted she was just herself as always. But everyone noticed there was a difference.

The Aldermaston had not publicly commented on the belief that he'd risen Celyn from the dead, but he'd allowed the misperception to stand. Indeed, several small comments he'd made, plus a somewhat uncharacteristic interest in her health, suggested to others that the stories were true.

Eilean started eating supper with Aisic every night, and sometimes Celyn even joined them if Ardys could spare her. She looked forward to it all day long, even though their talks were about nothing important. The girls from the laundry cast glances at them, as if curious about their friendship, and Rhiannon always had a friendly smile for them. Aisic seemed oblivious to the attention. He liked to talk, and Eilean enjoyed listening to him.

"We're starting another tunnel," he said that evening. "I guess the Aldermaston wants several. It's a lot of digging. Did you know that a village is going to be started soon?"

"I didn't," she answered, tilting her head. She saw the stubble growing on his chin and cheeks. The flecks of gold amidst the darker hairs fascinated her.

"It's true. I've heard there will even be an inn, a place where the wealthy can visit. It's hard to comprehend how quickly the abbey is going up now that the foundation stones are set. The walls are already nearly to the edge of the pit."

She'd seen that for herself during her walks, but she didn't say so. She liked listening to him. "I saw the starlings recently," she said. "There were so many, just like you said."

His brow knotted. "Oh."

"What's wrong?"

"I wanted to take you to see them," he said, looking down.

Her stomach wriggled with excitement. "I didn't know that." A nervous feeling came next, but she let the words out anyway. "We could still go together."

His chin lifted. "Tomorrow morning?"

"I'd like that," Eilean said.

"I'll meet you behind the kitchen before sunrise," he said. He looked pleased by the prospect. Then he stood up from his chair and reached down to help her up.

The feeling of his hand on hers sent a thrill up her arm and put the beginnings of a blush in her cheeks. "Tomorrow, then," she said.

"I look forward to it. But if we're to do that, there's some work I must finish tonight." He glanced at the table, stacked with their dirty dishes, and started to reach for them.

"Oh, let me handle them," she said. "It's no trouble at all."

He squeezed her hand and thanked her. Then he left, glancing back with a smile that made her heart flutter, and she took the dishes and went off to find Celyn. Her friend was finally sitting down to eat her own supper now that the crowd was dwindling. There was a delicious smell in the air—the scent of something sweet baking.

"What's that smell?" Eilean asked, dropping onto the bench across from Celyn after she deposited the dishes in the wash basin.

"There are so many apples that Ardys is trying to find new ways to cook them. She's making an apple pudding for the Aldermaston."

"It smells delicious. What's in it?"

"Apples, of course. Then a layer of flour, treacle, butter, oats, and a spice she's been saving from Tintern. I can't wait to taste it. She's made one for us to sample as well."

Eilean glanced toward the cooking area, where Ardys was hard at work. Loren leaned back on his stool, head propped against the wall, his eyes half-closed as he fell asleep. Mitching again. From the tall windows higher up the kitchen walls, she could see the first stars outside.

That soft, lovely glow filled her with contentment, and she reached over and squeezed Celyn's hand. "I'm so happy you are back."

Her friend's countenance fell.

"What's wrong?" Eilean asked, surprised.

"I feel so different now."

"What do you mean? Are you sick again?"

"No. I've never felt better in all my life. But something happened while I was gone." She looked down and picked at her roll.

"Tell me. I'm your friend."

"You're my best friend," Celyn said. "But I can't tell even you."

That was even more worrying. "Why?"

Celyn sighed, glancing back to where Ardys was working and then around at the rapidly emptying dining area. Only a few workers lingered, but she lowered her voice anyway. "I'm afraid of what you'll think of me."

"Nothing you could say would make me think less of you," Eilean promised. "Please. Tell me. Unburden yourself."

Celyn looked down at their hands, still entwined, then put her other one on top. "Have you heard about the apostate in Hautland?"

"A little," Eilean said.

Celyn's look became more somber. "I've overheard some of the mastons talking about it. They come and eat before the rest of the workers. I probably shouldn't be listening in, but I can't help it."

"What do they say?"

"There's a trial or something happening. They say he's going to be excommunicated. Then he'll be killed. He's an Aldermaston, Eilean. Why would they do that to him?"

"Even an Aldermaston can become a heretic."

Celyn looked at her and flushed, then looked away.

"Celyn? Talk to me."

"I can't."

"Please."

"I should get back to work."

Eilean gripped her friend's arm to keep her still. She had a suspicion of what Celyn was about to say, and something told her the words needed to be spoken . . . for both of them. "Please tell me."

Celyn looked ashamed and didn't raise her eyes. "Reckon our Aldermaston is one."

The words were said in a whisper.

"A heretic?" Eilean whispered back.

Celyn nodded and shuddered. "When I was dead, I saw and heard things, Eilean. They were too beautiful, too strange to describe. There were people there, beings of great power and wisdom. I knew things I'd never known in life. There was a city, a shining city. I wanted to enter, but they wouldn't let me. Not because I was a wretched. But because I wasn't a true maston. The guardian at the gate said there were few true mastons left. She told me pride had overrun the order."

Celyn looked up at Eilean, a pained crease in her brow. "And I knew as clearly as you sit before me now that Aldermaston Gilifil hasn't been true to his vows. That he cannot use the Medium at all, and yet he pretends to."

The words cut into Eilean's heart. She knew they were true, that this was the answer she'd been told to wait for.

"Please don't tell anyone," Celyn begged. "I can't tell Ardys. She would . . . she'd be so angry. *Shaw!* I can't believe I even told *you*. But I felt that I should. I'm sorry for putting this—"

"No," Eilean said, cutting her off. She looked into her friend's eyes. "I've had the same suspicion."

Celyn looked baffled. "Truly?"

Glancing over Celyn's shoulder, Eilean saw Ardys coming toward their table with a small baking cauldron she'd pulled from the oven with a metal hook. The kitchen had fully cleared out now, even the rest of the staff, and just the four of them were left.

"We'll talk later," Eilean said, nodding discreetly.

Celyn quieted, but she looked relieved. It was obvious she hadn't thought she'd be believed.

"It looks done," Ardys said with a pleased smile. "Come, Loren! Bring some spoons!"

Loren started awake and quickly rubbed his eyes. "I wasn't sleeping!"

"Of course you weren't." Ardys chuckled and set the steaming cauldron down between the two girls. The smell wafting from it was heavenly.

Loren brought four spoons, and the four of them began to dig through the thick layer of buttery crust to the spiced apples beneath. At the first taste, Eilean mumbled in delight, even though the apples were hot enough to burn her tongue.

"Oh, Ardys!" she said.

The cook smiled with affection and enjoyed her own taste. "Reckon the Aldermaston is going to like this. We have apple butter, apple bread, apple pudding . . . I'll even try and make apple soup!"

That sounded strange, but Eilean rather liked the idea. She and Celyn exchanged significant looks. No words needed to be uttered. They'd talk again soon. In the meantime, they could be comforted by the knowledge that even though their understanding of the world had been upended, they were not alone.

***

The next morning, Eilean rose early, dressed, and wrapped herself in a cloak before sneaking stealthily down the stairs. It was well before dawn, but she was so excited to see the starlings with Aisic she'd had difficulty sleeping. The dark and quiet castle was a little frightening, but she saw evidence of the fading stars through the windows. Dawn would be coming soon.

She went out the rear of the castle and nodded to the hunter who stood guard. It was Olien, one of the hunters whom she'd traveled with from Tintern.

"You're up early," he said in a neutral tone.

Glancing at the kitchen, she saw the light glowing from the windows. "Yes, it is early, isn't it?" she replied, hurrying toward the kitchen without giving a further explanation.

The turf was wet with dew, the air unseasonably cool, but her eagerness motivated her. She went toward the rear of the kitchen, bathed in shadow, and found no one there. So she began to pace, nervously listening for Aisic and hearing nothing but the clicking call of storks, Ardys's muffled voice, and the sound of cookery. It took a lot of loaves to feed all the workers, so the girls assigned to the kitchen were the first to rise.

She wasn't sure how long she'd been waiting when the sound of boots whisking through the grass announced someone was coming. Around the corner of the kitchen came Aisic, also wrapped up in a cloak.

"You're already here. Sorry I'm late."

"It's all right. Shall we go?"

They walked side by side in long strides, going around the new apple trees planted nearby, the same direction she'd gone on her previous journey. They spoke in low tones, not wanting to draw attention, but the coming sunrise made them plain enough to see. Some of the master builders were already walking around the pit in the distance, and the clank of hammer and chisels soon rose from the quarry.

There was a lot more mist that morning, so it wasn't clear whether the starlings had started swarming or not. She and Aisic spoke with the easy familiarity of friends now, and Eilean was grateful that he seemed to enjoy being with her. Sometimes, they walked so close that he bumped into her. She didn't mind that either.

As they approached the boundary Leering, she saw its eyes glow red and felt a tightening inside her stomach. Immediately Aisic slowed his pace.

"That's strange," he said. "Why is the Leering doing that?"

They approached carefully, Eilean's feeling of dread and fear increasing with each step. When they were about twenty paces away, a pulse of warning struck her mind.

"This doesn't feel right," Aisic said. He wiped his mouth, looking frustrated and fearful.

"Let's try going around it," Eilean suggested.

But they'd barely taken a few steps before she sensed the proximity of another Leering. The two were sharing magic, creating an invisible rope—a boundary.

"What is this for?" Aisic said with annoyance. He put his hands on his hips and huffed with anger.

Eilean reached out with her mind and revoked the barrier of fear the Leering made. It calmed instantly, although she still sensed a deeper underlying magic—the one that held the waters at bay.

"Huh?" Aisic wondered, then looked at her. "That was you, wasn't it?" He grinned. "Come on, then!"

He reached for her hand, and she let him take it, and together they hurried outside the border. The weeds got thicker as they walked, but she'd been there recently and knew they were getting close to where she'd seen the starlings.

"We're almost there!" he said, turning toward her with a smile.

Sure enough, the starlings began to swarm as they had before, although this time they were beyond the barrier rather than within it. It was the strangest sound, one that rushed back and forth as the starlings swept into the skies only to dive and twist.

"Reckon they're coming this way," Aisic said.

They were. Eilean felt a thrill as the swarm converged around them, coming so close it felt as if she and Aisic would be swept away. He quickly unclasped his cloak and spread it out on the grass and weeds. He knelt down on it and waved for her to join him.

She did, dropping onto her knees and gazing up with delight at the thousands of birds swooping overhead.

Aisic laughed and lay on his back so he could stare at them. He put his hands behind his head and grinned at the sight.

Eilean gazed down at him, feeling a surge of warmth and affection. Back in Tintern, he'd never taken any notice of her. Heart in her throat, she took his cue and lay down on the cloak so she could gaze up at the flock of starlings.

"I never imagined such a thing," Aisic said in wonder, his words reminding her of her own thoughts—although she knew he was talking about the birds. "Look, I reckon that's the leader!" He pointed, but there were so many birds, she couldn't tell which one he was pointing at.

She did feel the heat coming from his body and relished it. She wanted to sidle closer to him but pushed the thought away. A moment later, he edged toward her on the cloak.

"What does it sound like to you?" he asked.

"Like whispering. Like a whole town whispering at the same time."

And they stared at the view as the sun peeked over the hills at long last. Aisic turned toward her, propping his head on one hand and staring down at her face. The look he gave her was tender yet eager.

He was going to kiss her. He wouldn't even start by cushing her, which was what she'd imagined happening between them. She didn't know how she knew. But suddenly he leaned toward her, and their lips touched. She could feel the scratchiness of his stubble. It was a little ticklish, but she wouldn't laugh. This was her first kiss. It felt wonderful and strange and interesting all at the same time. He put his hand on her side, and she could feel the pleasant burn of his palm.

When he pulled away, he was smiling with something like victory. As though he'd won something.

"That was nice," he said.

She could still taste him. She wanted more. A quivering feeling came through her body, warming her all the way down to her cold toes. Yes, she very much wanted more kisses from him. And some cuddling and cushing too.

He tilted his head sideways, as if hearing something. Then he looked back the way they'd come, and his eyes shot wide.

"*Shaw!* It's Hoel!"

A spasm of dread wrenched inside her, and she immediately blushed a hundred shades of crimson.

War is delightful to those who have had no experience of it.

—Mícheál Nostradamus of Avinion Abbey

CHAPTER SIXTEEN

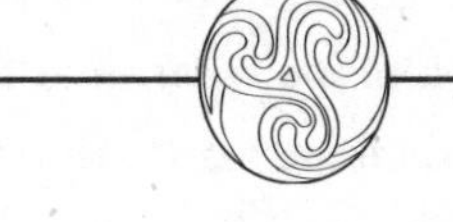

The Coming of Ten

Eilean hastily made it to her feet, and Aisic grabbed up his cloak before Captain Hoel reached them, eyes blazing with anger. The swarm of starlings continued to soar through the air, beneath the first morning rays, but the feeling of awe and wonder had been transformed into a sinking sensation of guilt and fear. Although they hadn't broken any rules other than leaving the barrier, she was embarrassed to be caught in such a position.

When the captain came, his words were strong and edged with accusation. "So it was you who disarmed the Leering?" he said, glaring at Eilean.

"I did," she replied, her throat thickening. Tears began to sting in her eyes. "We wanted to see the starlings."

"Didn't you think that the barriers might be there for a reason? Come on, both of you. Let's get back to them quickly."

Aisic looked embarrassed but not cowed. "What's the harm in seeing some birds?"

The captain shot him a look that silenced his question, then turned on his heel and started marching back the way they'd come. Aisic gave Eilean an apologetic look and then sneered at the hunter behind his back. She didn't think it was funny at all. The embarrassment of having been caught in a compromising position, by Hoel of all people, mortified her. Surely he had seen them do it. Her cheeks flamed even hotter.

When they passed the invisible boundary line, the hunter approached the Leering and placed a hand on the stone. The eyes began to glow red instantly, sending out a throb of fear. Eilean and Aisic backed away from it, for its power to affect their minds diminished with distance.

Captain Hoel seemed unaffected by the Leering, but then he was a maston himself. He walked toward them, his look intent.

"The boundaries are here for a reason," he said, somewhat softer but no less seriously. "Last night, a man was captured out here after he snuck past the ring of Leerings."

Eilean covered her mouth, flinching.

"Who was it?" Aisic asked.

"Someone who lives in the Bearden Muir. There are small settlements throughout this area. The druids have been rousing them to anger. We've learned they're forming a mob to ransack the castle."

"Shaw!" Aisic exclaimed.

A pit sank in Eilean's stomach. "Do you know when?" she asked.

"Three days from now. He'd wandered out of the woods in the dark and happened to pass the Leerings without seeing them. He was caught by Twynho and brought to the castle. Thank the Medium, Olien happened to mention that he'd seen you two wandering off. There are other enemies of the abbey out there, already gathered. Maybe fifty? Possibly more. They could have killed the both of you."

Aisic swallowed. "What are we going to do?"

Eilean's terror sharpened.

"There's no time for help to arrive. Most will hunker down inside the castle. We'll gather the men to help fight."

"I want to fight," Aisic said, stepping forward, clenching his fist.

Hoel looked at him with a smirk. "You might not feel the same eagerness afterward, but we need every boy and man who is brave enough. Go back and report to the master builders. We'll be training you all day."

"Will we get swords?" Aisic asked eagerly.

"You'd more than likely injure yourself with one, lad. Staves, pick-axes, scythes. We'll use what weapons we have. Now get going! And don't you ever leave the boundaries again without permission!"

Aisic was clearly chagrined by the scolding, but he nodded and then extended his hand to Eilean to escort her back.

"No, go on alone," the captain said, and Eilean's stomach dropped further.

Aisic shot her a concerned glance, but he obeyed the captain. She didn't blame him—he likely would have been thrashed if he hadn't.

Hoel watched him leave, then folded his arms and gave Eilean an intimidating look.

"I'm sorry for what I did. It won't happen again," she said weakly, trying not to cry in front of him.

"You left the boundaries before," he said. "You went into a grove of trees. Did you meet someone? Are you in league with the druids?"

The accusation shocked her. "No!"

"I wish I could believe you," he said with a strained sigh. "I've noticed you've changed since you came to Muirwood. And you are strong with the Medium. That much is obvious. Or are you only strong because you wear a druid talisman?" He took a step toward her.

"I don't have one," she said, backing away.

"You'll excuse me while I search you anyway. If you're in league with them, Eilean, you'd best be honest. Many people will die if they attack us. The peasants, trappers, woodsmen, and fools who are coming to rescue the apostate you've befriended."

Eilean was so stunned by his words, she couldn't find the words to refute them. "I'm not part of them!"

"You must see that your actions are suspicious. I'm told you were caught in the tunnel not too long ago. Did you tell Mordaunt about it?"

"No!" she said, feeling her eyes begin to water. A tear trickled down her cheek.

He approached her, and then she froze from fear as he began to search her. He checked her bodice first, touched her waist, her legs. She felt sick to her stomach as he performed his duty, treating her as if she were a rogue caught in a crime. He even examined her hair, moving it aside and then checking the back of her neck.

"I didn't want to do that," he said. "But I had to be sure you wore no talisman nor had the markings of one on your bosom."

Her cheeks were so hot she thought they'd catch fire. "Are you . . . quite done, Captain?" she asked in a shaking voice.

"You know nothing about the mob?"

"Nothing. I wouldn't have gone to see the starlings if I'd known about the threat."

"I'm still not convinced you weren't going to meet with the mob," he countered. "I wish you hadn't been chosen by the Aldermaston for this duty."

"I'm not disloyal to him," she said, though she felt a twinge of guilt in her heart because of her doubts about him.

"I hope not, for your sake. Truly. I'm sorry I had to be so forward with you, but my training teaches me to be distrustful. The commander of the Apocrisarius is Lord Nostradamus of Dahomey. He'd box my ears if I hadn't searched you. I only wish . . ." He pursed his lips and shook his head.

"What?" she asked. She'd never heard that name before, but judging by Captain Hoel's thoroughness and suspicious nature, she could only imagine the fearsomeness of the man who had taught him.

"Nothing," he said. "Let's go back."

"Tell me," she asked.

He tilted his head slightly. "Before we left Tintern, I asked the Aldermaston if you could join the hunters. I saw potential in you. I think you would have enjoyed the work. Starlings and all. But he was angry at me for even suggesting it."

His words once again stunned her speechless. Blinking, she gaped at him in confusion. "You . . . wanted . . . me?"

"Plenty of Apocrisarius are women," he said. "Trained to spy on kings in their courts. We need some in Moros right now, to be honest. It's not all skulking in the woods with bows and blades . . . although I think you'd excel at that too. But"—he sighed heavily—"it wasn't to be. The Aldermaston had another duty in mind for you." The look he gave her reminded her of how much he disagreed with Gilifil's decision.

She didn't know what to say. But hadn't she wondered if she would be asked to join the hunters the night she was summoned to speak with the Aldermaston? Had Hoel's conversation with the Aldermaston happened that very day?

Was her intuition perhaps something more? Had the Medium whispered those thoughts to her?

She felt a throb of confirmation in her heart. The sensation was small and subtle, but she clung to it.

What do you want me to do? she asked inside her mind.

All that came to her was the same message as before. *Patience.*

***

By the time they returned to the grounds, news of the danger had spread. The young men who had spent the previous day digging tunnels had been armed with makeshift weapons and lined up by the hunters for training drills. Those who had previous experience hunting were lent bows and arrows so they might practice against bales of hay.

Food stores from the Aldermaston's kitchen were being moved into the castle, and the defenses were staffed with watchmen. There were only two battlement walls spanning the main structures of the castle, and there were several people up there, marching back and forth to keep a watch from higher ground. She brought breakfast, late, to Mordaunt and told him the news.

"It makes sense to launch an attack now," he said with a shrug and look of indifference. "Once the abbey is built, it would be much more difficult. And if they release the Leerings controlling the rivers, then all the work will be flooded and ruined and they'd have to start over. Really, it's a clever thing."

"Did you ask the druids to do this?" she asked.

"How could I? I've been trapped here for a long time."

"But did you order it before you were captured?"

He chuckled. "Not at all. They see what's happening at court, how the mastons are taking over. Naturally they're rebelling. It's all very predictable. And what were you doing out past the boundaries this morning?"

He always seemed to know more than he ought. It wasn't fair.

"I was seeing the starlings," she said, but the stronger memory was of kissing Aisic. It made her lips tingle.

Mordaunt narrowed his eyes. "Oh? The starlings? You went alone?"

"I didn't," she answered.

"Celyn went with you?"

A feeling of shame washed over her, although it wasn't so potent as when Captain Hoel had happened upon them. "Not her. I went with a man I know from Tintern."

"A man," Mordaunt scoffed. "That was rather bold of you."

"We've been friends since . . ." She stopped. They hadn't been friends at Tintern, and it felt like a lie to say it.

"Hmmm? You've been friends for how long?"

"What does it matter? I was with him. We saw the starlings, and Captain Hoel found us."

Mordaunt shook his head. "I wouldn't risk your honor in such a way, Eilean. It's beneath you."

The hot feeling of shame turned into anger.

"Oh, there is her temper again," Mordaunt said. He looked her in the eyes. "Trust me, little sister. I've known young men and their hot passions. It will not end well for you."

"We didn't do anything . . . wrong," she spluttered. "We weren't even cushing."

He looked at her in confusion. "Is that another Pry-rian saying?"

"It's . . . it's a hug . . . except more . . . I don't know how to describe it. He kissed me, that's all."

He sighed. "I'm only trying to help."

"It doesn't feel helpful. I've liked him a long time. He's been lonely, friendless here."

"Why would that be?"

She tried to subdue her anger, but it got the better of her. "How would you feel being taken from your home and put somewhere unfamiliar? Torn from your friends. Faced with the unknown at every corner."

"Go on," he said. There was a look of understanding in his eyes that somehow only made her madder.

She wanted to shout, but she lowered her voice. "We've finally been able to talk. To really talk."

"You talk? Or he does?"

"Well . . . he does. But he never used to do that with me before. He's . . . interesting."

Mordaunt gave a noncommittal shrug. "Let's hope for the best, then. But most young men are rather selfish, Eilean. Their needs blind them to the needs or desires of others. If he wanted what is best for you, then I would encourage your feelings for him. I just fear your own feelings might be clouding your better judgment."

"And how would you know the first thing about my feelings?" she challenged.

He sighed again. "Because they are as plain to me as looking through a window, child. It is my Gift from the Medium. And my curse. I see people as they really are. Even your Aldermaston."

She gazed at him in confusion but not surprise. She'd had the thought before that perhaps he could read her mind. A throb of agreement came to her heart. Yes, the Medium had told her that before.

"You know my thoughts," she whispered.

Mordaunt went to the chair and sat down wearily. "Yes, Eilean. All of them. I already know about your experience in the Bearden Muir, although you didn't tell me. I know about Celyn and her doubts about the Aldermaston."

Eilean froze. "You know too much!" She feared his knowledge could get her friend in trouble. It could get both of them in trouble.

"A curse or a gift?" He sniffed. "How I see it, it depends on the day. But I'm on your side, Eilean. I've sensed your strength in the Medium since you first came here. I've offered to teach you. Willingly. Yet you resist because you doubt me. You think I'm going to corrupt you when all I desire is for you to achieve your potential. You are to be more than just a wretched."

"Can you see Captain Hoel's thoughts as well?"

"Of course."

"Is it true? Did he want me to become a hunter?"

"Yes. He sees potential in you as well. As does the Aldermaston." He steepled his fingers and rested his elbows on the table, leaning toward her. "What you must decide is whose vision of you do *you* wish to fulfill? Mine or theirs. It's up to you. Your thoughts will determine your destiny."

"My thoughts? How am I supposed to choose?"

"Let's consider the alternatives. Aldermaston Gilifil wants you to befriend me. He wants me to confide in you so *he* can find and claim *my* tome. He plots to become the next High Seer of Avinion in the future, and I am a mere stepping-stone in his ambition. If you follow him, you will be rewarded . . . if you never let him know that you know the truth . . . that his ambition has ripened into pride and the Medium shuns him now." Mordaunt smiled and shook his head. "Or there's the honorable Captain Hoel! Who sees your potential to become part of the Apocrisarius. The hunters of heretics. Seekers of the disobedient. He has his own designs as well."

"And you don't?" Eilean challenged. "You want me to free you."

Mordaunt shifted in his seat and rested his arms on the table. "I only want to do the Medium's will. I believe it sent you here to help me. But I do not see you as just a means to that end. I can discern that the Medium wishes you to do its will here. That your destiny is somehow wrapped up with this abbey. I feel it in my bones, although I cannot see what it means." He pointed his finger at her. "Your thoughts, powered by your dreams and ardent desires, can harness the Medium's power. You can do incredible things if you allow it to flow through you. If you seek to do its will, as I have."

A shout sounded from outside. Eilean rushed to the window and parted the curtain. A gasp escaped her as she watched people down below rush toward the safety of the castle. Looking to the east, she saw people marching through the wetlands. A whole host of them carrying pitchforks and staves. They were headed toward the castle.

Mordaunt appeared at her shoulder. "They've decided to attack early after their man was caught. Unfortunate. But which is it? The coming of ten? Or the coming of a thousand?"

Man is to man either angel or wolf. From my experience, it is more often wolf. Savage, cunning, constantly preying on the weak, the aged, the sick in order to cull the herd. But some people are angels who strengthen the weak, visit and honor the aged, and heal the sick. It is easy to mistake angels for being harmless, but in the tomes of the angels, called the Sefers, the angels carry swords. And their words are just as sharp.

—Mícheál Nostradamus of Avinion Abbey

CHAPTER SEVENTEEN

The Druid War

The few children at Muirwood Abbey were ushered quickly into the castle, along with the untrained women. Captain Hoel assigned two of his hunters to guard the castle and ordered stores of arrows to be given to them to aid in the defense. The young men, the mastons, and the aged had been conscripted to protect the abbey grounds.

Eilean brought Celyn, Ardys, and the kitchen girls up to Mordaunt's room for shelter. Loren had been conscripted to be part of the defenses, and his absence from the room made everyone feel even more on edge. Mordaunt was taciturn to the new guests, pacing back and forth in front of the window without attempting to speak to anyone.

As Eilean looked from face to face, seeing the fear and worry in her friends' eyes, she wished she had been trained as a hunter. A feeling of helplessness gnawed at her insides. What would happen if the castle was breached? What would the attackers do to the women inside?

"You will not be harmed," Mordaunt said to her in a low voice.

She turned, found him near her. His eyes were serious but comforting. Once again he had known her thoughts.

His words reassured her a little, but that awful feeling of dread continued to coil within her stomach.

A knock came to the door, making everyone start. Eilean went and stood at the crack. "Who is it?"

"Rhiannon. Let us in!"

Eilean opened the door and found the three laundry girls gathered there with tearful, worried faces. "Please!" Rhiannon begged. "Cimber said to barricade ourselves in a room somewhere. Cannot we come in?"

"Of course you can," said Ardys, who had come up behind Eilean. "Come in, hurry!"

Once inside, the three laundry girls glanced around before their fearful gazes settled on Mordaunt. He gave them a dismissive look and went back to the window.

Celyn offered the girls some bread that she'd brought, but none of them were hungry.

"How is this happening?" moaned one of the laundry girls. "I thought Muirwood would be safe!"

"The Aldermaston will protect us," said Rhiannon. "Believe that."

"What if we're overrun?"

"Hush," said Ardys. "The Medium is more powerful than those assailing us. Your friend is right. The Aldermaston will protect us."

Mordaunt snorted and coughed, earning a rebuking glare from Ardys. He didn't say anything, thank Idumea, but gave Eilean a knowing look before turning back to the window.

More anxious moments passed. Then Mordaunt said, loudly enough for all to hear, "They'll be breaching the ranks soon."

Almost at his word, the noise of shouting could be heard in the distance. The invaders were not hiding their approach but announcing themselves with shrieks and animal-like noises.

"Let's block the door," Ardys suggested. She organized the girls and carried the table and chairs in front of it.

After they'd done that, Eilean hurried back to the window.

Rhiannon and the laundry girls started weeping, which caused the younger kitchen girls to panic, leaving Celyn and Ardys to try to comfort them. Eilean, transfixed at the window, saw a horde of people rushing toward the castle, carrying staves, clubs, and sickles. The defenders were organized into groups, each one led by a hunter. Eilean pressed her fingers against the glass, her heart pounding in her throat. She saw Captain Hoel walking in front of them, bow in hand, giving them a little speech. If only she could hear it over the throb of noise coming from the invaders.

There were so many of them. Her insides began to tremble, but she clung to Mordaunt's promise that she wouldn't be harmed. Still . . . what if the druids captured her and took her and Mordaunt with them? It was impossible to know what would happen.

Her heart felt like a heavy weight in her chest when she recognized Aisic standing on the front lines, ready to fight. What if he *died*? The thought made her sick to her stomach.

The rushing mob came charging through the grounds, hollering and shouting and brandishing their weapons. Arrows began dropping the lead men, the twangs of the bows cutting through the chaos of battle. She watched men fall, watched them writhe in pain. Screams rent the air.

"We're going to die!" Rhiannon shrieked, shrinking to the floor and covering her ears.

Captain Hoel never missed a shot. Each time he drew back on the bowstring, someone fell. But there were too many. She watched in desperation as he was swarmed by attackers. Still he fought, swinging his bow to crack one of them in the head before drawing his gladius and plunging it into another. Some of those with him fled in fear back toward the castle. But not Aisic. No, her friend was one of the first to fight, and he knocked down several of the attackers with his pickaxe.

Eilean couldn't take her eyes away from the scene. In her mind, she pled with the Medium to protect her people. Then some of the mastons began to fall to the horde. Her heart ached as she witnessed the devastation in front of her, unable to look away. If only more could be done.

She felt a wave of power from the Medium, and moments later, water began to sweep through the fields. The rivers had been unleashed to defend the abbey. Eilean felt her arm hairs prickle as she watched the rippling waves pour through the fields and crash into the invading men, knocking them down in a rush.

Shouts and screams sounded from within the castle itself. She glanced at the door, frozen, and waited for the thunder of boots coming up the steps. When it came, the laundry girls began shrieking with terror.

"Quiet down!" Ardys shouted at them. "Do not doubt!" But Eilean saw the fear in the cook's eyes. Was the castle truly being overrun? How had they gotten past the barricaded doors?

And then Eilean remembered the tunnel leading from the pit to the castle. Had the enemies known about it? Had someone within the abbey told them?

She turned and looked at Mordaunt, and his slight nod confirmed her fear.

A hoarse, violent voice shouted in the hallway. "This way! Gorm them! Gorm them all!"

Mordaunt left his position at the window and came to the center of the room. The door began to shudder as it was struck, then the hinges splintered and broke. Eilean pressed back against the wall, her throat a knot of terror. The Myriad Ones were inside the castle. She *felt* them. They were driving the men to savagery.

The door shuddered again and broke open, knocking the table back and throwing the chairs asunder. One of the laundry girls fainted straightaway. Eilean stepped forward, trying to summon her courage, determined not to be a victim. She knew words of power. She would hold the villains off as long as she could.

Mordaunt glanced her way and held up his hand in warning. He shook his head no.

The mob broke through. A sickening feeling filtered into the chamber, causing a hush to fall over the panicked women and children. Eilean's eyes settled on one of the infiltrators, a man with glowing eyes, a snarling mouth, and black tattoos covering his face. He wielded a crooked staff beneath his black robe.

"There you are!" said the dark druid. "We've caught you at last!"

"Leave, or it will not end well for you," Mordaunt said calmly.

The dark druid sneered at him. "You will tell us where you hid it. Where is the Sefer Yetzirah? Where did you hide it, old man?"

"In a place where you will never find it," answered Mordaunt. "Leave, I warn you."

The dark druid lifted his crooked staff and stepped forward. The eyes of his companions were crazed with rage and bloodlust. She could sense the Myriad Ones inside them, compelling them to do and be their worst. "Like all the Twelve, you are squeamish about allowing harm to come to the innocent. I'll kill those waifs. I'll bash in their heads one by one until you *tell* me where you hid it!" He glanced at Eilean and grinned savagely. "Beginning with her!"

"No!" Ardys shouted in outrage.

Mordaunt stood immovable. "I will not tell you."

"Their blood will be on your soul!" shouted the dark druid.

Mordaunt looked at him and held out his palm. "On yours. *Ke-ev had.*"

The words of power invoked the Medium, and Eilean watched in astonishment as a wind seemed to blow from Mordaunt's hand and tear through the people clustered in the doorway and the corridor beyond it. The men crumpled to the ground and groaned in pain, blood blooming on their arms and staining their tunics. She had seen no weapon strike, but all of them had collapsed as if pierced with invisible swords. Some appeared dead.

The dark druid, facedown, lifted his head, his eyes no longer glowing. He'd dropped the crooked staff on the ground, and Mordaunt stooped and picked it up.

"Haz . . . rah . . . com . . ." The words came out of pale lips, choking for breath, wheezing with pain.

Before the words could be finished, Mordaunt twirled the crooked staff and struck the druid on the head with the knobbed end. The druid slumped—dead or unconscious—Eilean wasn't sure which.

Glancing cautiously out the doorway, Eilean saw that everyone in the corridor had fallen. Not one of them stood. Mordaunt walked to the opening and stood there, gripping the staff in his hand.

The scene was sickening, but it was reassuring that one utterance was all it had taken to destroy the attackers. No one else came charging up the stairs. Mordaunt turned and walked back to the window.

Ardys was gazing at him in fear and distrust. "He said . . . you were one of the Twelve. That's . . . that's blasphemy! They are *all* dead."

Mordaunt looked at her and said nothing. He directed his gaze out the window. "The attack is over," he said. "The waters came in time. The abbey has been protected by the Medium."

Eilean went to another window and looked out. Much of the horde had been struck by the rushing waters. Fear clutched her throat—had the defenders gone down with the rest of them?—until she saw Captain Hoel and his men rounding up the survivors.

When she saw Aisic helping with that effort, she smiled and leaned her forehead against the windowpane in relief.

***

"Eilean," said Captain Hoel from the doorway. "The Aldermaston wishes to see you."

A carpenter was fixing the broken door by candlelight. The dead crowding Mordaunt's room and the hall had been carted away, their bodies destined to be burned. Some mastons had died too, and their bones would be saved in ossuaries and buried in the cemetery.

From the window of the castle, which she'd spent most of the day peering out of, she could see the waters. They had not come up all the way, and the pit with the abbey foundation hadn't flooded.

Eilean looked at Mordaunt, who sat at the table, his crooked staff leaning against the wall. So he was one of the Twelve after all. And the dark druids had wanted his tome. Everything he'd told her was true.

Wonder unfurled within her. All this time, she had been serving one of the Twelve.

I'll bring you some supper when I come back, she told him with her thoughts.

He gave her a small smile and nod, and she followed Captain Hoel out of the room and down the steps. She had helped clean the blood from the floor, and her dress bore stains from the carnage.

"How many did we lose, Captain?" she asked as they jogged down the stairs.

"Too many, unfortunately. Olien was one of them." He sighed.

"I'm sorry to hear it," she said, meaning it. Although she hadn't known him well, he'd always been kind to her.

"So am I. The intruders knew about the tunnels. They knew how to get into the castle."

"I was thinking the same thing," Eilean said. "Are you going to find out who it was?"

He didn't answer, but he didn't need to. She could feel his determination, his rage. Horror filled her at the possibility he might think *she* was the traitor. Surely he wouldn't have mentioned it to her if he did, would he?

When they reached the main floor of the castle, she saw knights in armor standing outside the door to the Aldermaston's chamber. She hadn't seen any of them in the fighting.

Hoel noticed her confusion. "These are the sheriff of Mendenhall's men," he said. "They got word of what happened, and the sheriff himself brought fifty men to help defend the abbey. But the battle was already over. Their men can't cross the waters until they recede, but we brought some of them over on rafts."

"Where is Mendenhall?" she asked.

"It's a castle about a league from here. This castle was under its jurisdiction until the king named it an abbey. The sheriff's going to take the prisoners we captured back for the king's justice."

"What will happen to them?"

Hoel gave her a knowing look. "They'll be hanged for breaking the king's peace."

Eilean shuddered. "Did you capture any of the druids who led them?"

"All but the one who died upstairs," he said pointedly. He sighed. "We would have welcomed the chance to interrogate him."

The door to the Aldermaston's study opened, and a man stepped out, middle-aged with a scar on his left cheekbone. His hair and beard were gray, but the knotted cords of muscle in his arms suggested he was a powerful man. He looked at Eilean first, then at Captain Hoel.

"Wish we had come here sooner, Captain," said the man, whom Eilean assumed was the sheriff.

"So do I. It's an unfortunate loss."

"Heard some of the lads did well, though. I've offered the Aldermaston some additional protection for the abbey while we hunt down any who got away. Any of the wretcheds seem promising? Could use some more guards in the ranks if you can recommend any. Will pay them too, even if they're under eighteen."

Hoel pursed his lips. "Several. But the best was a lad named Aisic. No one took him down. He fought hard."

"That's the kind of lad I like," said the sheriff. "I'll have my captain ask for him. Any others?"

The thought of Aisic leaving so suddenly made her inwardly cringe. It was purely selfish, though. She knew he'd been dreaming of exactly this sort of opportunity, and she was happy for him. But would he come back? Even if he did, his feelings for her might change . . .

"Everyone else is needed to work. Thank you for offering more guards."

The sheriff nodded thoughtfully. "You held off a rabble with naught but a handful of hunters and some ill-equipped laborers. Well done. I'll be sure the king knows of it."

Hoel gestured for Eilean to go in to the Aldermaston. Their conversation interested her, and she was loath to leave it, but she did as he bid. When she entered the study, she found the Aldermaston slumped in his chair. Some cold bread and cheese sat on a tray on his desk.

"Did they ransack the kitchen?" she asked him.

He nodded. "Took off with some stores that we didn't have time to move, and then they—and the food—perished in the flood. Winter will be here too soon. We'll need help."

She looked at him inquisitively.

"What happened upstairs, Eilean? How did those men die?"

After licking her lips, she answered him simply enough. "He spoke a word . . . and they perished."

"Did they say what they wanted? Ardys said they asked for something, but she couldn't remember the name. It was a strange word to her. Do you recall?"

"They were looking for the Sefer Yetzirah. I think that's what he said. Do you know what that means?"

The Aldermaston's eyebrows rose. "I do, actually. You know of the tomes written by the Twelve? Men like Ovidius?"

She nodded.

"Ardys also claimed the men said Mordaunt was one of the Twelve. Did you hear that absurdity as well?"

"I did." She pressed her lips closed, knowing it was not absurd at all.

"Why would one of the Twelve forsake the maston order and become a druid? It makes no sense." He shook his head in disgust before returning to their previous discussion. "There are other tomes you likely haven't heard of, ones not from this world. These are tomes written by the Sefers, the angels. There is one written by the Sefer Raziel. Another by the Sefer Hamalakh. One is called the Book of Secrets. Another, the Book of Lore. The Sefer Yetzirah is called the Book of Creation. It's the most powerful one of all. And the one that was stolen from Avinion. Mordaunt refused to disclose where it's hidden?"

"He did." She paused. "Those druids weren't like him. They were dark druids."

"There's hardly a difference, Eilean. I'm grateful none of you were harmed."

She looked at him, sensing his guilt and shame for failing to protect the abbey.

"Why did the flood come, Aldermaston? Did you summon it?"

"I did not," he said, and she knew he was being truthful.

"Then how did it happen?"

"One of the mastons sacrificed his life," answered the Aldermaston sadly. "His blood was shed by an attacker near one of the boundary Leerings, which invoked the defenses. We were all saved because that happened."

"Who was it?" Eilean asked in concern. Her heart ached at the loss. Still, she couldn't help but wonder why the Aldermaston hadn't sacrificed himself if such a gesture had been needed.

Maybe, because the Medium no longer heeded him, he couldn't have done it.

"It was Critchlow," he said sadly. Anguish furrowed his brow.

It was shocking news. Had Critchlow been asked to do it? Had he offered himself?

She didn't have answers for either question, but it felt as if the world had spun on its axis, revealing that everything she'd thought she knew was wrong.

"Is there anything I can get you?" she asked him.

He looked her in the eye. "Just the Sefer Yetzirah, Eilean. Do whatever it takes. Or Critchlow will have died for nothing."

She didn't like that he'd put such a gargantuan task on her shoulders. But she nodded meekly and left his study. Although she knew she should find food for Mordaunt, her heart sent her searching for Aisic. When she found him, he was already with the sheriff's men, who were joking and laughing with him. Someone had brought him a horse. The sight made her throat tight with emotion. Her eyes were welling with tears, and she didn't dare cry in front of the soldiers.

Whether Aisic noticed her standing afar or not, she didn't know. But he left shortly afterward with the sheriff's men.

Her feelings as raw as if Ardys had taken to them with a grater, she made her way to the kitchen, only to discover Loren had been injured during the attack. He hadn't been hurt badly, however, and Ardys and a few others were seeing to his care. Eilean stayed as long as Ardys would allow her, then fetched some scraps of food and brought a tray upstairs to Mordaunt. The carpenter was gone, the door fixed.

She shut it behind her and put the plate on the readjusted table for him.

"Your thoughts are firm, child," Mordaunt said. "I could feel them as you came up the stairs."

"I want you to teach me," she said. "I want to learn everything."

Rarely do great beauty and great virtue dwell together. I have recently returned to the Holy See of Avinion from journeys abroad. There is still no report of the whereabouts of Utheros. He is in hiding, and I cannot believe he has not gotten help from some prince or lord in Hautland. The High Seer has authorized use of the Cruciger orb to hunt him down. It is a curious device, a most valuable gift from the Essaios—the makers of worlds—that uses the power of the Medium to locate lost things. But although it points us in the right direction, our path is not clear. There are border skirmishes in Hautland between those who support the heretic and do not want him to be made a martyr and those who realize that cancers must be cut out before they spread. I've called off the hunt, for now. The hunter is patient. The prey is careless.

I was pleased to see tremendous progress made on the construction of Muirwood Abbey. The troubles from summer have been quelled and many druids were imprisoned for their role in the attack. King Aengus (they pronounce it Anguish . . . how absurd) has ordered the sheriffs of his realm to provide protection to Muirwood and other construction projects, and so we've seen immense progress at Muirwood, and foundations have been started at Billerbeck to its north, Augustin to its east, and Ceaster to its south. Those projects will take years to complete, but the bones and shell of Muirwood should be finished by the start of winter, allowing the interior to be worked on during the cold.

The Aldermaston of Muirwood is a wise steward of the faith. Because his wretcheds and helpers do not all hail from the same abbeys, they clad themselves differently, and many skirmishes resulted from the styles of their tunics and kirtles. The Aldermaston has done away with such differences. Both the male and female wretcheds wear green wool with black-and-white trim. They all look similar now, and the regional differences have been abolished. He has also taken care to increase the formality of his people's speech, putting an end to slang words. Captain Hoel tells me that one of the girls at the abbey, the one guarding the druid Mordaunt, has been especially influential in shifting attitudes. All seek to emulate her. It's really a clever thing the Aldermaston has done. It breeds unity and contentment instead of rivalry.

But wretcheds will always be wretcheds, even if they are fair of face, like the one Gilifil assigned to watch over the prisoner. Interesting girl. I couldn't get much out of her. She didn't talk like the others, though. Not that it matters. They're all born from seeds of sin and carry a predisposition for the same. That is why the abbeys free the wretcheds from their servitude. A spoiled apple will, in the end, pollute the entire barrel.

And speaking of apples—the variety that grows at Muirwood continues to be quite popular at court. The abbey gardeners have planted a new orchard and intend to press the fruit into cider to sell throughout the realm. Ingenious.

—Mícheál Nostradamus of Avinion Abbey

CHAPTER EIGHTEEN

The Mists of Muirwood

The candle had burned out again, but Eilean didn't awaken to darkness. The Leering she had carved into the stone of her small cell glowed softly. It gave off just a trickle of magic, not enough to rouse the awareness of anyone living on the main floor of the castle. She lifted herself on her elbow and smiled at the face she had made—the one Mordaunt had helped her with.

She rose from her pallet, stretching her arms, and quickly brushed her hair. She pulled the green dress on over her chemise and tugged on her shoes. She took the burnt-out candle and then, with a thought, extinguished the Leering as she left.

She entered Mordaunt's room and found him standing at the window, a silent sentinel to the goings-on at the abbey's construction.

"Good morning," she greeted him. In the months since she'd begun studying in earnest, she'd lost her Pry-rian accent and now spoke as they did at King Aengus's court. It was a more polished manner of speaking, with fewer slurred words, outbursts of emotions, and wasted sounds. It had taken time, but now her ears were attuned to it, and she'd discovered that others at the abbey had begun to copy her manner of speaking. Every day Mordaunt shared stories about the different courts, who was in charge and what they were like. She knew the word of power that allowed her to speak and understand different languages, and under his tutelage, she'd learned to speak them so well she could convince a nobleman from any country that she was of their social class.

"I'd forgotten how misty these lands are at this time of year," he said. "Look outside. You can barely see the abbey even though it is so near. Some monsters prefer the fog."

Eilean joined him at the window. The fog was so thick around the grounds that only the shadows of stone could be seen. In the east, there was a brighter smear in the clouds, but the sun could not penetrate the mist.

"There is a myth of one such monster in Pry-Ree," she said.

"Are you sure it is only a myth?" he asked with a grin. "This part of the kingdom is known for morning fogs. It happens every year at this time."

"Is there a word of power that drives away mist?" she asked.

"Yes. But the more useful word is the one that summons it. It is especially useful in times of war when there is a need to surprise or escape from an enemy. The word is *Vey-ed.* That could obscure a single person. But when you need to cover a larger area, you would say it thus: *Vey-ed min ha-ay-retz.*" When he taught her new words, he swayed one hand up and down to mimic the rise and fall of his voice as he spoke them. The other hand he closed into the null gesture, which allowed the words to be spoken without invoking their magic.

She made the null gesture herself, the crossing of her two middle fingers over the outer ones, forming a V shape. It was an easier gesture to do with her left hand, for some reason, but it worked equally well with either hand.

"Vey-ed min ha-ay-retz," she repeated.

"Flawless, Eilean. You really have an ear for it now." He gave her a pleased smile, which made her feel grateful and honored. He was a good teacher. She'd spent the summer learning the ways of the Medium, how to coax it to come when she needed it. How to carve Leerings, although that took a lot of time. Now fall had descended on the grounds, and the starlings were almost gone.

He turned back to the window, his countenance brooding again. He had been doing more of that lately. Something was troubling him. Something he hadn't shared with her.

"What is it?" she asked him. "Is it the confinement? I've asked the Aldermaston to let you walk the grounds, but he continues to forbid it."

"I know, little sister," he said. "That's not what troubles me."

"Will you tell me?"

He didn't look at her, his eyes gazing out at the mist. "The last time I used those specific words of power was to help a king seduce another man's wife."

That was not what she'd expected him to say. "That does not sound like something the Medium would want."

He sighed. "You are right. I've told you the story about the two rival kings. That which we conceive in thought and marry to desire becomes *real.* The Medium makes it so. Even if it isn't good for us. It will allow something you ardently desire to become your curse, even after you've stopped heeding its whispers. The night the one king disguised himself as his foe, there was a great mist that was summoned to aid in the defeat of his rival. The mist allowed him to slip unnoticed from the camp and pursue the other man's wife. It also caused confusion in the battle that followed."

She looked at him, remembering the story. Two rival kings, fighting like wolves. "The king's Wizr transformed him," she said slowly. "I remember."

He sighed again. "I was the Wizr. I was also the one who concealed the child from being slaughtered."

She gazed at him, not with judgment, but wanting to understand. "But if you knew it was against the Medium's will, why did you help him?"

"I refused him three times because I suspected what would happen, but he could not be persuaded against his own folly. His will was strong. His lust was powerful. In the end, the Medium delivered up his desire . . . and then unleashed a flood of consequences. Sooner or later, little sister, everyone sits down to a *banquet* of consequences." There was bitterness in his voice, a haunted wrinkle on his brow.

"Where is the child?" she asked. "The one you hid in a pigpen?"

"He is no longer a child. A man grown. A king. An emperor."

"You mean the Holy Emperor of—"

"No," Mordaunt said, cutting her off. He turned and looked at her. "It's as I've told you, child—there are more worlds than this one. And there are ways one can cross between them. That child of the pigpens became king. And that king is turning out to be as proud as his father. I see the same ambition. I dread the same outcome. He was the king I served before Aengus. Before I was banished from that other world."

She felt a bubbling sensation inside her chest, a keen sense of interest and deep wonder. "Is the Medium part of that other world too?"

He looked at her. "Yes, although they know it by a different name there. While I am a prisoner here, I fret at what might be happening to my friend. Whose counsel does he heed now that I'm gone? What choices is he making? What consequences will heap as a result?"

"How did you get banished?" she asked him.

She watched the muscles of his mouth twitch. Her words must have triggered painful memories. "The woman I trained betrayed me. I taught her, as I have taught you. And she used that knowledge against me."

She pitied him. Sympathy bid her put her hand on his shoulder. "I am sorry for you. Why would she do that?"

"I don't know her true reasons," he answered. "Her thoughts were so guarded, so controlled. I've never met someone with stronger self-control. She's become a powerful Wizr, and I can do nothing but worry about my friend." He tapped her hand, still on his shoulder. "That is *my* burden to carry, Eilean. Not yours. For now, the Medium wishes for me to languish in this prison. I am grateful for your friendship. Your kindness to me."

"Let me bring you some breakfast from the kitchen," she said. "I'll get the brazier going first. It's cold in here."

When she left the castle, the mist seemed to cling to her skin, her eyelashes. The whole grounds were shrouded, and not a soul could be seen tromping through the grass. Maybe others had slept in? Thankfully the kitchen was so close she wouldn't have to wander and risk getting lost. She entered through the back door and found the kitchen helpers working to prepare breakfast.

"Did you see the fog outside, Eilean?" Ardys asked wonderingly. "I've never seen anything so thick. It's like a pudding out there."

"Only not as sweet," Eilean answered.

Celyn looked up from the rolls she was cutting and smiled at her. Her dress was identical to Eilean's. All the helpers at the abbey wore the same attire now. Each boy had two tunics and each maiden two dresses—green with black at the hems and cuffs, along with a trim of white. It was an unnecessary expense, to be sure, for all their clothes had been perfectly fine, but the Aldermaston was creating an image of Muirwood. He intended to run it like a lord ran his castle.

She assembled a tray for Mordaunt, grabbing two rolls, which she slathered with honey, some slices of cheese, a pear, and some mashed apples with treacle stirred in.

"Guess who came by the kitchen last night?" Celyn asked, wiping her doughy hands on her apron.

"You're implying I should know or could guess," Eilean answered.

"Aisic."

That was a surprise. After being chosen as one of the sheriff's men, he'd been taken to Mendenhall for training in arms and had been gone for the entire summer.

"He's back?" Eilean asked with eagerness.

Celyn raised her eyebrows. "He's got a leather tunic, sturdy boots, and a sword at his hip if you can imagine it. I didn't even recognize him at first, he's gotten so big. His nose is crooked, like it was broken."

Her heart seemed to skip a beat. "Did he ask about me?"

"He did, in fact. I told him you'd already had supper and had returned to the castle. I take it he didn't visit you?"

"No. Do you know where he's staying?"

"The soldiers are all staying in the village down the road. The one that's bringing stores and supplies for the abbey. They're guarding it too."

Eilean bit her lip and felt a flush start on her cheeks. She hadn't seen him in months. The last time they'd been alone together was that fateful morning they'd snuck out to watch the starlings. He hadn't attempted to seek her out after that. She'd watched him leave without a backward glance. And yet . . . she couldn't blame him for having ridden eagerly into his new life. Nor could she deny the truth about her own feelings.

"I'd like to see him again," she admitted.

"I knew you would, Eilean." Celyn paused as if thinking, then added, "He's changed. And so have you."

That nervous feeling of anticipation wriggled in her stomach. "I'll see you for supper."

"Yes. I hope so." She looked around the kitchen. "I'm going to miss it here."

Eilean was startled. "Where else would you go?"

"I can't stay here, Eilean," Celyn whispered. "I have to get away from this place. It's . . . it just feels *wrong*. I can't tell Ardys or Loren. They'd be heartbroken if they knew how I really felt. I'm not going to stay past my service."

The thought of her friend leaving was painful. But Eilean and Celyn shared a secret the others didn't know. They'd confided in each other about what Eilean was learning from Mordaunt. Not the words of power but the truth that Mordaunt was on the Medium's side.

And Aldermaston Gilifil wasn't.

***

The mist cleared before midday, and everything looked normal again after that. All summer long Eilean had watched the abbey grow out of the pit like a stone plant reaching for the sky. It was taller than the castle and had a series of spires, buttresses, and slate-shingle roofs that formed a cross shape around a central tower that lifted high above the other wings. The main facade was made of ornate stonework, and it led to a door embedded with Leerings that had not yet been activated.

Occasionally noble visitors rode in from the king's city of Moros to observe the abbey's progress. In anticipation of more visitors, carpenters had already started and finished building an inn nearby. There was money to be made, trade to be conducted, and Muirwood would be the first to enjoy the benefits of King Aengus's conversion to the maston rites.

Now that the abbey's exterior had been built, the stone masons were working on fencing that would surround the main part of the abbey grounds, and they'd begun constructing the learners' quarters. There were no more tents, for small cabins had been erected to provide the workers with shelter before winter arrived.

Another feature that had been finished was the cloister—the walled garden where the learners would come to study the art of reading and engraving tomes. A tree had been planted at its center to provide shade. It could be seen from Mordaunt's window, but neither he nor Eilean spent much time looking out anymore. They studied together for hours each day, Eilean learning history, dialects, and alphabets for the languages she'd magically learned to speak.

There was no aurichalcum to practice on, but Mordaunt had a prodigious memory, and he taught her the words of Ovidius and other members of the Twelve, who had been the first disciples of the maston order. The dark druid had accused Mordaunt of being one of the Twelve, and she'd learned for herself that it was true. His stories about other kingdoms and worlds had come from many lifetimes of experience. He did not sleep because he did not require sleep. Nor could he be killed by weapons or fire. But he *could* be imprisoned. And for now, it was the Medium's will that he should remain so. And that was enough for her. She had no remaining doubts about him.

"You've worked hard today," he said. "No . . . how do you say it in Pry-Ree . . . no *mitching*. Before we finish, let's test your memory. Name one of the precepts of Ovidius."

"We are slow to believe that which, if believed, would hurt our feelings," she said. "That is one of my favorites."

"Aye. He was a good man, a good friend."

It still amazed her that he knew the people who were written of in the tomes. That he *was* one of the people who was written of in tomes.

"His wisdom can be hard to bear, but there is always truth in it."

"I know it," he agreed with a chuckle. He leaned back in the chair and folded his arms. "He once warned me that someone who says o'er much 'I love not' is in love. I learned that one myself, to my regret. I couldn't believe, at first, that anyone so beautiful could love an odious man like me. And then I let it blind me. The heart is treacherous. Remember that, lass."

She'd been thinking about Aisic all day, even though she'd tried not to.

"You're warning me," she said, looking down.

"I suppose I am. Feelings are powerful. They can sweep someone away like a bit of bark on a stream."

She looked at him. "Like the king you served in that other world."

He spread out his hands. "I'm only telling you what I've learned from difficulty and sadness. Most men want a lass who will give them what they want and not what they need. You have many admirers, Eilean Donnán. More than you know."

She wrinkled her brow. "Eilean Donnán?"

"It's an old name, an old story. Donnán lost his head, let's just say. Don't lose yours."

"I'll bring you your supper," she said, pushing away from the table.

"I hope it is fish stew and pumpkin bread. Ardys is a marvelous cook."

"I'll tell her you said so again," she said with a smile and then left and hurried down the steps.

The Aldermaston had some new visitors who had arrived during the day, and she recognized the emblem on their tunics as being from the northern lands. The Earl of Forshee? Yes, that was it. She nodded to one of the knights standing guard outside the Aldermaston's study and passed out the back of the castle toward the kitchen.

She heard muffled voices from behind her and barely made out the whispered words, "You're right, she *is* fair!"

Eilean turned midstride, and saw four soldiers standing against the wall of the castle. Aisic was already stepping away from them, his thumb hooked in his scabbard belt, and he approached her with a cocky smile.

"It's good to see you, Eilean! I'm back from Mendenhall now."

Over his shoulder, she saw the other soldiers jabbing each other and laughing, watching the two of them with great interest.

Something felt off about his greeting. The excitement she'd felt all that day began to wither.

"Celyn told me you had returned," she said more formally.

His eyebrows lifted. "You hardly sound like yourself, Eilean." He lowered his voice. "Are you unwell?"

"I am very well," she answered. "I have to go get supper right now."

"Can I join you? Like in old times?"

She knew Celyn had been wanting to talk, to unburden herself about her decision to leave, and something in Aisic's eyes disturbed her. He was looking at her with an almost greedy expression. Like she belonged to him. And it was clear he'd been telling tales to his friends too.

"I don't think so," she said, turning away and walking swiftly to the kitchen.

She heard the other soldiers laughing, and her ears burned.

Many problems can be avoided through careful planning. That is why I train the Apocrisarius to be watchful, vigilant, and act soon instead of late. Prevention is better than a cure. I've been examining the druid prisoners brought here by Captain Hoel of Muirwood. The metal talismans they wear around their necks enable them to circumvent Leerings. These amulets, if you will, bind them to the Myriad Ones, which they interpret as primal spirit creatures of the forest and not the malevolent entities they truly are. It seems we saved Moros just in time, before it fell under the dark power of Ereshkigal, the Queen of the Unborn.

—Mícheál Nostradamus of Avinion Abbey

CHAPTER NINETEEN

The Power of Thought

The next day brought the same sequence of fog as the previous one. There was something about the Bearden Muir that invited mist as the air cooled day by day. She had tried to talk to Celyn the evening before, but Ardys kept interrupting them, asking why they were talking so quietly, so they'd agreed to meet in the afternoon for a walk in the brief lull prior to the work required for supper. Now that the soldiers had joined them, it took a lot of work to feed so many mouths.

Eilean and Celyn walked arm in arm, away from the construction happening at the abbey. It would take a generation for the abbey to establish itself, to form its own industry, to build itself up to the point where it could sustain itself year after year. By the end of the first generation, there would be multiple forges, inns, streets, and learners who had begun to raise their own children.

"When you said you need to leave Muirwood, where do you mean to go?" Eilean asked, guiding her friend toward the new apple orchard, which was yielding the final fruits of the year, much smaller than the first harvest.

Celyn gazed down at the trampled grass. There was a single gardener there, collecting the fallen apples and putting them in a wheelbarrow. But he was too far away to hear them.

"Something's wrong, Eilean. Not just here, but with the maston order. Look at how they've persecuted that Aldermaston in Hautland. Uros? Is that his name?"

"Utheros," Eilean said. "He was excommunicated."

"For daring to speak up," she said. "What did he say against the High Seer? No one knows. I haven't heard anyone talk about what Utheros did, only that he should be punished for it. Was he pointing out valid concerns? You asked where I want to go. Part of me wants to go to Hautland. To hear the other side of the story. But what can I do about it? I don't speak that language. I don't even know how to get there."

"I know where Hautland is," Eilean said quietly.

"You've seen the Aldermaston's maps?"

"No, Mordaunt taught me. He helped me learn their customs and way of speaking. The abbeys in Hautland have very tall spires. It is a harsher tongue. It sounds a lot like coughing."

Celyn grinned and bumped shoulders with her. "We should go together, Eilean. I don't think I'm brave enough to go by myself. You can teach me some of what you've learned. My thoughts are bigger than a kitchen now. Reckon it might be because of what happened to me when I was sick. And what you've told me about the Medium."

"I wish they would let more wretcheds become learners," Eilean said. "Mordaunt thinks I could pass the maston test now. He's sure of it."

"How would you ever afford a tome?"

Eilean shrugged. "That's the thing, Celyn. I can't right now. But if I put my mind to it, the Medium will come up with a way to make it happen. Maybe the Medium is telling you to leave?"

Celyn sighed. "I wondered at that. I wish I was as brave as you."

"I'm the one still afraid of the dark, remember?"

"Do you still tuck your toes under your blanket each night?"

"Of course! I know it's silly, but I can't help it. Just the thought of not being covered makes me fearful. But I'm less afraid now than I used to be."

They were circling back around toward a copse of young oak where some of the wretched boys were sitting and eating their midday meal. Fleetingly, it reminded her of their days at Tintern, back when things were less complex. But she didn't long for those times—she'd learned too much, come too far.

Four soldiers approached the lads, and she was taken aback to see Aisic was one of them. They were far enough away that she couldn't hear what was being said, but Eilean could see the soldiers' threatening posture. They wore leather tunics with buckles and straps, high boots, bracers that also had buckles on them, and stiff collars. Each of the soldiers had a sword belted to his waist, and they glared down at the lads sitting beneath them. One of the wretcheds stood up quickly, then they all got to their feet.

"They're going to fight," Celyn warned.

Eilean agreed. The two groups were roughly comparable in size—about six laborers to the four soldiers. Aisic pointed his finger at the one who'd stood up first and then shoved him backward into the tree. Eilean's stomach twisted with concern.

The fight broke out immediately. And it ended almost as fast. The four soldiers made quick work of their opponents, who had none of the training the soldiers had experienced. Aisic gripped the first of the wretcheds, the one he'd approached, by the hair and smashed him in the face with his fist and then kneed him in his male parts, making him collapse to the ground in agony. One of the soldiers had another man's arm twisted around, making him cry out.

Eilean and Celyn clasped hands and hurried along, not toward the scene, but toward the kitchen, which brought them parallel to the fight. They were close enough now that Eilean could make out the young men who'd been attacked. They were the same ones she'd seen humble Aisic in the pit when he'd first come to work at Muirwood. Back then, she'd been powerless to help him. Now, she had the ability to stop a fight with a single word, but she'd been warned by Mordaunt not to do so publicly.

All these months Aisic had harbored his feelings of revenge. And now, with the change in his status and situation, he was declaring his dominance. This fit with what Mordaunt had told her about the hierarchy at the abbey. The strong competed for positions of strength and intimidated others they considered beneath them. This one fight would alter the situation and put Aisic and his fellow soldiers on top.

It disgusted her, but she recognized why he'd done it.

The soldiers clapped each other on the backs, rejoicing in their victory. One of them noticed her and Celyn walking and nudged Aisic and pointed at them. He turned and saw them, but he didn't change his stance. He looked proud of what he'd done.

She lost respect for him because of it.

***

At dusk, she left the castle again to get supper for herself and Mordaunt and again found Aisic waiting for her outside the castle. This time, however, he was alone.

She kept walking toward the kitchen, but he hurried to catch up with her.

"Are you cross with me?"

She arched her brow at him. "I saw what you did to those boys this afternoon."

"I'm glad you saw it," he said, puffing out his chest. "Those were the same lads who knocked me on my arse that day in the pit, and they've lorded it over me ever since."

"It *did* seem like you were enjoying yourself."

"What's the matter, Eilean? I can defend myself now. Why shouldn't I?"

She kept walking, but he grabbed her by the arm and stopped her.

She nearly flung a word of power at him to knock him down. Instead, she clenched her jaw and turned to give him an icy look. "Let go, Aisic."

"I've wanted to talk with you, Eilean. But you've been treating me like I have the pox ever since I got back. That's clean off."

She tilted her head. "We're talking now. But let me go."

He did, holding up both hands. "This isn't how I thought it would go between us."

"Is that my fault?"

"No! I'm sorry. I just . . . I thought you . . ." His voice guttered out, and he looked frustrated.

"You didn't even say good-bye to me, and you've been gone for months." She paused, stopping her words because her accent was starting to drift back to Pry-rian. That happened when people were upset, Mordaunt had told her. It was important to always maintain self-control. When she spoke again, she was more precise with her words. "I've changed, Aisic. And so have you."

He jutted his chin at her. "I'm better now. Stronger."

"Stronger doesn't mean better."

He scowled. "Is it because I'm not a hunter? Is that it?"

She wrinkled her brow. "What in Idumea are you talking about?"

"I just want a chance, Eilean. A chance for things to be the way they used to be. To be friends again." His frown turned into a grin. "Well, a little more than friends. I've thought about that morning on the moors. Our kiss."

Her cheeks were beginning to flame.

"You enjoyed it too, admit it! Come, lass. Why be enemies?"

"We're not enemies."

"Good. I was afraid you'd tossed me off."

"I don't want you fighting the other wretcheds. It doesn't make you strong. It makes you no better than they were, and you didn't like it when you were on the losing end."

He held up his hands. "All right. I can see that. Would it please you, then? I want to please you, Eilean."

She sighed, seeing the contrition in his eyes. It melted the remaining resistance in her heart.

"I have to get Mordaunt's supper and bring it to the castle."

"I'll not bother you. But I'll be waiting outside the castle tomorrow night. And the night after that. And after that." He gave her a promising smile.

"Good night, Aisic."

"Good night, Eilean."

She walked the rest of the way to the kitchen, a smile lifting her mouth, and the flutter in her chest only increased. In the dimming light, he had looked very handsome in his soldier's armor. Very different from the dirt-stained young man working in the foundation pit. He was indeed changing. Everything seemed to be.

Once inside the kitchen, she basked in the warmth from the ovens and the wonderful smell of baking pumpkin loaves, listening to the commotion of people eating at the trestle tables crowded in there. Another kitchen was being built to accommodate the learners and teachers who would be coming after the abbey was built.

Celyn came up to her, breaking her from her thoughts. "Have you heard the news, Eilean?"

"I don't think so. What is it?"

"The Aldermaston is going to have a maypole constructed. He said next spring, at Whitsunday, the abbey will hold a dance."

"Why did he choose Whitsunday?" Eilean asked.

"Because he thinks that is when the abbey will be finished. He says there will be a big celebration every year, with a special festival that everyone takes part in. Even the wretcheds."

Maypole dances were very popular in Pry-Ree, so bringing that custom to Moros sounded enchanting. But there was a nagging feeling in her heart that neither she nor Celyn would be there when it was time to celebrate.

"That sounds like a wonderful tradition," Eilean said. "If he puts up the maypole now, there will be a chance to practice before winter."

"Surely." Celyn gripped Eilean's hands. "Ardys made pumpkin bread. Can you smell it?"

"Yes. Mordaunt will be happy. He was asking after it." She got the tray and loaded it with stew, a few slices of the fragrant pumpkin bread, and then added a syrupy cherry tart to go with it. Departing the kitchen, she walked back to the castle and climbed up to his room.

"Is that what I think it is?" Mordaunt asked as she lowered the tray before him.

"It's the right season. The pumpkins will only keep until winter begins."

She sat down opposite him and took a nibble from one of the slices. A little butter added to the flavor.

"I heard the Aldermaston is going to start a tradition after the abbey is built. A maypole dance at Whitsunday."

The druid gazed at her. "Do you know about the origin of that day? How it started?"

"No. It's been a holiday from working for as long as I can remember. A feast day."

"It is a remembrance from the early days. After the emperor-maston and Safehome disappeared, the Twelve were left behind to establish the maston order and spread it throughout all the kingdoms. But before we did, we waited for a sign from the Medium. It came, like the rushing of a great wind. Not a wind that rattles branches. It was a spiritual wind that we felt within us—a sign from the Medium that the time had come. We were given the Gift of Xenoglossia then. You have that Gift too now."

"The gift of languages."

"Aye. How could we share with other kingdoms if we could not speak in their tongues? I've had a strange feeling lately, Eilean Donnán. The same feeling I had before that whispering wind came on the first Whitsunday. The Medium is going to speak to us again. It is going to speak to the entire world."

She stared at him in surprise. "Another sign? Like the one back then?"

He nodded, gazing at her from across the table. "And I fear what it may say. There has been so much decadence in the maston order. So much pride. It may be a warning of the Blight. Be ready, Eilean. Be ready to listen when you hear it."

Suspicion is the cancer of friendship. That is why I teach the Apocrisarius to respect their fellow hunters but not befriend them. To be vigilant, one must be suspicious always. For even those we esteem most can harbor secret wickedness.

—Mícheál Nostradamus of Avinion Abbey

CHAPTER TWENTY

The Mind of an Enemy

"No, I don't think I'll stay at Muirwood," Aisic said, twisting a bit of grass between his fingers.

He and Eilean sat amidst the apple trees in the shadow of the castle. There was no more fruit to be had—the final harvest was done. He leaned back on one elbow, gazing at the little green strand he'd plucked. She sat down near him, arms crossed over her knees.

"Where will you go?" she pressed. Lately, she had felt a pull to leave the abbey herself. Maybe it had started with Celyn's feelings of foreboding that she was meant to leave and go to Hautland. Eilean had thought on it often, and she felt a tug on her heart in that direction too. It wasn't a specific command from the Medium. Just a growing sense that her time at the abbey was limited. That she would not be there to see the project completed.

Aisic flung the strand away and lay back, clasping his hands behind his head. "Moros City perhaps. I heard the king is going to wed a Dahomeyjan bride, and she will need her own guard."

"I thought only knights protected the royals?" Eilean asked.

"I could be a knight," he said proudly. "I just need some coin, is all. If I serve as a solider for a few years and save my wages, I could do it. Don't think I couldn't."

"I believe in you," she replied, looking down at his handsome face as he gazed up at the branches of the apple trees. A feeling of warmth grew in her chest. He'd sought her out every day as he'd promised. His duty ended before sunset, so these stolen moments together were becoming more frequent. She knew she needed to fetch supper for Mordaunt, but she enjoyed Aisic's attention.

"You could be whatever you desire to be," she said earnestly. "If you *want* it enough. If you do not accept defeat."

"I do want it," he said, looking at her. "What about you? Are you going to stay at Muirwood?"

That was a sobering question. "I don't think so."

"Weary of wearing a kirtle and slaving over a heretic?" He had a mocking smile as he said it. "You could do better yourself. Maybe you could serve the new queen?"

He might be jesting, but Eilean believed she could. Speaking Dahomeyjan would be a simple matter, thanks to the fluency granted to her by the word of power for understanding and speaking languages, and she knew more about court than Aisic did. Mordaunt had been a close friend to King Aengus, after all, and he'd drilled the names of the noble families into her head repeatedly.

"He's not a heretic," she said, looking away.

"He's a druid, of course he is!"

He's one of the Twelve, Aisic. The knowledge squirmed in her heart, and she longed to share it with him. Maybe she should trust him with a little information and see how he reacted? Because she really wanted to trust him. If she and Celyn were to leave Muirwood, perhaps Aisic could go with them as their protector? Would he do that? The thought made a warm feeling spread inside her.

"He's a maston," she said.

Aisic snorted. "So was Utheros, and now he's being hunted by the High Seer. It's a wonder they haven't caught him yet. And burned him."

"They've tried," Eilean said. "But some of the princes of Hautland have protected him. He's in hiding. But what were his crimes? Do you know? Did any of the sheriff's men talk about it?"

"Why should they share something wicked? He was found guilty. That is enough for me."

"What if he's not guilty? I'm troubled we haven't heard what he was accused of."

"We're about as far away from news as one can get. The Bearden Muir isn't exactly a crossroads for information."

"I hear a lot in the castle," Eilean answered, keeping her tone neutral.

"I'm sure you do," he said. She noticed his hand move closer to hers.

He tore loose another bit of grass.

"I should be going," she said with a sigh.

"Stay a little longer," he coaxed.

She watched him take the bit of grass and then, with a mischievous twinkle in his eyes, put it in her hair. She quirked her brow at him. He smiled apologetically before plucking the grass and flicking it away. He scooted a little closer to her.

She stood up and brushed off her hands. "I have to go."

A look of disappointment flashed in his eyes. "You don't have to."

"*Good night*, Aisic," she said and started to walk away.

As she reached the edge of the trees, she heard some laughing and noticed some of Aisic's soldier friends at the edge of the trees. She flashed them an annoyed look. Had they been watching them from the trees? She would have seen them if they'd been nearer.

One of them nudged the others and pointed to her. Another bowed at her like a knight paying respect to a lady. Then they buckled under a fresh wave of laughter. Annoyed by their foolish display, she walked away, ignoring them, and went to the kitchen to get supper. The sun had already set when she walked around the side of the castle. As the full view of the abbey loomed before her, she was impressed by the expertly finished exterior. But inside, she knew it to be still empty, save a few completed rooms. It struck her that it was like the current state of the maston order. Lovely to look at, but empty inside.

Celyn was too busy to talk, so Eilean fetched Mordaunt's meal and took the meal back to the castle. When she arrived in his room, he was gazing from the window again, but he paused to glance her way before looking back outside.

"The season is changing," he said. "Before long the snow will come."

"Does it snow much in this part of the kingdom?" she asked.

"No, not much. The farmers still plant winter crops. And the snow isn't thick enough to stop riders journeying through the realm from crossing through this land."

Eilean set the tray down on the table. "Are you going to test my knowledge again? See what I remember of geography?"

He turned and gazed at her. "You're in love with that boy," he said with a frown of disapproval.

"I wouldn't declare my feelings to be *that* strong," she said. "But I do care for him. I always have."

Mordaunt nodded. "And you wonder if you should invite him to go when you and Celyn leave."

"Are we leaving for Hautland, then?" she asked with a chuckle.

"You both think about it loudly enough," he replied. "Would you bring that soldier with you if you could?"

There was no point in hiding her thoughts from him. "I don't know if he can be trusted. But I would feel safer if he came with us."

"Do you trust my judgment, little sister?"

"You know I do."

"He's not the one for you," Mordaunt said.

A pang of disappointment struck her. They were too young to marry, yet she'd hoped there would be more of a future for them. Someday. "I see."

"You've known each other since you were both children," Mordaunt said. "There is a special familiarity that comes with such intimacy. Yet you are far more capable of deeper feelings than your soldier."

"We're both very young still," Eilean reminded him.

"Aye, lass. You remind me of something Ovidius said. 'To be able to say how much love is love but little.' He knew the ways of the heart. Better than anyone."

Eilean sighed and gestured to the tray. "Are you not hungry?"

"I am always hungry," he confessed with a grin and started to work on the meal she'd brought. Her own appetite had faded with his words. She didn't doubt him—he knew so much—rather, she pitied herself because the boy she'd desired in secret for so long wouldn't be hers. Instead of pining, she went and filled the brazier with logs and watched as the tongues of flame began to dance amidst the pile.

"Is there a word of power that can make someone fall in love?" she asked, half out of curiosity. If there were one, surely it would be against the Medium's will to use it.

"Oh, words are the only way to make someone truly fall in love," he answered with a chuckle. "But no, there is no spell. A talisman can create false feelings, but those are only temporary. It is against the will of the Medium to force anyone into love. It must always be coaxed." The way he said those last words made her turn her head and look at him.

He was staring off in the distance, lost in a memory.

"You're thinking of the woman who betrayed you," she said.

"Yes."

Eilean straightened and went back to the table. "You love her. Don't you?"

"There are different kinds of love, Eilean. But yes, I loved her as a mentor, a friend. Betrayal is one of the deepest pains. Even after she did what she did, I cannot banish those earlier feelings. Love is powerful, Eilean. Be wary when someone seeks your heart."

"I will trust you in this," Eilean said. She could spurn Aisic if she had to. His pride would be injured, but he would move on to someone else. One of the laundry girls most likely. That thought caused a spike of jealousy to stab through her chest.

Mordaunt gave her a knowing look and then went back to eating again.

***

Her decision to set Aisic aside in her heart made him all the more determined to win her. After her meeting with Mordaunt, she'd pulled him aside and told him that however much she cared about him, it would be best if they kept apart, only she'd said it kindly, which he'd taken as encouragement. Whenever she walked to the kitchen to fetch Mordaunt's meal, he'd follow her and demand to know why she'd changed toward him. So she became more forceful in her rejection. Her words inflamed him. She could see it in the flare of his nostrils, the anger burning in his eyes. He didn't come the next day, or the day after that.

When he did come again, he looked so miserable that her heart ached in sympathy. The anger was gone. He begged her to tell him what he'd done to upset her. He'd done nothing, of course. But that answer didn't satisfy him. She watched his misery grow, and it tortured her too. Only pure determination could make her stay fixed on her course.

And then he stopped coming entirely, and that felt even worse.

The fog began to lessen as the rains started. Water dripped from everywhere, and the turf became sodden and full of muddy stretches. The second inn, dubbed the Pilgrim, had been finished just in time. Fewer people wandered out of doors as the interior work continued inside the abbey. She could see the lights shining from behind the stained-glass windows.

After getting Mordaunt's tray for supper, she left through the rear doors of the kitchen. She was heading back to the castle when someone shoved her and knocked her down. The whole tray upended and spilled the food onto the muddy ground.

"Watch where you're going, lass," said an angry voice from behind her.

"You shouldn't have done that, Flint," said another. "He'll be furious!"

"I don't care. She's putting on airs, acting like a lady, but she's nothing but a wretched."

"Be silent, you fool!"

Eilean had mud soaking her knees and hands, and when she stood, she glowered at the two young soldiers behind her. Both were friends of Aisic's. One of them stared at her angrily, and the other held him back. They both walked off, leaving her to fend for herself. She went back to the kitchen with the filthy dishes, and Ardys was outraged when she heard what had happened. She helped Eilean clean her hands and wipe the mud from her dress.

Celyn came up to them. "Do you want me to bring supper to him instead?"

"Would you mind?" Eilean asked. Celyn had spent time with Mordaunt as well, with Eilean there. She'd listened to his stories avidly but had never heeded his gentle offers to elevate her speech.

"I'd be happy to." She fetched a fresh tray and left, while Eilean and Ardys continued to work on the stain. The dress would need to be washed on the morrow.

Aisic came into the kitchen, a worried look on his face, and then hurried over to her. "Did that idiot Flint knock you down?" he demanded.

Eilean sighed. "He was the one."

A fierce look flashed in his eyes. "I'll knock him down!"

"No," Eilean said, shaking her head. "Let it be. It's only a little mud."

Aisic ran his fingers through his wet hair. "The blathering idiot," he grumbled.

"It's all right," Eilean soothed. "No harm is done."

"Have you had any supper?" Ardys asked him.

"I grabbed a bite at the Pilgrim," he said. "No offense, Ardys. The soldiers were told to start eating there. The cook is decent, but she's not as good as you."

Ardys dipped the muddied rag in a basin of water and squeezed it. "You can eat here anytime you'd like, Aisic. But your friends can't."

"Thank you. I'll make sure it doesn't happen again."

"Good lad. Well, that's about all we can do tonight, Eilean. You'll have to wash it proper in the morning."

"I will. Thank you, Ardys."

"I'll walk you back to the castle," Aisic offered.

After what had just happened, she was grateful for the kindness. They went out the back door of the kitchen. It was full dark by then, and the thunderheads concealed the moon and the stars. Rain dripped from the shingles of the kitchen and splashed in puddles at the base of the building.

"Here," Aisic said, holding up his cloak to cover her.

When she ducked under it, she could smell him and the leather armor he wore. It was a wonderful scent. They tromped together toward the castle.

"Have you been to the Pilgrim yet?" he asked.

"No. Is it nice?"

"Oh yes. Once the abbey starts bringing in learners, it'll be impossible to get a room there. Did you know there's a tunnel connecting the abbey and the inn?"

"No," Eilean said.

"The Aldermaston had it done. I heard about it from some of the lads who dug it."

"Why would he want a tunnel going to the inn?"

"Who knows? Maybe he wants to get away now and then? Do you want a drink of cider? They sell it at the inn. We could get a cup together."

"If you want cider, we can get it from Ardys for free."

"Oh." His voice throbbed with disappointment. "We don't have to go."

"Maybe tomorrow," she offered as they reached the door to the castle.

His eyes brightened, and a hopeful smile twisted on his mouth. "I'll wait for you at sunset?"

She knew she should say no—that it would be even more painful later—but her heart spoke for her.

"Yes."

A disease that is not rooted out will quickly spread. We have confirmed reports that the heretic Utheros has begun to organize his deviant thoughts into a new branch of the maston order. Some are proclaiming him the new High Seer. The holy emperor is outraged by this falsehood and has summoned the royal council as well as Tatyana Dagenais and all the resources of the powerful Dagenais family. We travel to Paeiz through the Apse Veils to meet in council. Hautland is a mountainous country with heavily fortified castles. It will not be an easy conquest.

But conquer it we shall and crush this heresy into oblivion.

—Mícheál Nostradamus of Avinion Abbey

CHAPTER TWENTY-ONE

A Raven's Knowledge

"Tell me again the significance of the Dagenais family," Mordaunt asked, leaning forward, his hands clasped before him on the table. When he sat this close, she could easily see the tufts of gray hair above his ears. It gave him the appearance of a middle-aged man, not one who had lived and witnessed the world for so many centuries.

Eilean thought for a moment. "The Dagenais family are from Paeiz. They helped found the holy empire. They were a trading family at first, from Antimo."

"Good, lass. From what abbey did Tatyana become the High Seer?"

"She was the Aldermaston of . . ." Her memory began to fail, but then it came to her. "Sumeela! Sumeela Abbey in the mountain valley."

"Yes. But it didn't happen by chance, my dear. Her choice of position was quite calculated. Although the kingdom of Sumeela is high in the mountains, it is known for the simpleness of life. There are many shepherds in Sumeela."

"Are you saying she served there to create the appearance of humility?"

Mordaunt gave her a crooked smile. "Exactly. And it helped boost her family name and their incredible fortune and power. You told me you've met the High Seer. She has been in that position for many years and has consolidated her power in Avinion, the place of the Holy See. Her influence and wealth help prop up the holy emperor." He entwined his fingers together. "The maston order combined with political authority. That is a dangerous alliance. Why?"

"It wouldn't be dangerous unless the order became corrupted. Wouldn't the Medium desire that kings be faithful?"

"And if the order *did* become corrupted, how would the Medium seek to heal it?"

She stared at him. "By calling a new High Seer."

Mordaunt smiled. "You have a raven's knowledge, Eilean."

"You mean I'm as smart as a bird?"

"It's a druid proverb. To have a raven's knowledge means to have the most powerful Gift of all. The Gift of Seering, to see the future."

"I can't see the future," she said.

"Not in the literal sense, but the more you can judge a person and their passions, their interests and desires, the better you can predict what will come. That is the closest thing to the Gift of Seering in our world. The mastons believe the High Seer has this Gift, that it comes with the calling. But it is a title only. That Gift from the Medium is exceedingly rare."

He looked over her shoulder. "Someone is coming."

She rose from the table and fetched the broom so she wouldn't appear to be slacking in her work. Not long after, she heard a knock on the door, which startled her because she hadn't heard footsteps.

She opened the door to find Captain Hoel standing there. His cheeks were flushed, his eyes narrowed with anger and concern. He looked past her to Mordaunt, sitting at the table, and gave the prisoner a derisive look.

"The Aldermaston wishes to see you, Eilean," he said.

"Oh," she answered in surprise. She put the broom away and then went back to the door. Captain Hoel was glaring at Mordaunt still, looking angry enough to do him harm. She slid past him, but he followed her out of the room and shut the door behind them.

They went down the stairs together, but he caught her arm before they reached the bottom and pushed her against the stone wall. The threat in his eyes made her shrink with fear. His hand was still fixed to her arm, just above the crook of her elbow.

"I'm giving you a warning, Eilean," he said in a low voice. "Do not play Mordaunt's game. He's using you, and it will not end well for you when it's over. You are nothing to him but a means of escape."

His grip wasn't painful, but it was firm. She tried not to let her fear show in her eyes. "What game do you mean? I'm doing exactly what the Aldermaston asked me to do."

"He asked you because he knew Mordaunt would influence you. He thought it more likely the druid would confide in you if you seemed to take his side. And you *have* been influenced by him. I can hear it in the way you speak. Your Pry-rian accent is all but gone."

"Is that a serious crime, Captain?" she demanded.

"No. But it is evidence that you've been corrupted. I've held my tongue long enough. When you start walking on a road, be certain you know where the path leads. The road you are on leads to your destruction."

Again, it felt as if he'd struck her in the stomach with his words. Sweat began to bead on her brow.

"I don't know what you're talking about, Captain. I've done nothing but follow orders."

He shook his head and released her arm. "The world is a very big place, Eilean. There is much you do not know. Go to the Aldermaston, but be mindful of what I said."

With a nod, he sent her on her way. She rubbed her arm where he'd squeezed her, troubled by the encounter, and by the time she reached the Aldermaston's study, she was trembling. But maybe that was his purpose, to rattle her. Or, more likely, Captain Hoel knew more than he let on.

She rapped softly on the door, and Aldermaston Gilifil bid her enter.

He sat behind his desk, a scroll of parchment in front of him, a broken wax seal nearby. As she approached the desk, she saw the sign of the maston order on the discarded wax.

"You sent for me, Aldermaston?"

He steepled his fingers. "It looks like our time with our prisoner has come to an end," he said with a disappointed sigh. "Since you have been unable to discover the location of the hidden tome, the High Seer feels it is her duty to extract that information through other means of . . . persuasion." He sighed. "I'd really hoped to prevent that."

"What will they do with him?" Eilean asked worriedly.

"As I understand the High Seer's intention, he will be kept shackled in a cell in a dark dungeon. Here, he's enjoyed Ardys's excellent cooking, a spacious room, and even pleasant companionship"—he gestured toward her—"but soon those privileges will seem but a wonder, a dream. I wish, I truly wish this could have ended better for him."

Eilean felt sick again. "I cannot make him tell me, Aldermaston. I've . . . I've done as you asked. I've befriended him, and he's taught me so much."

"Yes. I know. You've done the best you could. But it wasn't enough. Captain Hoel has grown suspicious of your loyalty. The High Seer may wish to speak to you in person, but I don't think you have anything to fear, child. You are not a heretic yourself, even though you've been near one."

She swallowed. "Is the High Seer coming here?"

"No. You needn't worry about it, Eilean. When the time comes, you will know what to say. You've always been strong with the Medium. Maybe they will let you learn at an abbey when this is all done. Who knows? Anything is possible." As he said those words, she felt even more confused.

"What am I to do, Aldermaston?" she asked, her voice barely above a whisper.

"If only you could have gotten the tome," he said with a hint of rebuke.

***

"You look troubled," Celyn said to Eilean. They'd met at the rear of the kitchen.

Eilean quickly related what had happened to her that day. The sun was still cheerful, but it was setting earlier and earlier now. The storm clouds of the previous day had been chased away, but the rain had brought out new smells.

Eilean paced nervously, her arms folded tightly over her chest. "I feel like I'm a rabbit in the first grip of the snare," she said. "If I try to run, it'll choke me."

Celyn put her hand on Eilean's arm, stopping her. "Reckon we should leave Muirwood. We've been talking about it for a fortnight now, but I'm serious. Let's get away. I don't want anything to happen to you, Eilean."

"What would they do? I've done exactly what the Aldermaston said."

"But he's wrong. And we both know it. If they need someone to blame . . . they'll blame you, not him. I feel strongly about this, Eilean. We should go away."

"You want to go to Hautland."

"I do," Celyn said forcefully. "They have a port in Bridgestow. We could walk there, then take a ship to Hautland. I have enough coins saved to buy us passage."

"You'd leave Ardys and Loren? Just walk away before our service is done?"

"I would," Celyn answered firmly. "We're nearly of age. We would be leaving Muirwood anyway in the spring. Together, you and I."

"I wish we had someone else to help us. I wish Mordaunt could escape and come along."

"The Leering binds him here," she said. "You've said it yourself."

"I could try to break it."

Celyn shook her head. "They would know. And then you'd truly be in trouble. I will gather some food and blankets for both of us."

The prospect of leaving terrified Eilean. Part of her had depended on the structure of belonging to an abbey. The protection and guidance it offered. But as Celyn spoke, she felt a strong feeling of rightness about their plan.

"What if we could talk Aisic into coming with us?" Eilean suggested.

Celyn's brow wrinkled. "Reckon he would?" Her tone implied doubt.

"I don't know. I'm supposed to go to the Pilgrim Inn with him today."

Celyn squinted. "I don't know, Eilean. I'm not sure telling one of the sheriff's men where we're going would be wise."

"I wouldn't tell him unless he was willing to come. I'd feel better if we had someone who could protect us."

Celyn gave her an arch look. "Is that the only reason? Because I know you can protect us better than Aisic ever could."

She put her face in her hands. "I don't know. I'm confused."

"Eilean!"

She lowered her hands and turned to see Aisic approaching them both. "I was going to wait outside the castle, but I saw you talking. Would you like to go to the inn with us?" he asked, nodding to Celyn.

"I can't," she said. "I'm needed for supper."

"That's right. I forgot."

Celyn gave Eilean a warning look.

"I promised him I'd go," she said in an undertone. "I'll come back after to get Mordaunt his supper."

Celyn nodded wordlessly and slipped into the kitchen.

"I'm glad we're talking again," Aisic said when they were alone. He looked eager about something. Giddy was probably a closer description. "I thought I'd done something to offend you."

"I've never hated you, Aisic," Eilean said. She started to walk alongside him, folding her arms tightly over her chest, afraid he might try to take her hand. Afraid she'd like it.

"You once liked me," he said. "Admit it."

She didn't want to speak the truth that she'd *always* liked him, though he had not always treated her with interest. She remembered the friends he used to work with back at Tintern. What were they doing now?

"It won't be crowded this early." He gazed toward the sinking sun. "The hills are lovely tonight."

As they walked together, side by side, she felt a strange certainty that it would be wrong to ask him to go with her and Celyn. It would make their relationship more complicated if he came. Mordaunt had told her that Aisic was not the man for her, and she trusted his assessment.

But if she *did* go away, this might be the last time she saw Aisic. That thought filled her with sadness.

"Are you unwell?" he asked.

"Not really," she answered.

"The inn has a stable. We have two horses there in case we need to ride to Mendenhall to bear a message to the sheriff. Do you know how far away that is?"

"It's to the east, I believe," she answered. "At the edge of the Bearden Muir?"

"How'd you know that?" he asked, his brow lifting.

She knew much about the land, even though she'd never journeyed it. "I like knowing things," she said. "You know how to ride a horse?"

"I do, and I'm fair at it. The brown one is called Captain. He's my favorite. Do you want to meet him?"

"I'd like that," she said. It did not take long to reach the Pilgrim Inn, which was not far from the wall that was being built to separate the abbey from the village. The wall was still low enough to step over. Other buildings had been constructed too, and there were many tents to protect from the weather.

"This is going to be called High Street," he said as they approached. "That's the road to Mendenhall there." He pointed, then shifted his finger. "That one goes north to Bridgestow."

The inn was two stories high, and a sign bearing the image of a bearded man with a staff and script hung from a bracket above the door. The stables were in the rear yard, so Aisic took her there, helping her avoid some of the larger mud puddles that befouled the street. When they reached the door of the stable, she could hear the nicker of horses and smell the pungent aroma of manure and the sweet scent of hay.

"Our horses are in the back of the stables," Aisic said, raising his voice. It was well kept, with harnesses and saddles hanging from pegs on the wall. The main aisle had been broom-brushed, and the smell of oats wafted from an open barrel as they walked past it. He took her hand and guided her into the deeper shadows. There were eight stalls in all but only the back two had horses in them.

Aisic went to the nearest stall and then began to stroke the withers of the horse and croon to him.

"Aye there, Captain. Aren't you a strong lad?" He let go of her hand and continued to show the horse kindness. Eilean was a little frightened of the animal because he was so large, but she touched his neck.

"Always let him see where you are," he said. "He'll get used to you soon enough."

"He's a beautiful animal," she said, feeling in awe of his size. He could carry them both easily. The hide was feathery soft. He grunted but not in a menacing way.

Aisic nodded toward the next stall. "That other one's called Blackie. Reckon you can understand why by looking at him. But he's got a bit of a temper. I wouldn't go near him."

She continued to stroke the majestic animal, who nuzzled into her touch.

"Captain *loves* his apples, I'll tell you that," Aisic said, hands on his hips. "Too bad the season is over already." He came and stood next to her while she stroked the animal.

"Have you ridden a horse before, Eilean?" he asked her.

"Of course not. Why would I have?"

"There's something about it," he said, his eyes intense. "The feeling . . . it's like flying. Reckon you'll like it."

She had a suspicion he meant something else entirely. A little worried nudge seemed to push her, only it was something she felt in her mind, not her body. She should leave the stable.

"Supper, then?" she asked brightly and then backed up when he stepped toward her.

"If you want," he said, reaching for her hand again.

She started to walk, but he stopped her with a soft touch to her hair. She turned and looked at him quizzically. What did he expect from her?

"You are so lovely," he breathed. "It makes . . . it makes my heart hurt. Eilean, why do you torment me so?"

"I'm not trying to torment you, Aisic," she said, shaking her head. The feeling that they should leave grew stronger.

"Then why did you kiss me when we were out in the moors?" he asked, coming closer. "You liked me then. I know you did. I think about it all the time. I've thought about it over and over. You love me, Eilean. I know you do. And I'm for you. Only for you."

He gently pushed her into the empty stall next to Captain's, and then he was touching her, his mouth pressed to hers. She was shocked by the sudden display. Her feelings surged with fire in such blazing intensity that she couldn't even think.

"Eilean, Eilean," he groaned, kissing her cheek, then her neck. Again, he wasn't trying to cush with her—he was going not for a tender show of affection but something stronger, more possessive.

It felt intensely pleasurable, but something was wrong. There was passion, yes, but it was too urgent, too soon. She tried to push him away, to put space between them, but he responded by leaning against her, bringing her back into the wooden railing of the stall. And then she lost her balance, and they both fell into a patch of hay. It was prickly but not unpleasant. But he was on top of her, and his hands were beginning to explore her.

"Aisic," she said, pushing against him to get him off her.

"My love, my dearest, I know you want this. I've been dreaming of this moment . . ."

"Get off me," she insisted, determined to leave the inn and his companionship. She'd thought she wanted him, but everything felt terribly wrong. This wasn't what she'd imagined him doing. He was thinking only of himself, his own desire.

"You can't mean that," he said huskily and gazed at her with a look of possessiveness. "You want this. You *want* it." Like he *owned* her. Then he dropped his face down to smother her with kisses again.

"Kozkah gheb-ool," she whispered, invoking the words of power.

The Medium jolted through her and shoved Aisic from her, flinging him into the wooden partition on the other side of the stall. She heard boards cracking, and Aisic slumped into the hay on that side, stunned and dazed.

Eilean hastily got to her feet, and as she did, so did Aisic's friends, who had been hiding in the shadows across from them. They looked at her with fear in their eyes, fear and surprise. With the power of the Medium surging through her, she knew their thoughts, she understood their intentions. They'd hidden in the stable before she and Aisic had arrived, because he'd promised them that he could woo her. The plan had been for them to watch for a while before coming out of their hiding places when she was in a compromised position. So they could laugh at and mock her. So they could have this secret to hold over her.

It wasn't love that had brought her to the stables. It was revenge.

And she had ruined the fun. She could sense their desire to humiliate her. Their will to dominate her. One of them took a step toward her, his hand opening to seize her.

She glared at them all.

"Kozkah gheb-ool," she whispered again, and they flung from her like leaves in a wind.

A desire to be observed, considered, esteemed, praised, beloved, and admired by his fellows is one of the earliest, as well as the keenest, dispositions discovered in the heart of nearly all people. Concealed talent brings no reputation. Utheros's youth is also his downfall. Everybody detests an old head on young shoulders.

—Mícheál Nostradamus of Avinion Abbey

CHAPTER TWENTY-TWO

Chosen

Eilean didn't stop at the kitchen first. Her heart was on fire with fury, and her body was weak from invoking the words of power. She felt slightly dizzy, but she hurried from the Pilgrim and was grateful for the dark to hide her burning cheeks. The knowledge that she would have been taken advantage of, made a fool, if not for Mordaunt's teachings filled her with gratitude and relief.

She entered the castle, hastening up the steps. Her breath was labored when she reached his door and opened it, and then she leaned back against it, palms flush against the wood, trying to compose herself.

Mordaunt looked at her curiously, but she could almost feel his thoughts entwining with hers. She held nothing back, reliving the awful moment in the stable so that he could picture it himself.

Finally, after her gasping had subsided, she said, "You knew this would happen. You warned me against him."

"You heeded me at first," he answered solemnly. "But every woman wants to be desired. I don't blame you, Eilean. I'm glad they didn't harm you. That was their intention."

She lowered her head, the weariness making her want to curl up on the bed and fall asleep.

"I trusted him," she said with bitterness. "And he betrayed me."

"People's trust in each other is blind, child. Motives are unseen. Brooding thoughts concealed."

"But not from you," she said, giving him a grateful smile.

"In the country of the blind, the one-eyed man is king," he said simply. "I don't claim to have the Medium's omniscience. And knowing the thoughts of others is a gift as well as a blight."

"It must be so," she said. "I think . . . I have some of that blight within me. At the end, when I felt the Medium's power was coursing through me, I understood their intentions. That's why I defended myself."

"You did well, Eilean. And yes, the Medium can reveal the thoughts and intentions of others when it chooses."

"Why didn't you warn me more strongly against Aisic?" she asked him, her heart aching. Aisic had lost her respect now. Utterly and totally. There was no way for him to redeem himself in her eyes.

He sighed. "It was better for you to learn through your own experience. I knew it would happen, sooner or later. You must be on your guard. Most men are like him. They are greedy, selfish creatures interested only in proving they are better than other men. A woman who shows interest is a prize to be won. But they are rarely satisfied once a conquest is made. They'll seek another. It is fear that drives them, and hate—but usually they hate themselves most of all."

"That is awful, Mordaunt," she said, shaking her head. "Can none be trusted?"

He tilted his head to the side. "Can a *pethet* be trusted? Some but not all. I have been in this world for many, many years. I have seen this sad tale repeat over and over again. What you want is someone who'll both desire you and listen to you. Someone you can trust not to take advantage of you. Both those goals conflict. You want the warmth from the fire but not to be burned. Yet some feelings are so powerful they must be banked and cooled by a dozen restraints. The tomes teach this. *I've* taught you this. You weren't burned by the fire. But you almost were. Now you are not quite so blind."

"I hate those soldiers," she said, shaking her head. She felt unsettled, as if she'd just learned the world was darker and more unsafe than she'd imagined.

"Do not let that hate fester in your heart. You learned an important lesson. Heed that lesson. Learn from it. There are some honorable men, but they are exceedingly rare."

She gazed at him. "You have never tried to hurt me," she said simply.

"I have only tried to help you, little sister," he offered. "I brought you here."

His words stunned her. Her mouth opened, but no words came out.

"We don't have much time left together, Eilean. I've tried to prepare you as best I could."

"Prepare me for what?"

"My thoughts brought you here. I pleaded with the Medium to send someone whom I could entrust with my tome. I fixed my thoughts on that single purpose. Having been betrayed myself, you can imagine that it was not easy for me to banish my desire for revenge and succumb to the Medium's will. My thoughts summoned you here. It was manifest to me clearly when you arrived."

"But what of Aldermaston Gilifil?" she asked.

"It has always been your choice, Eilean. I am willing to entrust you with my tome if you will do the Medium's will with it."

"But what is the Medium's will?" she pleaded.

"You already *know*. It has been coaxing you for months. It has been preparing you for this moment, this time when you must forsake Muirwood Abbey and visit the broader world."

He was right. She *had* known. But fear had kept her from embracing the thoughts. Celyn was better prepared than she was.

"Your friend has already submitted to the Medium's will. She will go with you."

Terror coiled inside her stomach like a snake. "I'm afraid to."

"I know. I can feel it. You would be incredibly foolish if you weren't afraid."

"What must I do?"

"How can I tell you that? What could I say that wouldn't terrify you further? Your path will be revealed one step at a time. The Medium reveals itself in its own due time. All you must do is follow where you feel impressed to go."

In her head, she heard those whispers from months ago. *Patience. Patience.*

She looked down at the floor, sick to her stomach and physically weak. "I'm supposed to go to Hautland."

"See? You already knew. Are you willing?"

She licked her lips. "What will happen if I refuse?"

He arched his eyebrows. "You know this as well."

"I'm not as wise as you," she countered. "Tell me."

"What did Captain Hoel warn you of? I know his thoughts, just as I know yours."

"He said the road I'm on leads to my destruction. That it would not end well for me."

"If Captain Hoel finds out that you have invoked words of power and injured some of the sheriff's soldiers, what will his duty compel him to do?"

Eilean blinked rapidly. "He serves the High Seer, not the Aldermaston." Her stomach shriveled even more.

"He's part of the Apocrisarius. He will hunt you like he did the druids of the Bearden Muir."

Would Aisic and his fellow ruffians talk about her? Of course they would. Revenge had been their motivation all along. What better way than to accuse her of being a heretic.

"I think I'm going to be sick," she whispered. She'd hoped that she and Celyn could wait to leave the abbey until their service was complete, but that was no longer possible, both because of the soldiers and because Mordaunt needed her to retrieve his tome and keep it safe.

"Do you need to use the garderobe?"

"I cannot escape Captain Hoel and his men."

"Careful, Eilean Donnán. Don't lose your head to fear. You lack the experience and training to elude hunters of the Apocrisarius. Their skills and abilities far exceed your own. But you, little sister, are stronger in the Medium than any of them . . . well . . . except the captain, perhaps. He is very strong. With the Medium guiding you, you shall succeed in anything it asks you to do."

"But what will happen to you?" she said with pangs of dread. "The Aldermaston said . . . he said they were going to send you to a dungeon."

"None of that matters. I've been in chains before. We must do the Medium's will."

"That's not *fair*," she said, pushing away from the door. "You are one of the Twelve! Why would they do this to you!"

"You feel sorry for me?" he asked with a kindly smile.

"Of course I do!"

"You will come to learn, Eilean, that suffering is the greatest teacher of all. If it is the Medium's will that I wear chains instead of a chaen, then so be it. I am never truly alone." He reached out and gently pinched her chin. "And it will give me pleasure to know that you are fulfilling the Medium's purpose. That you are doing your part to break the iron grip of a fallen order. An order that has laid claim on the eyes, ears, and imagination of the world. That can still charm and bewitch the simple and the ignorant. I wonder how Utheros ever saw through it."

She was still trembling inside. How could she do such an enormous thing? She was only a wretched.

Mordaunt smiled again. "Do you not think the Medium has tried to persuade the learned, the powerful, and the strong that things need to change? But the learned, the powerful, and the strong won't change until they have to. The humble, the meek, the patient, the persevering—they are the ones who get things done. Even a simple oak tree can bring down a wall with its roots."

Although she was still fearful, she accepted her fate. "I will do it."

"Bless you, child. I knew you would. Would you kneel, please? I would like to give you a Gifting to help you on the journey that lies ahead. And I will give you a new name. One that will help you become who you are meant to be."

"I've never had a Gifting before," she said.

"Then it is long overdue. Kneel, please."

Eilean did, and she bowed her head. She felt Mordaunt's hand rest against the back of her head. The hand was warm, powerful but gentle.

"Eilean Donnán, through the Medium I Gift thee with diligence. No matter how many times you stumble and fall, you will rise again and keep pressing on. You have always had a clear mind, a sensitivity to the Medium. You will need it on this first of many journeys. You will continue to be sensitive to the promptings of the Medium, and your heart and mind will be filled with light and truth. You will set your feet on paths that lead to righteousness, and your heart will be more devoted to the ideals of Idumea than those of this world. Your new name is Gwenllian Siar. Your name means *blessed flax*. Remember where you came from."

As he spoke the words, a series of tingles went down her neck and the backs of her arms, making the hair stand on end. It sank deep into her bones, all the way to her toes. Comfort and peace dispelled her fear.

"I also give thee the Gift of Knowledge. Druid lore is only passed from one druid to another. It must never be written on aurichalcum, parchment, or stone. There are certain oak trees, deep in the forest, which contain spirit creatures called the Dryad. You will recognize these trees because of the mistletoe clinging to their branches. You only need to find one of them in the Bearden Muir to be led to the others. My tome is buried beneath one of these trees, guarded by a Dryad named Gwragith Annon. Remember her name. Gwragith Annon. The other Dryads will lead you to her. Approach her tree alone, for she will not appear if other mortals are with you. Kneel before the roots with your eyes closed. Do not look at her, or she will use her magic to steal your memories. After she has tested you, you may see her for yourself, and she will guide you to the tome. Other items to ease your journey are stored with it—coins from different lands and a talisman that will protect you from the Myriad Ones until you become a maston yourself. Take the tome where the Medium directs you. If you safeguard it, then it will not be taken from you by force. But if you fail in your purpose and neglect it, you will be captured by your enemies. I will send you off with the same words of wisdom I was given before leaving on my quest as a wayfarer. 'I send you forth as a sheep in the midst of wolves. Be as wise as a serpent and as harmless as a dove. By Idumea's hand, make it so.'"

Eilean opened her eyes and felt tears welling there. Grateful for Mordaunt's wisdom and help, for the feeling of peace that had settled upon her, she stood and embraced him.

When she pulled back, she saw a look of pain in his eyes. "Bless you, little sister. May the Medium bless you on your journey."

"Will we see each other again?" she asked him.

"I don't have a raven's knowledge, lass. I had hoped that the Medium would impress me to give you the Gift of Seering, but it did not. Only one of a few have ever been blessed with that Gift." He cupped her cheek. "Be diligent, Gwenllian Siar. That Gift will serve you even better."

Eilean heard the sound of footsteps coming up the stairs, but she didn't feel afraid.

"It is Celyn," he said. "She's worried you never came."

Eilean went to the door and opened it, surprising Celyn on the other side. Her friend held a dinner tray clutched in her hands.

"You didn't come for supper after leaving with Aisic," Celyn said, her brow furrowed. "Rhiannon told me what the soldiers planned to do to you. They did something similar to one of her friends. I t-told Captain Hoel to try and find you. I didn't know you'd be up here. I was so worried."

Eilean turned back and gave Mordaunt a knowing look. Captain Hoel was already on his way to the stable. Soon he'd know about what she'd done.

"We must go, Celyn," she said. "We have to leave Muirwood tonight."

King Aengus's bride will soon arrive in his kingdom. She has passed the maston test with great aplomb and, as I understand, solemnity. I must admit partiality, of course, as she hails from my native Dahomey. Rarely do great beauty and great virtue dwell together, but the eldest daughter of King Tristan is a great beauty and devout in her beliefs. This marriage alliance will provide a strong foundation for the maston order in Moros. Perhaps her time at the island abbey of Dochte will prepare her for ruling an island kingdom. That grand abbey, built centuries ago, is the most distinguished abbey in Dahomey. It is built atop a small island that is accessible by sea when the tide comes in and by land when the tide goes out. All the princes and princesses of the realms study there.

—Mícheál Nostradamus of Avinion Abbey

CHAPTER TWENTY-THREE

Whispers in the Bearden Muir

After sharing a final dinner with Ardys and Loren, they left Muirwood after dark, hand in hand, and started on the road toward the port town of Bridgestow. Celyn had gathered a single pack with provisions to last a few days. They both wore cloaks and their old wretched dresses from Tintern Abbey since the Muirwood ones were so distinctive it would be easy to recognize them as wretcheds from that place.

They'd cut through the fledging cider orchard and into the woods, knowing they'd meet up with the road before too long. They did, and the compacted ground was easier on their feet. It would also leave less of a trail for the hunters to follow.

"How long do you reckon it will take for Captain Hoel to find us?" Celyn asked nervously.

"They could overtake us tonight if they wanted to," Eilean answered. Darkness was still oppressive to her, but her courage had been bolstered by the Gifting.

"That soon?"

"But they won't. If they suspect we're going after Mordaunt's tome, they'll let us seek it. Our greatest danger will come *after* we've retrieved it."

"I hadn't thought of that. How do we escape them, then?"

"I can disguise us to appear as strangers to them. I know how to summon fog and storms. It will be even easier this time of year. But even so, we won't succeed on our own. We'll need the Medium's help."

"Then we have nothing to fear," Celyn answered boldly. She squeezed Eilean's hand. "It was hard slipping away without saying goodbye to Ardys and Loren. My heart hurts, but I know we're doing the right thing."

"I'm just glad I'm not doing this all alone."

"I'll never leave you," Celyn promised. "You can help us both speak like Hautlanders, right?"

"Yes. I don't know how we'll find Utheros, but we will. The Medium has urged me to be patient. Planning one step at a time is enough."

"The Aldermaston will be furious," Celyn said. "I hope we don't have to face him after this is over."

"That would be dreadful."

They continued in silence, feeling the chill of the night air come down on them as they traveled along the road, moving fast to put as much distance as possible between themselves and the abbey. Soon they could see their breath. Wagon wheels had worn ruts through the middle of the narrow road, and they'd each picked a stripe to walk on during the journey. They had been walking for a while before they heard a horse coming toward them at a gallop.

"He's riding fast," Celyn warned as they ducked into the scraggly trees that lined both sides of the road. The moon hadn't risen yet, so the darkness was full, though there were plenty of stars visible in the sky above. The branches, gnarled and twisted and thick with moss, provided them with ample cover.

The rider stormed past their place of concealment. The moment of excitement faded, and the two girls left the woods and started down the road again.

"Could you tell who it was?" Celyn asked.

"I think I saw a sword at their side," Eilean replied. "It might have been one of the soldiers."

"If it was, then they're going to Mendenhall," Celyn answered. "Maybe they're reporting what happened at the stables."

"Part of it, anyway," Eilean answered, for she felt quite sure they would neglect to mention that they'd intended to humiliate and shame her. She clutched the cloak hasp at her neck, and they quieted as they continued.

When the moon rose above the trees, it was much easier to see their way. The sounds of the woods reminded her of the frightening trip they had taken to reach Muirwood. A long time had passed since then, another change in the seasons.

"I'm getting cold," Celyn whispered, her teeth chattering.

"Do you want to stop and rest?"

"No. Let's keep going. I'm trying not to think about what's happening back at the abbey. Captain Hoel must have told the Aldermaston already. By morning, everyone else will know." She shook her head. "I'm still furious about what those boys were going to do."

"I'm glad Rhiannon told you," Eilean said. "She's kinder than the others. I hate that I was so wrong about Aisic." And yet, some of her fury had abated during the long, cold walk. They were doing what they were meant to do, and although the sudden change in her reality was difficult to process, she felt a strong sense of determination driving her forward. It was the Gifting she'd been given.

The sounds began to change toward dawn, birds chirping to greet the day.

"The fog is coming," Celyn said in awe, pointing up.

She was right. Eilean had been so focused on moving her feet forward that she hadn't noticed the tendrils curling around the tops of the trees. The stars were invisible now.

A thought came that they should leave the road and find a place to rest.

"It's almost dawn," Eilean said. "Let's rest for a while. We've walked far enough."

"I *am* tired," Celyn agreed.

They left the road and found a spot beneath a fallen tree. The trunk would help conceal them from anyone going down the road. After refreshing themselves with food and a little bit of water, they pressed close to each other to share warmth and fell asleep.

***

When they awoke midmorning, the fog was finally dissipating. Eilean had slept well, although she still felt a bone-deep weariness. Beetles of some kind were crawling along the edge of the tree trunk. Celyn stretched and yawned, and they both ate some bread and nuts from the supplies she'd brought.

Glancing at her friend's old dress, Eilean said, "They'd be done with the flax harvest by now at Tintern."

"I miss those days," her friend said with a smile. "It was hard work, but it felt good seeing the sheaves stacked at the end before they were made into linen."

"I miss the flax when it flowered," Eilean said. "Those little blue flowers covered the fields as far as you could see."

"There's beauty here too," Celyn said, gazing at the Bearden Muir. "It's just different."

They rose and brushed off the bits of earth and scrub that clung to them.

"Do we still take the road?" Celyn asked.

Eilean gazed at it and listened to her feelings. She had the impulse to take it a little farther. It posed a slight danger, but not enough of one to warrant using magic to change their appearances. Each time she used magic, it drained her, and she needed to stay as strong as possible if they were to get away.

"Let's follow it for a while longer," she confirmed, and they went back to the road and started walking again. Clouds gathered overhead, blotting out the sun, but the day was warm and pleasant. As they continued along, they spoke about their lives together and shared stories. Every now and then, Eilean would glance back suddenly, wondering if she might catch sight of one of Captain Hoel's hunters. But if they were being followed, their pursuers took pains to conceal themselves, and Eilean didn't feel any warnings from the Medium.

Before midday, the road reached a stone bridge supported by two arches, one narrower than the other. The arches joined at an outcropping of rock, covered in moss, showing that the river, when swollen, would split and drain to either side. They walked across it, stopping midway, and looked down. Water rushed beneath the steeper arch, but the other was bone dry.

"Someone could hide under that one," Celyn said, pointing to the dry ground.

Eilean rubbed her hand along the rough stone railing. "I think this is the river that fed the lake of the abbey," she said. "It's flowing away from Muirwood." Leerings had been put in to divert the waters so as to drain the lake.

"I see a fish down there," Celyn said.

Eilean got the sense that they should leave the bridge and the road. They hadn't encountered anyone at all that day, but their luck wouldn't hold out much longer.

"I think we should leave the road for now."

"Which way?" Celyn asked.

Eilean furrowed her brow, trying to get a premonition from the Medium. *East* was the only thought that came. She pointed, and the two girls left the road and entered the thick vegetation again. Before the bridge was out of sight, she looked back at it and thought she heard the sound of a wagon coming.

"Do you hear that?" she asked.

Celyn listened, then nodded. "A wagon."

They plunged deeper into the vegetation, until they heard only the whispers of the Bearden Muir. Eilean studied the moss-thickened branches of the trees as she wove her way through them. She was looking for oaks, which were everywhere, but none of them had clumps of mistletoe hanging from the branches.

They wandered eastward through the early afternoon, and the trees became less dense. While the sun was still falling to the west, they reached the edge of the Bearden Muir, approaching a set of hills. In the crook of those hills was a small farmstead with a tiny cottage and smoke drifting up from the chimney. There were some cows grazing in the yard as well as pens with other animals.

Celyn looked at her. "They have a well," she said. "Maybe we could refill our water?"

Eilean listened to her heart and felt no danger, so she nodded, and both girls tromped through the soft meadow to the cottage.

A man with an axe came around from the side of the cottage and saw them. He called out, and then a woman emerged from inside the cottage, wiping her hands on an apron. The two stood next to each other and watched as Eilean and Celyn approached.

"Could we use your well to get a drink?" Celyn asked brightly.

"You're not from these parts," said the man with the axe with a distrustful look. "Your speech is strange."

"We just wanted some water, please," Eilean asked, matching their accent in her own speech.

The woman gave the man a little shove. "They're harmless, Adain. Of course you can. Help yourself."

The man sniffed and then nodded.

Celyn thanked them, and she and Eilean went to the well. Their reluctant host lowered the bucket it, filled it, and drew it up with bulging forearms. While they filled their flasks, the man studied them suspiciously. "What are you two doin' all alone out here?" he asked.

"Adain, leave them be," said the lady. Turning to them, she said, "You worked at the abbey, didn't you? Did they let you go?"

Eilean and Celyn exchanged a glance.

The woman gave them a probing look. "There's more to it than that, isn't there?"

"It's none of our concern, Madge," said Adain.

"Hush, Adain. They're good girls. I can tell. You didn't just leave the abbey. You ran away from it."

Celyn glanced at the ground.

"One of the sheriff's men attacked me," Eilean said truthfully. "I got away."

"See, Adain! I knew it. You got away, and your friend came with you." A protective look filled her eyes. "Those soldiers are ruffians, the lot of them. Where are you going? Do you have anyone to help you?"

"Madge!" said the woodsman with surprise.

"Hush, I'm only going to help them a little. You stay the night with us. No one leaves my cottage hungry."

Eilean felt a prickle of reassurance from the Medium. "Thank you. Thank you both. Can we help with some chores?"

The woodsman huffed and then walked over to a pile of wood and began assembling pieces to cut.

"Can either of you cook?" asked Madge. "That would help."

Celyn grinned. "We both can."

The cottage was a one-room structure, made of stacked and mortared stones and a thick thatched roof. While the woodsman made work of the woodpile, the two girls helped inside. Eilean tidied, and Celyn helped with the meal and showed herself Madge's equal in making bread while the older woman prepared some stew. Adain came in at sunset with some logs for the fire, and Madge set aside small wooden bowls for them to eat from and spoons carved from wood.

It was a delicious stew, the bread was fresh and hot, and they enjoyed the meal together by the warm fire, Adain grunting with satisfaction at what he was eating.

"It's good, really," he said, waving what was left of his bread after Madge told him that Celyn had made it.

Some of the farm animals began to make noises, and the farmer set his bowl down.

"Hello? Is anyone there?"

The voice came from outside. The woodsman quickly rose to his feet, grabbing his axe as he went to the door, and Eilean and Celyn looked at each other as he went outside.

Madge gave Celyn and Eilean a motherly nod. "You're safe here. Don't be frightened." Nonetheless, she got to her feet and followed her husband to the doorway, peering out and blocking their line of sight. Adain said something, then the newcomer, and Madge proceeded to wave them both in merrily.

"Of course you can!" she said, waving. She smiled at the girls. "It's all right. It's safe. It's just a druid."

Well is it said that the most disadvantageous peace is better than the most just war. The kingdom of Hautland is fractured into rival factions. Treachery abounds. The emperor's army was expecting support from Earl Glott, but at the last moment he switched sides and now defies the emperor and the High Seer, risking not only his own destruction but excommunication. Every attempt to infiltrate and discover where Utheros is hiding has been thwarted. Though the ancient device known as the Cruciger orb affirms he is still in Hautland, we cannot get near him by land or by sea, so the device has been sent back to Avinion. The emperor fears that if he draws all his strength to attack Hautland, he leaves his rear vulnerable to encroachment by Dahomey. Such is the tangled web we live in. But the Medium will prevail despite the fickleness of princes.

—Mícheál Nostradamus of Avinion Abbey

CHAPTER TWENTY-FOUR

Stright

Eilean and Celyn exchanged another worried look. Was it one of the dark druids? One whose eyes turned silver when he used his talisman? The only way in or out of the cottage was through the front door, so the girls could do little other than watch as the druid was welcomed inside.

Although younger than their hosts, he looked a few years older than Eilean and Celyn. He didn't have much by way of a beard, and his garb showed he was used to living off the land. A few woad tattoos crisscrossed his neck and the edges of his eyes, and Eilean noticed the chain around his neck and the symbol of the talisman against his chest, similar to ones she had previously seen. When he saw them, he nodded in greeting and then sat down on the rush matting on the floor and waited for his food.

"We don't see many druids these days," the woman said, producing another wooden bowl and spoon.

"There aren't many of us left in the Bearden Muir," he answered. "Not after the uprising."

"Heard about that," Adain said worriedly. "Nasty business."

"It was nasty business," the druid agreed. "Were you caught up in it?"

"One of them dark druids came by and tried to rouse us up. The Medium warned us of the danger, so we didn't open the door to him. He banged on the door and tried to force it open, but it wouldn't budge. Eventually he left."

"I'm sorry that happened," said the young man. "Most of the dark druids have been rounded up and imprisoned by the king's command."

"Did they come after you?" asked the woman.

"They did. But I can go to ground like a fox," he said with a smile. He nodded to Eilean and Celyn. "These your daughters?"

"No, travelers . . . like you."

"I'm Stright," he said to them.

"It's nice to meet you," Eilean said, not giving her name in return.

"Do you want to stay the night as well?" Madge asked him.

"Oh no, I wouldn't trespass. There are men about, roving in the woods." Although he said it to the woman, Eilean had the impression that his words were meant for her and Celyn. Her friend squeezed her hand.

The druid rose after finishing his stew. "I'll be going. Thank you for the hospitality."

"You're welcome," Madge said. "Can you leave a blessing on our cottage?"

"It would be my pleasure," said the druid. He clasped the talisman and bowed his head.

Immediately, Eilean felt the Medium's gentle presence filter into the cottage. It was nothing like the feeling she'd experienced after the dark druid's attack in the Aldermaston's kitchen. Mordaunt had told her that the two types of druids were very different, and here was the proof. This man wasn't a maston, yet he could access the Medium.

Stright lifted his chin and smiled at the couple. "A spirit will watch over your cottage tonight. Leave some berries for it in the morning, and it may linger for a few days. Peace be with you."

"And also with you," said the farmer with a look of reverence.

The druid gave another wave and disappeared into the night.

"It's a shame really," sighed the woman. "Most druids, like that young fellow, are quite helpful. I don't see why them mastons want to drive them off."

"Can you blame them?" snorted her husband. "After a group of them attacked their new church?"

"It's called an abbey, dear."

He tossed up his hands. "I want to go look around. He said some men were roving about. I took it as a warning."

"You'll frighten the girls with that talk. All will be well. A spirit is watching over us."

The farmer looked down, thoughtful, then nodded. "I'll put the crossbar over the door. Just in case."

The fire was stoked for the night, and Eilean had no trouble falling asleep. In fact, she drowsed off immediately.

***

The next morning, the couple fed Eilean and Celyn some porridge. The girls helped with some chores to show their thanks and then departed to continue their journey. The woodsman was busy at work sharpening his axe on a whetstone and repairing a bucket, but he nodded to them as they left.

"Where do we go next?" Celyn asked.

Eilean felt they should return to the Bearden Muir.

"We go back into the swamp and begin looking for oak trees."

There was no sign of Captain Hoel or any of the hunters, but Eilean had no doubt they were nearby, hidden from sight and watching to see where the girls would lead them. That didn't alter her resolve.

As they entered the dank forest again, the air grew chill, a stark contrast to the warm fire in the cottage's hearth. Following the Medium wasn't like following a trail. Eilean only had a vague sense of where to go. It was like being led by the hand as a child.

Before midday, they found an oak tree with unmistakable wreathes of mistletoe hanging from the branches.

"It's beautiful," Celyn said admiringly.

Eilean agreed. "Mordaunt said that only I should approach it. The Dryad won't come out if there are two of us."

"I'll wait over there, then," Celyn agreed and walked over to a smaller oak, sitting against it and putting her back to the one they'd found.

Eilean walked around to the other side of the oak so that she was facing Celyn's direction. She rubbed her palm against the ridged bark of the tree, taking in its tangled branches, its scent, and the pleasant sounds of nature around her. What was she supposed to do next?

Following her intuition had worked for her up until now, so she relied on it again. Kneeling by the tree, she reached out and touched it again. She bowed her head and waited.

I am here to speak with you, she thought. *I will not harm you.*

She waited and waited. After her knees started aching, she sat down, hands on her lap, and just waited. She felt no rush. In fact, she sensed any impatience would keep the Dryad from emerging. With the breeze making her even more uncomfortable, she raised her cowl to cover her hair as she continued to sit and wait, letting out thoughts to show her intentions, her wish to protect the Dryad from harm.

A twig snapped behind her, and she nearly turned around abruptly, but she remembered Mordaunt's warning not to look upon the Dryad before she passed her test. If she did, she would lose her memories.

Eilean closed her eyes, which made a prickle of apprehension go down her back.

"They are coming," whispered a woman's voice.

She felt a strong urge to look back, but she squeezed her eyes shut and clenched her fists. A tickling itch went down her neck.

"The hunters are coming for you." The whisper came a second time.

"May I speak with you?" Eilean asked.

"They will catch you. They will torture you until you tell."

"I will say nothing to them," Eilean answered. "I need your help."

"Run!" said the hushed voice.

Eilean felt herself at the edge of panic, but she held firm. Another crack. Somewhere in the distance a raven croaked. Eilean's breath came faster, but she kept her eyes shut. She could sense a presence behind her now, and it felt as if she were about to be attacked from behind. It took every portion of willpower she possessed to remain fixed in her spot.

"I will not harm you," Eilean said. "Please talk with me."

"Your thoughts are powerful," said the Dryad. "Look on me, and we shall speak."

"I will not," Eilean answered. "You will steal my memories."

"You are not a druid."

"I am not. But I learned from one."

"Do you serve the dark druids?" Eilean could feel the disdain in the soft, musical voice.

"I do not. I serve the druid Mordaunt."

"Who is that?"

"The druid of Muirwood," she answered. "The one held captive."

Silence. The pressure to look was receding. Weariness came over her, but she remained alert.

"Who do you seek?"

"I seek the Dryad Gwragith Annon."

"The mother tree?" whispered the voice. "How do you know her true name?"

"I was sent to find her," Eilean said. "Will you help me?"

"No."

"Please," Eilean said.

"No."

The feeling of the Dryad's presence vanished. She heard the raven croak again, the sound diminishing as it flapped away.

***

"It's getting dark," Celyn said after they'd spent the rest of the day marching through the swamp. They'd looked for another oak tree with mistletoe and found one, but it did not respond at all. The tree felt *closed* to her, or perhaps it was nothing more than a tree.

There were no cottages, no peasant hovels. There was just the impenetrable Bearden Muir. Eilean's legs ached from walking, and her shoes were wet from the journey. What she and Celyn both needed was a pair of sturdy boots.

Eilean sighed. The situation felt hopeless. They had wandered around the Bearden Muir all day, and it felt like they'd gone in circles. The sun was setting on what was sure to be a cold, dark night.

"Let's find shelter," Eilean said. They'd have to make their own.

They'd been following a trickle of a stream for a while, and without any other guidance, they decided to stay close to it. They'd found some thimbleberry bushes during their journey, and they'd eaten the slightly sour berries and brought some more with them. The bread Celyn had brought was getting hard, so they ate that first and saved some of the bread the woodsman's wife had sent with them for the next day.

When they found a pleasant spot for their shelter, they collected twigs and smaller branches and built a nest for their fire. Once they were finished, Eilean held her hand over the twigs. *"Pyricanthas. Sericanthas. Thas,"* she whispered.

Flames began to spurt within the nest of twigs, and the mass began to crackle and hiss. Light came from the tongues of flame. They fed the fire some dried moss as well, and soon their little campfire was glowing in the encroaching darkness. Once it was stable, they began to nibble on the old bread.

After finishing the humble meal, Celyn asked, "I wonder why the Dryad refused to help?"

"Because I told her *I* would help you."

The voice came out of nowhere and startled Eilean and Celyn out of their wits. It was Stright, and he suddenly stepped into the firelight. He held up his hands in a calming gesture. "Sorry for frightening you."

Eilean couldn't speak for a moment. "Have you been there all this time?" she asked.

"No, I just approached. I was curious about how the two of you were going to start a fire. A bit of flint perhaps? But no, you put your hand over the twigs, and they burst into flame. Do you have the fireblood?"

"I don't know what that means," Eilean admitted, certain he could see the confusion on her face. There was little point in lying.

The druid's eyes narrowed. "I didn't sense it in you. I was just curious. I told the Dryad that I would lead you to the tree you seek. She said you already knew her true name."

"I do," Eilean answered.

His brow furrowed. "How?"

"Mordaunt told me."

His lips pursed. "Mordaunt is not his true name. When he was captured by the mastons, they did something with their magic. None of us can say his true name anymore. Whenever we try, our . . . our . . ." His voice choked off, and a look of frustration contorted his face. "See? It's strange magic. Unnatural."

"Why do you want to help us?" Celyn asked warily.

"Because you look very lost, and there is still a group of men hunting you right now. They're not close enough to hear us talk, but they can see us—especially now that you've lit a fire. You know these men?"

"They are the hunters of the abbey," Eilean said.

He nodded. "They are. And you've fled the abbey?"

"Yes. We cannot go back."

Stright studied them with serious eyes. "Why do you seek the mother tree?"

"Why should we trust you?" Celyn asked.

"Actually, I'm trying to decide whether I can trust *you*. Many druids have been abducted by those men. Not all of them are dark. A friend of mine was taken away, and I haven't seen him since. I've heard rumors that the mastons . . . *burn* those who do not believe in their form of magic." He kept control of his features, but Eilean could sense his anger through the Medium's power.

She also sensed she could trust him. The Medium had put him in their path, just as it had the woodsman and his wife at their little farm.

"We seek something Mordaunt hid at the tree. He sent us to retrieve it."

"His golden book," the druid said. "I've heard that he was once a maston."

"Yes. We seek it. Will you help us?"

He sighed and rubbed his mouth thoughtfully. "How will you get past the hunters after you have it? That's what they're after, isn't it?"

"It is," Celyn agreed. "We will get past them."

"How?"

"With the magic Mordaunt taught me," Eilean said.

He scratched the back of his neck. "I came across your tracks yesterday. A spirit creature had followed you, and it led me to the farmer's cottage. I warned you about the hunters so that you'd leave during the night. Instead, you chose to leave at dawn for all the world to see." He chuckled. "I've been following you . . . and them . . . all day. But I told the Dryad I would help you, and I keep my promises. You have my word as a druid."

"Is that an oath?" Eilean asked.

"Yes. And our oaths are sacred to us. If I were to forswear myself, then I would lose the trust and respect of all the spirits of the Bearden Muir. They cannot abide dishonesty. My talisman would be useless to me. So yes . . . I'm being truthful."

"Thank you," Celyn said. She nodded to Eilean to signal she trusted him too. "We'll share our food with you."

He quirked his brow. "I won't object to that."

As Celyn began to rummage through the pack for more bread, Stright's attention was diverted. A large, triple-winged moth was dancing over the flames of their fire.

Stright stood. "The morrigan wolves are coming," he said warningly. "They caught your scent at last."

Eilean shuddered. She'd grown up hearing stories of the morrigan wolves, but had been told they hunted people because they were blighted with the Myriad Ones.

"Do we need to build the fire more?" Celyn asked with concern.

"There is only one kind of fire they fear," he said, standing tall. The light from their camp highlighted his determined features.

Eilean heard the words that he spoke in his mind as if he'd whispered them aloud.

Pyricanthas. Sericanthas. Thas.

Wreathes of blue flame began to swirl around Stright's hands.

There is only the power of the Medium. Any claims of the existence of another magical power are the deepest of heresies. Even the Myriad Ones and their abominations use the Medium, only they use it in a way that is twisted, evil, and dangerous. Some say there are people who use ancient magic, bound by talismans, that derive from other worlds and commune with the spirits of the woods. This is a falsehood. It is but another deception of Ereshkigal. When interviewing these folk, who are convinced in their hearts they are right, it is difficult to persuade them that what they hold dear is an abomination. But truth will prevail in the end. It always has.

—Mícheál Nostradamus of Avinion Abbey

CHAPTER TWENTY-FIVE

The Crooked Path

The wolves came silently.

Celyn gripped a burning torch made from a log in their fire, her face pale with fear. She and Eilean stood back-to-back, facing opposite directions so they might defend each other. Stright's hands continued to ripple with bluish flames, which sometimes flickered orange, yellow, and even green. Taking a deep breath, Eilean reached for the power of the Medium and felt a calmness ripple beneath her growing feeling of dread.

And then the wolves attacked.

Stright lifted his hands, his legs slightly bent in a pose of defense, and flames shot from his hands into the front line of charging wolves. Eilean turned at the sudden glare and watched as the beasts were enveloped in blue heat and instantly charred to ash.

"That way!" Celyn warned.

Eilean looked and found another group loping toward her, snarling and ravening. She sensed chaos and mindless hunger as the morrigan wolves came at her.

"Kozkah gheb-ool," she whispered and felt the Medium tingle up her arms.

The wolves were thrust away from her, yelping as they struck the invisible boundary. She felt the strain of the magic sapping her strength, but she held the boundary she'd set, watching as the wolves began to circle around it, their snouts snapping, their fangs bared.

Another jet of flames struck that group as Stright sent his druid magic into them. Some managed to evade the blast, but many were consumed by the magical fire.

Celyn waved her torch, trying to scare one off. "It's a big one," she gasped.

Sweat trickling down her face, Eilean glanced back at the wolf prowling on Celyn's side of the barrier. Maybe it was the leader, for it snarled and padded forward aggressively. It radiated an aura that caused fear. In the firelight, its eyes seemed silver.

Eilean extended her arm, ready to summon the silent knives that she'd watched Mordaunt conjure when the dark druids attacked Muirwood.

An arrow beat her to it. The wolf barked in pain as the shaft pierced its chest, the wound oozing red blood. It had been struck directly in the heart. The wolf tottered, yowling, then collapsed.

The captain's hunters had joined in the defense.

More arrows whistled from the darkness of the woods. Another group of wolves rushed them from the opposite side, and Stright pivoted with both arms outstretched, sending battering rams of flames into their midst. Growls of warning turned to yips of pain, and the wolves began to slink away. Another arrow thudded into fur. Then another.

She heard the metallic screech of a blade, followed by a cry of pain that was distinctly human and the ripping sounds of a wolf ravaging a man. Then the wolf shrieked in pain and fell silent.

The crushing darkness began to ebb as the wolves retreated, and Eilean watched in fascination as the triple-winged moth lighted on Stright's shoulder. He looked into the gloom with wariness, his fingers still glowing and sweat dotting his face.

"Cimber is hurt," ghosted a voice from the dark. Eilean recognized it as Twynho.

A grunt of pain could be heard. "Got my arm when I drew my gladius." She recognized the voice as Cimber's.

Someone swore under their breath. "Tend him." That was Captain Hoel.

Stright raised his arms as a shadow flickered into being at the edge of the firelight. Captain Hoel approached, bow in hand, an arrow pulled back and aimed at the druid's chest.

Eilean stepped in front of Stright, putting herself in the path.

Hoel relaxed the tension and dipped the tip of the arrow down.

"Captain, tend to your men," Eilean said.

He was closer now, enough so that his face was visible in the firelight and the glow of Celyn's torch. He looked furious, absolutely enraged, but also worried.

"Come back to Muirwood," he said, fixing his eyes on hers.

"I have not done what the Medium has sent me to do," she answered.

"The Medium?" he said, his mouth tightening with disbelief. "Are you that far gone? You cannot see this for what it is?"

"I'm afraid you are the one who misunderstands, Captain Hoel. I can tell the difference between darkness and light. I know what it feels like."

He closed his eyes as if she'd uttered dreadful lies. Then he looked at her again with a fierceness she found terrifying. "It's not too late to turn back," he whispered. "I know where your path is taking you. What will happen to you. Please. Trust me."

Stright stepped up next to her, his hands glowing brighter.

"No," she said, putting a hand on his chest to block him.

"They've captured many of us," Stright said, his voice throbbing with anger and anguish. "They've no mercy."

Hoel stared at the druid with a look of disgust. "What of your fellows who attacked the abbey?"

"They were not my kind," Stright answered.

"And I'm supposed to know the difference when someone is trying to gut me with a sickle?" Hoel shot back. His gaze softened a little as he turned back to Eilean. "Come home to the abbey. I can offer my assurance you'll be treated fairly."

"Don't listen to him," Stright said. "They'll send you to their special *courts.* You may as well die here with the wolves."

Hoel took a threatening step forward, and Eilean shook her head. "Captain, if you come any closer, you'll regret it. You cannot touch us through the barrier I've put up. Please don't try."

The strain of holding that spell was making her eyelids heavy, but she remained erect and used her words to try to calm the situation.

"If you go further, I will hunt you," Captain Hoel said. "I will do everything in my power to bring you to justice. But it doesn't have to be that way. You've been tricked and misled."

"I haven't, Captain. I follow the Medium's will."

"What you *think* is its will," he countered.

"Mordaunt is one of the Twelve," she said. "He's one of the *founders* of the maston order."

"He's only a druid," Hoel snapped.

"No shame in that," Stright said defiantly.

"By Cheshu," Hoel sighed, shaking his head. "I should just kill you now and bring the women home."

"You could try," Stright said solemnly.

"But those aren't your orders," Eilean said, feeling the Medium pulse within her, helping her know his thoughts and warning her that the spell would soon cripple her if she didn't release the magic. "You were told to follow us until we reached the tome."

His mouth quirked, and then he shook his head. "You don't know my orders, lass."

"I think I do," she replied. "Tend to Cimber. I'm sorry he was hurt."

If she held up the barrier any longer, she was going to pass out from the strain, but Hoel didn't need to know that. She let the magic go, releasing it as she would a bird that had willingly rested on her outstretched palm. The power faded, gently, peacefully. She forced herself not to show signs of weakness.

"Go, Captain," she said. "You follow your orders. I will follow mine."

"This isn't going to end well," he said, frustrated. "I tried to warn you."

"You did. I accept my fate, whatever it is."

An image flashed through her mind—an image from *him*, although she doubted he'd shared it intentionally. A stone cave carved with Leerings, engulfed in flames much hotter than the ones Stright had summoned.

A look of pity came to the captain's eyes. His brow softened. "I'm sorry for that," he said. "I believe you've been deceived by a heretic and an apostate. But remember that you *chose* it." He pointed at her. "You chose it," he repeated even more softly.

"We all have choices." She remembered something Mordaunt had once told her. Looking Hoel in the eye, she said, "Sooner or later everyone sits down to a *banquet* of consequences."

"Enjoy the feast," he said, taking a step back. She sensed that his determination equaled her own. As an Apocrisarius, he had been trained to be distrustful, to be wary of deception and constantly look for it in others. And he was totally convinced that she had been misled.

"Do your duty," she said. "While I do mine."

"You won't like it when I do," he said with a pained look. "We'll be watching during the night. Rest well."

"We don't need your protection," Stright said. "There are spirit creatures guarding us. And they will protect us from *you* as well."

Hoel bit his lip, probably trying not to snort. "If that helps you sleep better, druid. I care not."

He gave Eilean one more glance, although this was no pleading look but an expression of resignation. They were enemies now, and he was probably right.

She wouldn't like it when it came time for him to capture her.

Just like he wouldn't like it when she defended herself.

***

When morning came, Stright quenched the coals of their fire and carefully buried the ashes to make it look as if they hadn't slept there. There was no sign of Captain Hoel or any of his hunters, but then Eilean hadn't expected there to be. Had Cimber been sent back to Muirwood to recover from his injuries?

A fat, black bumblebee droned near Stright, but he didn't shoo it away. In fact, he held out his palm, and the bumblebee landed there. Celyn and Eilean gazed at him and then at each other, wondering at the druid's strange powers.

"The hunters are still nearby," Stright said. "They're just watching us."

"Did the bee tell you?" Celyn asked with open curiosity.

"It did, but it's not a bee. It just appears that way to you."

"The hunters won't interfere until we have the tome," Eilean said. "Show us the way."

He folded his arms and frowned. "I don't relish the idea of leading them to another Dryad tree. The Dryads' greatest defense is their secrecy. If the hunters got the notion, they could cut the oak down and destroy her power. It would affect all the other Dryad trees in the region."

"They don't know about the Dryads," Eilean said. "Nor would they believe in them. They will only be looking for the tome."

"After you have it, where will you go?" Stright asked.

"We're leaving the kingdom," Eilean answered simply.

"That's probably for the best. Those hunters are relentless."

Eilean had originally hoped Aisic might join them on their journey to Hautland, and not simply because she'd fancied him. She'd hoped for protection. It amazed her that the Medium had provided someone else to help them make their way through the Bearden Muir. Was Stright supposed to continue with them? Would he if they asked? She didn't want to broach the subject without first discussing it with Celyn.

They left the camp and began walking northwest. They spoke as they moved along, and the druid told them about himself. Stright was a wretched too, although there'd been no abbeys in Moros when he was abandoned, so he'd been handed off from family to family. Occasionally a druid would visit the family he was staying with to request a meal or a place to bed down for the night. They'd intrigued him, both because they traveled so much and so freely and because of their power. At the time, druids were trusted to resolve disputes, and the most powerful and wise among them were chosen by rulers as advisors. He'd heard of the fame of King Aengus's druid and chose to become one himself. And then the mastons came, and suddenly Mordaunt's name was never to be spoken again.

They stopped midday at a little hovel in the swamp, a small dwelling made mostly of sticks and thatch occupied by a hermit that Stright knew. The old man shared his lunch—a watery broth full of mushrooms. It tasted absolutely horrid, but it was food, and she and Celyn accepted their portions gratefully. Stright did most of the talking with the old man and left another blessing on him and his hovel before they left.

They reached another Dryad tree later in the day, and Stright said he would commune with the spirit creature to warn Gwragith Annon they were coming. This time, Eilean waited out of sight with Celyn while Stright spoke with the Dryad. She could sense a prickle of magic from the Medium when it happened and another when the communication was over.

All her life, she had believed that the Medium could only be controlled by those associated with the maston order. But she'd gotten it wrong. Their guide had been kind and pleasant to the hermit as well as the woodsman and his wife. He embodied many of the maston virtues. So it made sense that the Medium favored him. It was a person's acts and intentions that drew the Medium closer.

Stright came to them. "We'll be there tomorrow," he said. "I've never spoken to the mother Dryad before, but she has a great reputation in this region. All spirit creatures hold her in deference. It's no surprise that Mordaunt entrusted her with his things."

"I'm excited to meet her," Eilean said.

"We've been traveling together for a while, and I still don't know your names," Stright said. "Is it important that you keep them secret? I know that true names can bring power. That you even know the mother tree's name is itself a strange thing. Mordaunt must trust you a great deal to have shared that information."

Eilean turned to Celyn, who nodded.

"We were both given names at Tintern Abbey, where we were foundlings," Eilean said. "My name is Eilean. Mordaunt used to call me Eilean Donnán. But he also gave me another name. A new name. Gwenllian."

Stright smiled. "And what's yours?" he asked Celyn.

"Celyn," she answered. "I . . . I don't have a new name yet, but I suppose I'll need one as part of our disguise."

He crossed his arms and then tapped his mouth. "In druid lore, the Holly King and the Oak King battled for dominance and formed a treaty whereby each rules half of the year. That is because the oak is majestic during spring and summer but loses its crown of leaves in the winter, and holly is most vibrant in fall and winter. How about Holly since we are venturing into that season?"

Celyn smiled. "I like it. Gwenllian and Holly."

"And Stright," Eilean said. "That's an interesting name."

"It means *the right path*," he said. "Druids don't get lost. You know, the oak you're looking for is the source of the river that floods the Bearden Muir. That's what gives the tree its name. Gwragith Annon means *Lady of the Fountain*."

I came to this position of trust through diligence, assiduity, and temperance. My predecessor in the Apocrisarius was more inclined to trust than I. This has given me a reputation that is not entirely undeserved, although it is an undeniable truth that in passing judgment, almost every person is influenced not so much by truth as by preference. I'm satisfied that while my conduct may not be totally without reproach, my skills serve the noblest of causes.

—Mícheál Nostradamus of Avinion Abbey

CHAPTER TWENTY-SIX

The Druid Past

The path they followed continued north, winding through the inland valleys thick with trees. Another thunderstorm came before noon, bringing a tempest of rain with bouts of hailstones, from which they sought shelter beneath the canopy of leaves. Eilean gazed through the twisting maze of trees, unable to spot the hunters pursuing them, but she had no doubt that Captain Hoel and his men were out there, following their footsteps like shadows. She could have ended the storm with a word, but she didn't want to drain her energy too soon.

She'd need it to escape the hunters.

"How long have there been druids?" Celyn asked Stright as they hunkered beneath the protective boughs. Rain dripped through the weave of branches, dampening their cloaks, but at least it wasn't too cold.

"How old is the world?" Stright answered with an enigmatic grin.

"I don't know. At the abbey, we were taught that beings from another place created this one. And that two individuals, the First Parents, were given dominion over it. The Garden of Leerings protected them from wickedness. But the man and the woman were disobedient, and the Leerings turned against them, driving them out."

Stright's face quirked with confusion. "Whether that is legend or truth, I cannot say. The history of the druids is passed down from person to person. There is no written record—it must be told and then memorized."

"Will you tell us something of it?" Celyn asked.

He paused for a moment, as if considering her request, then said, "There are connections between the worlds through magical portals. We believe there is a spiritual realm called Mirrowen. It is a nexus between the worlds, full of spirit creatures. When they visit the mortal realm, the weaker spirits' forms change. The moth, if you remember. That was not a moth, but a spirit creature." He reached into his shirt and withdrew his talisman, holding it out for them both to see. "This allows me to see them as they really are. To commune with them, thought to thought." His look became more serious. "Thoughts are powerful things."

"The maston order believes that too," Eilean agreed. "Everything begins with a thought. So the druids originally came from Mirrowen?"

He shook his head. "They came *through* Mirrowen. There were two individuals, a husband and wife, named Isic and Phae. Maybe they are the First Parents you mentioned."

"Aisic?" Celyn asked, looking at Eilean.

"It's a common name, surely," Stright said. "Phae was Dryad-born, and Isic was immortal. They passed through Mirrowen to visit other worlds, but they did not return. Eventually other druids went searching for them. When the searchers found this world, they began to teach the people of our ways. To show that harmony with the world was the right way to live." He spread out his hands. "Men build castles to protect against other men. Would it not be better if men no longer preyed on each other?"

"It would be better," Eilean agreed. "But I'm not sure it is possible."

Stright shrugged. "Men like that captain, the one who hunts us, think of things in terms of boundaries, kingdoms, and laws. In truth, we are but caretakers. This land doesn't *belong* to King Aengus. It belongs to everyone. We are all but stewards, not kings."

"How long have the druids been here?" Celyn asked.

Stright leaned back against the trunk. "We have been here as long as the maston order. Maybe longer."

"Has there always been a conflict between the two groups?" Eilean wondered.

"Not always. This used to be one realm, not fractured as it is now. When the maston order was young, we spoke up in their defense against the tyranny of emperors. Some druids even joined the maston order to learn more about it. When Emperor Incessant III joined the maston order . . . this was several centuries ago . . . he named the Medium as the true source of magic in the world. The Aldermastons of his day became very powerful, and once their power was absolute, they began to persecute others. The druids retreated to Moros and Pry-Ree, where we had started."

Eilean listened with great interest, although she couldn't be sure which parts of the story were true and which were only legend. The Medium neither validated his words nor recoiled from them. She didn't believe that Stright was trying to deceive them, but he had studied and learned the ways of the druids, so naturally he saw the world through their eyes.

"I'm sorry your people have been persecuted," Eilean said, reaching out and gripping his forearm. "There are factions within your order, are there not? The dark druids?"

"Yes. Not all spirit creatures are benevolent. Just as day wars with night, so the druids have a dark side. There is a duality in all things. But the spirits I commune with warn me when dark druids are nigh. It is usually easy to avoid them because they tend to live in caves, in fixed places. The rest of us prefer to roam about and travel. I would love to travel the rest of the world, only I dare not for fear of persecution."

Celyn looked down at her feet, and in that moment Eilean could sense her thoughts. She wanted to invite Stright to come with them to Hautland.

She'd had that same idea earlier, but nothing had come of it. This time, the Medium pulsed inside her, impressing upon her that he *should* join them.

Eilean withdrew her hand from Stright's arm and pulled Celyn closer. Their gazes locked, and Celyn's eyes shone hopefully.

"We are going to Hautland," Eilean said. "There is an Aldermaston there, one who has defied the High Seer of Avinion. He's been excommunicated, but some of the rulers of Hautland have hidden him. The maston order has become corrupt, and the leadership must be changed." She lowered her voice. "You could travel with us."

Stright stared down at the ground and fell silent. "If I did, my life would be in jeopardy."

"Think on it. You would be safer there than you would be here."

"I know little of maston politics," he said. "I will seek permission from the druid council. If they grant it, then I will go."

"How will you ask them?" Celyn asked with curiosity.

"I'll show you," he replied. He held the talisman in his palm and lowered his head. A few moments later, a little thrush came swooping toward them and lighted on one of the branches of the tree. It trilled a pretty song down to them.

Stright looked up at it, smiled, and nodded, and then the bird swooped away.

"I take it that wasn't just a bird," Eilean said.

"No. We spoke by our thoughts, and it will seek out the leader of the druid council to deliver my message. I told him about you and what you've asked me to do."

Eilean squeezed Celyn. She was confident that the Medium would work its will on all of them.

"The rain is finally letting up," Stright said. "Shall we go? There is a hill nearby. We'll be able to see where we're going from the summit. We're almost there."

"One more question," Eilean asked. "How is it that you can summon fire into your hands?"

"I have the fireblood," he answered. "There is a certain tree in Mirrowen that contains a variety of fruit, each of which bestows an ability. One of those fruits is the Gift of Ambition, and ambition and fire are two sides of the same coin. Long ago, the fruit used to be cursed, but it is cursed no longer. The power passes down from parent to child, which is how I inherited it. There are words I must say in my mind to tame and control the flames. They are secret, so I cannot share them. When I saw you summon fire from your hands, I wondered if you had the fireblood as well."

"I don't know who my parents were," Eilean said. "Perhaps one of them was a druid, like you."

***

The hill was harder to climb than Eilean had hoped, but the view from the top was well worth the struggle. From the summit, she could see the lowlands of the Bearden Muir stretching out to the south and, in the distance, Muirwood Abbey and the village. Squinting, Eilean could even see smoke coming from the kitchen flue.

"Shaw," Celyn whispered in wonder, pointing at it. The castle where Mordaunt was held prisoner was so much smaller than the grand abbey.

Stright folded his arms, his mouth twisting into a frown. "They dammed up the river and took over that beautiful valley. They built it up very quickly, and they're not done." He sighed. "I don't know how my people can fight such magic."

Eilean imagined how it must seem to him. The natural land had been indelibly altered so that people could live and thrive there.

"It is still beautiful, only in a different way," she said.

"Begrudgingly, I agree," he said, his frown easing a little. Then he turned around and pointed to the northwest. "That's the town of Bridgestow. You can barely see it, but it's yonder at the edge of the sea. Now follow the valley halfway there." He shifted his finger. "Do you see the crags and peaks?"

"Yes."

"That is Sedgemoor. There used to be a palace down there, but it's rubble now. There are abandoned quarries they dug up for stone."

"What happened?" Celyn asked.

"A king had claimed that part of the land, but he was too near the Dryad tree, and he didn't know it. There is a gorge through those rocks. You can't see it from here, but I've been there before. The mastons carved Leerings at the mouth of the gorge to divert the water. Now they've turned it into a single river that goes around the moors instead of right through them. That is where we're going. The mother tree is in that gorge."

"Will we make it there by nightfall?"

"We will, but the Dryad will not speak to us at night. She will only come out when her power is strongest. At midday."

"Is there another way out of the gorge?" Celyn wondered, her eyes widening in worry. "If there isn't, then Captain Hoel and the others will be waiting for us to come out."

Stright wrinkled his brow. "There's no exit on the other side. The rocks are steep, and we'd need wings. We'll have to pass back the same way and fight our way out."

Eilean felt her stomach tense. She didn't want to fight Captain Hoel, and not because she thought she would lose. She didn't want to hurt him or the other hunters. But she would if they gave her no other choice.

"How far into the gorge is the oak tree?" she asked him.

"It'll be a long walk. And we have the current to contend with as well. We'll have to cross the river multiple times to reach it."

"And no one lives in there?" Eilean prodded.

"Not anymore. Some cattle farmers used to use the land and water, but the mastons drove them off. I haven't been into the gorge since they put the Leerings there." He paused. "There are many of us who think the Leerings have eyes so they can see."

Eilean shook her head. "They're just stone. Unless you touch them, they cannot see you."

"And the mastons would know if we tried hammering the faces off the stone?"

"Yes. And the Leerings themselves probably have built-in defenses." She turned back toward Muirwood, wishing that Mordaunt were with them. He didn't deserve to be imprisoned, not there or in a dungeon. A pang of sadness struck her chest. If there was any way she could help free him, she would.

"We need to think of a plan before we go into the gorge," Celyn said. "Are there any spirit creatures that can help us? We've seen moths and birds and the like. Are there any larger creatures? Like maybe a bear?"

Stright chuckled. "Oh, yes. But I wouldn't *dare* try to summon a Fear Liath."

"What is that?" Eilean asked.

"One of the most powerful and dangerous spirit creatures. Solitary. They don't come out in daylight because it is the only time they are vulnerable to weapons. Their magic can draw a fog about them, which makes them nigh invincible. They're savage. Only the dark druids try to control them, and that doesn't always end well for the druid. They feed on fear. Just seeing the shadow of one can transfix someone with terror."

"It sounds like the monster of the Myniths," Celyn said. "You remember, Eilean?"

"I thought those were tales made up to frighten children," she answered.

"You've heard about them?" Stright asked.

"Yes, in the other abbey we came from," Celyn said. "The Aldermaston said learners and wretcheds should never wander into the mountains or stay out after dark because there was a monster in the mountains. On foggy days, Ardys, the cook, said we should stay inside the abbey grounds because the monster was hunting."

An idea began to form in Eilean's mind. "Captain Hoel and his hunters are from Pry-Ree." She looked toward the gorge and the craggy peaks. "And I know how to summon fog."

An unscrupulous intellect does not pay to antiquity its due reverence. Were it not for the Twelve who inscribed their knowledge of the Medium meticulously on tomes of aurichalcum, their secrets would now be lost to us. We do not blame them for their faults or the weaknesses of their writing. Their words set the stage on which we play our turn today. I do not think they expected the order they founded would become the governing power. They were probably too meek to realize its potential.

—Mícheál Nostradamus of Avinion Abbey

CHAPTER TWENTY-SEVEN

Into the Gorge

A slow drizzle had persisted throughout the afternoon, but it eased as they reached the farthest edge of the Bearden Muir. The sun sank over the rocky crags of the valley gorge. It looked as if some enormous beast with stony scales lay beneath the green turf, a monster so vast it could step on a village and crush it beneath its paw. The water exited the gorge, burbling and lapping against tangled rocks and roots. The water was fresh, and Eilean crouched low to fill her palms and drink from it. The water was warmer than she'd expected and tasted a little of iron.

"I think we should camp just inside the crags," Stright said, arms folded, his damp hood covering part of his face. He turned his neck to look at them. "That way, we can see the hunters when they come."

Celyn looked back the way they'd come, at the maze of trees and marsh grass. "How far off do you reckon they are?"

The druid shook his head. "We've not seen them at all since the wolves attacked us. They've kept their distance on purpose. They want us to claim the tome so they might steal it from us."

Eilean stood up and shook the droplets from her hands. "I think your counsel is good. We should make camp a little ways past the entrance and watch for them. We'll build no fire tonight. In the morning, we'll seek the Dryad tree."

Celyn pursed her lips. "I hope your idea works."

Eilean nodded. "So do I. Let's go in."

The waters were full of rocks and stones that had broken off from the upper part of the gorge and tumbled into the stream. Some of them were knee height or even higher. They followed a gravelly path on one side of the stream, until the way bent sharply and they were forced to cross the stream to the other side.

Eilean felt the magic of a Leering up ahead—the first she'd sensed since leaving Muirwood.

"Look," Stright said, pointing.

The boulder sat in the middle of the stream, as tall as the druid himself. It seemed to have tumbled down from the heights like all the other rocks, but the lower half had been eroded because of the steady rise and fall of the stream. The face of a bearded man had been chiseled into the stone.

"It looks like Aldermaston Gilifil," Celyn said as they approached it warily.

She was right. It *did* resemble him. And seeing it there put a pang of unease in Eilean's chest, as if the Aldermaston himself were glowering at them. The eyes were glowing faintly, revealing that its magic was active.

"It's an abomination," Stright said with disgust. "To use rocks to contain magic."

"Is it any more of an abomination than using a talisman?" Eilean asked him. "Magic comes in many forms." She moved closer, wanting to touch the Leering and discern the nature of its magic. Her hand lifted slightly.

"Eilean, don't," Celyn warned.

She stopped herself, her fingers just shy of the rough stone. She could feel the power trickling from it.

"It's here to help divert the water from the Bearden Muir," she announced confidently, close enough to discern that much.

"Is that all it does?" Celyn asked.

"I can't tell without touching it. But if I do, I think someone from the abbey would be able to sense me. Let's go farther upstream since there's no longer any path ahead."

The three of them plunged into the river, feeling the cold at their legs. The gorge rose dramatically, and soon the jagged cliffs were blocking in on each side. After they went in, the stream turned again, and they lost sight of the Leering behind them.

"How about that little ledge of rock?" Stright said, pointing. "I think all three of us could fit on it." The chasm was getting darker by the moment, and the fading sun brought a chill to the air.

"I agree," Eilean said.

The three of them scrambled up onto a smaller boulder and used it to reach the outcropping. There was still moss and turf on top of it, so it wasn't uncomfortable, and there was room for all three of them to stretch out.

"I will summon a spirit to watch over us," Stright said, sitting cross-legged on the moss. He bowed his head, and Eilean felt the warmth of the Medium course through her as he made his silent petition. She could *feel* it—not the words but the intention. He had protective feelings toward her and Celyn. Especially Celyn. Eilean was surprised at the insight, but she kept it to herself.

Stright's brow furrowed. "I cannot hear them." He looked up at the sky, which was a deep violet now. "Nor do I sense any spirits in the area."

Eilean nodded. "I wonder if the Leering is keeping them out of the gorge."

"It could be that, or something else might be keeping them out," the druid said. "I don't sense any danger, though."

"We'll have to take turns keeping watch," Celyn said. "Hopefully the wolves don't come back."

"We're high enough that they won't," Stright said in a reassuring tone. "But I agree. Let's split the watch. I don't want the hunters getting past us."

"I'll take first watch," Eilean offered. She trusted that the Medium would warn her if they came too near. There were words of power she could use to help in the vigil, but she didn't want to drain her strength, knowing she'd need to be at her fullest if the ruse didn't work and they had to fight their way out of the gorge.

"What is your plan for tomorrow?" Stright asked.

"After we've found the Dryad tree, I'll summon the fog to hide our movements. Then the two of you will wait out of sight while I commune with the Dryad and get the tome."

"She'll talk to you," he said with a nod. "She has to because you know her true name."

"As we leave the gorge in the thick of the fog, I will create an illusion to make it seem like I'm the Fear Liath. If they shoot with their arrows, I know a shield spell that will block them. I can also create a feeling of gloom and terror. The only problem is that using so much power will weaken me. If it goes on for too long, I'll pass out. That's why I need your help in case that happens."

Celyn took Eilean's hand and squeezed it firmly. "We won't let it happen. I promise."

They opened the pack and withdrew some food to share. During the day, they'd found more berries as well as some tubers Stright had dug up from the swamp. They ate quietly as darkness settled over them.

Eilean faced the way they'd come and could see, even in the darkness, the stream as it flowed to the mouth of the gorge. Her eyes had adjusted to the dark, and even though the hunters could walk very quietly, she felt confident that she'd be able to spy them coming.

Stright touched her knee and whispered, "Wake me when the moon reaches directly overhead. I'll take the next watch."

"Very well," she answered.

"And I'll go last," Celyn offered.

The two of them hunkered down, covering themselves in their cloaks. Celyn used the pack as a pillow, her back to them, and Stright lay facing her.

Again, Eilean sensed his devotion to Celyn, his appreciation for their growing friendship. He was looking forward to traveling with them, but she also sensed his fear of being captured. It was strange how the Medium worked inside her. The little flashes of insight and emotion were small, but she'd grown to recognize them for what they were. To *trust* them.

Eventually her two companions fell asleep, and she was left alone to watch the stream. Determined to stay awake and vigilant, she kept her mind focused by reciting some of the sayings Mordaunt had taught her. It made her think of him, and how he would have enjoyed being outside, free of his prison. Her heart ached for him.

If the Aldermaston spoke truly, then Mordaunt would be taken to Avinion to languish in a cell. Even though chains could not hold him—for he knew the words of power that could unlock things—if there was a Leering to bind him, he would not be able to escape as long as that stone stood.

And stones could last for a very long time.

***

A gentle hand shook her shoulder. Eilean awoke, blinking, hearing the lapping of the stream. She'd awakened Stright as directed, but it was Stright who had wakened her, not Celyn. The change in hue in the sky showed her it was nearly morning.

She gave him an inquisitive look but dared not speak.

"All is well," Stright said. "There was no sign of the hunters. None at all. And Celyn was resting so peacefully, I didn't wish to wake her. I didn't mind taking a double turn." He gave her a slightly chagrined look.

Eilean sat up and then shook Celyn awake next.

Her friend yawned and stretched. "Is it my . . . ? No, it's almost dawn." She looked at Stright. "You should have woken me."

"I'm sorry," he said, but that was all.

They ate the last of the bread they'd gotten from the cottage. Thankfully, Bridgestow was about a day's journey away, and they could replenish their supplies with the coins hidden with the tome. She also had confidence in Stright's ability to forage.

After eating the sparse meal, they climbed down the rock. Eilean's dress and shoes were still damp. Their clothes were also in need of a good scrubbing, but it was not the time to attend to such things. As the sun brightened the sky, it revealed the stone faces of the gorge on either side, revealing hidden colors. It was a beautiful place. A hallowed place.

They walked farther up the stream, knowing they were still some distance from the Dryad tree. Her leg muscles ached from the constant days of walking, but she felt strong and determined that no aches or soreness would undermine her journey. Another large boulder had crashed midstream ahead, and they circled around it, for it was larger than a cottage. Trees grew inside the chasm, on sandbars thick with grass. A mother skunk and her growing kits wandered the opposite bank, but they were no threat and kept trundling through the brush across from them.

The chasm seemed to close in on them overhead as they went deeper into the gorge, although the stream conversely widened. Trees were everywhere on the edges, thick and untamed, as were gorse bushes and wildflowers. The air smelled clean and crisp.

At last, they reached the end of the gorge. The rocks led upward as if part of a man-built stairway, and water continued to cascade down the smoothed faces. A towering oak tree, absolutely enormous, crested the top of those rocks, its massive roots wrapped around the edges. Some of the leaves had already shed, but there were clearly clumps of mistletoe hanging from the branches.

Eilean turned and looked back downstream. There was still no sign of the hunters. But Stright was likely correct. The hunters' best chance to intercept them was to wait for Eilean and her friends to come out. There was no other way out of the gorge.

"It's nearly midday," Eilean said, excitement and nervousness bubbling within her. "Why don't you two wait there, in the scrub." She pointed to the place she meant. "I'll commune with the tree. After I have the tome, I'll summon the fog to help us escape. Wait for me."

Celyn smiled and nodded, and Stright led her into a patch of scrub so dense they both disappeared from sight. Eilean, alone, began to climb up the wet steps to the Dryad tree.

The water soaked her, but she was warm enough it didn't matter. They could change after this was done. She had to be careful lest she lose her footing, but she clambered up the steps and approached the roots and majestic boughs. As she looked to the edge of the gorge, she caught sight of a series of caves. And she felt another Leering.

Curious, she started toward it, but she immediately felt a throb of warning from the Medium. She should not go there.

Eilean hesitated, wondering why the mastons had put another Leering deeper into the gorge. What was its purpose? But that feeling of curiosity was met by another small warning.

She obeyed it.

As she approached the base of the tree, she knelt on the turf. On the far side, water burbled from the oak tree as if the tree itself were a fountain of water, which made perfect sense given the translation of the name. She clasped her hands and tried to push away her doubts and fears.

I would speak with you, she thought. *I was sent here to meet you.*

The rushing sound of the water seemed to grow louder as she waited patiently. She listened to the sound, felt its mesmerizing power. Weariness made her head droop a little more, but she did not press the Dryad with her thoughts. She would wait until the mother tree was ready to speak with her.

You came not alone.

The thought whispered in her mind, although it was not hers.

I have two companions with me. A druid named Stright, who is faithful to your ways, and a cherished companion named Celyn. I came at the behest of someone who told me about you.

Silence was her answer. She waited, feeling a growing ache in her knees, but she endured it. Hands clasped, she opened herself to the Medium's power, willing to do what she had been asked to do.

You came not alone.

Eilean felt uncomfortable. *Was I supposed to leave them behind? They cannot see us from where they wait.*

A light breeze came and rustled the branches. She felt a few dry leaves come fluttering down on her head.

Your companions are already captured, child. They were waiting for you here. They watch you even now. You came not alone.

A sick feeling wrenched inside Eilean's stomach as she realized what the Dryad had been trying to tell her.

The hunters were already there.

Captain Hoel was watching her, waiting to see where Mordaunt had hidden his tome.

The maxim that every first-year learner is taught is "All destiny begins with a thought." That is the acorn that transforms into a mighty oak. But thought, without plan, without action, yields nothing. I teach my hunters to think like their prey. To understand them in wit and substance and to imagine what they would do and then act ahead of that knowledge. It is my maxim that if you keep thinking about what you want to do or what you hope will happen, you don't do it and it won't happen.

—Mícheál Nostradamus of Avinion Abbey

CHAPTER TWENTY-EIGHT

The Medium's Roar

How had Hoel known she'd be there? In a flash of insight from the Dryad, she understood that Captain Hoel and his hunters had been ahead of them, not behind. Disappointment clubbed her in the stomach, and worry began to twist her insides. This was the trap. She had led them to the hiding place of Mordaunt's tome.

She began to tremble with the fear of capture, of failure, and of *death*. The Medium had guided her to this point. Would she fail already?

In her mind, she imagined Mordaunt looking at her angrily. *You knew it wouldn't be easy. You must prevail! Only* pethets *quit. I Gifted you with diligence. Use it!*

Eilean rose from her kneeling position, her knees aching from the time she'd spent there. Although she was tempted to glance behind her to see if she could glimpse the hunters, she denied the urge, not wanting them to know they'd been discovered. If they'd already captured Celyn and Stright, then she was her friends' only hope of rescue. Were there five or six hunters in all? She didn't know, but Cimber had been wounded. Had he gone back to the abbey, or was he part of the group still?

Summon the fog.

The whisper of thought came from the Medium.

She unclenched her fists and uttered the words of power in an undertone. *"Vey-ed min ha-ay-retz."*

The words danced on her tongue, and she felt the magic first as a prickle and then as a surge. The initial gust made her dizzy, but she centered herself. There was another word of power, *apokaluptis,* which could unveil a disguise. She considered using it now, to see if it would reveal the hunters, but its purpose was to lift illusions if someone's true form had been rendered invisible or distorted by magic. If Captain Hoel's concealment were not illusion, then the word wouldn't work, and she'd be drained further.

Tendrils of mist began to swell from the water cascading from the roots of the oak tree. Her words had invoked them. She stood there waiting as the fog rose, kissing her skin.

She had the impression that Captain Hoel was concealed by the other Leering, the one she'd been warned not to approach.

"Can we talk, Captain?" she said, projecting her voice toward the intersection of the gorge.

She waited, not certain if he would respond. The mist continued to swell around her, sheathing the oak and the rocks in the fleece. A shadow emerged from the crevice, holding a long bow with an arrow nocked but not drawn back. She recognized the curl of the cape, the leather armor, and the bracers covering the muscles on his forearms. His hood was down, his expression unreadable. He stopped atop a small boulder, looking down at her.

"I warned you, Eilean. You didn't listen."

He looked so powerful, so confident and determined, that her hope began to wilt. Yes, she could unleash a blizzard of invisible blades at him. But the thought of cutting him down with magic was abhorrent. And her friends might be executed immediately if she tried.

"I am following the Medium's will," she said as firmly as her quavering voice permitted.

"I know it seems that way to you," he said.

"How did you get ahead of us?" Eilean asked. She started to walk toward him, to leave the tree behind her.

"I've been to this gorge before," he answered, gazing up at the steep cliffs. "I learned about it from druids we've captured and questioned."

There was something off in his answer. He wasn't telling her the full truth.

"Then why did you follow us?"

She felt the power of the Leering radiating from behind him. As she came closer, she felt fear chill her bones. It was a protective Leering. One that prevented passage. Was there another way out of the gorge after all? A cave, perhaps?

"Where is the tome, Eilean? I know Mordaunt hid it here."

"I'm not giving it to you," she said. "I've been entrusted with it."

He sighed and tilted his head. "You cannot leave this place without my permission, Eilean. The Leering you passed, the one with the Aldermaston's face carved in it, did you notice it?"

"Yes."

"It will prevent you from leaving. This is your prison, just as Mordaunt is bound in his castle." He hopped off the small boulder and came closer to her. "Be reasonable. If you cooperate, there may still be a chance to resolve this peacefully. The High Seer wants that tome. It belongs to the maston order."

"It belongs to the maston who wrote it," Eilean said.

"I'm doing my *duty*," he said firmly. "And I'm not leaving this place without that tome."

The mist swirled around him now, but they were close enough to see each other clearly. When she glanced back, however, only the shadow of the tree could be seen through the thick, swirling air.

"The Aldermaston cannot use the Medium," Eilean said. "He's powerless. His pride has blocked it. Please, Captain. Release my friends."

His brows quirked with disbelief at her words, but he didn't acknowledge her claim about the Aldermaston. "I won't do that," he said simply. "I'm sending Celyn and the druid to Avinion. You're the one whose knowledge I seek. I'm a patient man. You will find my will quite immovable."

What he said was true. She could sense his implacable thoughts.

But again the question nagged at her. "How did you know we were coming here?"

She saw a flicker of his thoughts as the truth rushed through his mind. And then the Medium confirmed what she'd seen.

Her eyes widened. "You saw a vision of it," she whispered. "You have the Gift of Seering."

Anger flashed in his eyes, his mouth turned down in a stark frown. He had kept this secret for a long time. Indeed, he hadn't told *anyone*. How must that have affected him in his life? He served the Apocrisarius, which served the High Seer. And he could see the future, but the High Seer could not.

"I do," he confirmed, his voice throbbing. "It is a curse more than a gift."

"I imagine it would feel that way," she said.

"Did Mordaunt tell you?"

Eilean shook her head. "The Medium did. Come with us, Captain. Help us."

He snorted. "You mistake me in every way, Eilean. I once thought you'd be a hunter, because of a vision I saw. But I was wrong. What I've seen in your future, I wouldn't wish on anyone. But I saw you with the tome. I know you got it from this place. Show me where it is. *Now.*"

Deliver us from this man, she thought to the Medium.

In response to her thought, she received a distinct answer, the thought a whisper in her mind: *Release the Leering at the cave. Be not afraid.*

She obeyed. With a thought, she released the Leering, just as she had snuffed out the ones at the border of the abbey.

The instant the power guttered out, an overpowering rush of fear came from the cave beyond. It bound her bones in place, made her mouth drop, and then a roar split the air. This was no elk bugling in the night, but a terrifying roar that made her feel every bit of her helplessness and vulnerability.

"What have you—!" Captain Hoel barked, whirling around, drawing the arrow feathers back to his ear.

A thick, hulking shadow emerged into the mist, crunching on the gravel and snuffling with a bearlike snout.

Hoel loosed the arrow and drew another one so fast his arms were a blur. The arrows thumped into the shadow before clattering noisily onto the rocks.

Another ear-splitting roar came, and Eilean sank to her knees in terror.

Hoel shot the great beast again, getting the same result, and then tossed down his bow as the creature charged him.

"It's loose!" he shouted at the top of his lungs. "Get out of here!"

The Fear Liath was a thing of nightmares, all bristly gray fur, massive paws ending in dagger-long claws. It was three times the size of Captain Hoel, yet it moved with surprising speed. Its paw swiped at him, but he dodged the blow and drew twin gladiuses in his hands. One strike, then another, proved those blades couldn't pierce the hide. The monster barked in his face, fangs slavering, and Eilean could do nothing but stare in shock and horror at what she'd unleashed.

Hoel was knocked over by the next rush, and she saw those horrible claws rake down his body. A cry of pain escaped him, but he didn't draw back. He stabbed at it again and again, then groaned as his bones began to crack under its awful weight. The beast bit into his body, and Eilean squeezed her eyes shut, unable to watch, unable to comprehend what the Medium had asked her to do.

She cowered, trembling with fright, listening to Hoel choking in pain. She heard whistles from the mist. Then the sound of an arrow launching.

"Back, you demon!" cried Twynho.

Eilean's head popped up, and she turned and saw the hunter rushing forward, a look of desperation on his face. He shot at the Fear Liath again with his bow, but the arrow bounced harmlessly off his hide.

"Captain!" Twynho shouted as he beat at the monster with a bow.

"Go!" Hoel groaned in agony.

Twynho's eyes blazed with fury and fear. He threw his bow and reached for his gladius, but no sooner had he done so than the Fear Liath lifted and attacked him next. Eilean watched as the hunter dodged the charge, vaulting over the monster to get away. But the creature turned and swiped with its jagged claws, catching Twynho across the middle and shearing through his leather armor.

Twynho went down instantly, dazed, twitching and convulsing in pain. His eyes were wide with shock and incomprehension.

The Fear Liath turned to Eilean.

"Ghe . . . bool," she stammered. But in her fear, she'd said it wrong. She felt the fetid breath snort against her face. *"Gheb-ool."*

The Medium encased her in a shell of power. The Fear Liath snuffled against it, a deep growl in its throat. Then it lifted onto its haunches and let out another bellowing roar and loped into the mist toward the tree and the waterfall.

Anguish and fear roiled inside her. Twynho lay motionless. She released the word of power, feeling her energy sapping fast, and went to Twynho. He stared vacantly, his chest neither rising nor falling. She touched his throat, trying to feel for the throb of his heartbeat, but it had stilled.

"Oh no," she groaned in sadness.

She went to Captain Hoel next, found him quivering in pain, gasping. He had blood on his lips, staining his short beard.

"Can't . . . breathe . . ." he gasped. He looked at her in panic, his eyes wide, his whole body racked in agony.

She put her hand on his chest, lightly, and uttered another word of power. *"Anthisstemi,"* she whispered. It was a word of power for reviving strength. It would not heal his wounds, but it would grant him vigor. Maybe that wasn't a mercy.

A cry of fear sounded from farther away. She gazed down at Captain Hoel, her eyes wet with tears. "I'm sorry," she said. "I didn't know it was there."

He looked at her with feverish intensity. She could only imagine the agony he was in.

"Can't . . . kill . . . it . . ." he gasped. "Hide."

She understood his thought. The beast was trapped in the gorge as surely as she was, though it could now roam at its pleasure.

"Captain, I wish . . ." Words failed her. He'd never treated her like a wretched, like someone not worth saving. She didn't want him to die, but unless his wounds were tended to, he would.

"I'm sorry," she said again, brushing a kiss against his forehead. Then she hurried to the oak tree and knelt before it.

Please, can you heal them, Gwragith Annon? I didn't mean for that monster to come. If there is anything you can do to heal their injuries, I would be grateful.

A soothing power settled over her shoulders. *I cannot raise the dead. But the injured can be healed. If you command me to see to them, I will do so. But know this. If you heal the captain, he will hunt you.*

Eilean felt the tears rolling down her cheeks. What did the Medium want her to do? She felt no assurance either way, as if the choice, in the end, were up to her.

Heal him, please, she begged.

So be it. Your fate is entwined with his. Take the tome. It is hidden beneath that stone.

In her mind, she saw an image of a stone close to the tree.

Get the tome before your friends perish. Do not look at me.

Eilean hurried into the mist, away from the bodies of the two hunters. She heard shouts still, and another cry of anguish. It terrified her to think Celyn and Stright might be in harm's way. The boulder was flat but rounded on one side, stacked atop another one. Eilean fell to her knees and began to push it. It was heavy. Too heavy.

"Kozkah," she said, invoking another word of power. She felt strength surge into her arms, and she shoved the boulder aside, but another wave of dizziness struck her as soon as it moved. Planting her palm on the stone to support herself, she looked down at what had been revealed—a stone box. She opened it and found a shoulder pack containing a bulging bundle. There was also a scabbard with a raven symbol on it that sheathed a glimmering sword.

From the corner of her eye, she spied a woman in a dress walking toward Captain Hoel's body. She had the feverish urge to look at the woman, for the glimpse she'd seen had astonished her, but she turned her head, deliberately staring into the hole. She picked up the sword in its scabbard and then hoisted the heavy pack.

Her strength was fading rapidly. Spots of black began to form in the corners of her vision. She'd used too many words of power too quickly. Dizziness washed over her, blinding her a moment.

But the feeling faded a little as she stared into the box. The sword and pack had rested on a folded set of gray robes, the kind greyfriars wore, not the same pale shade of the Aldermastons'. Greyfriars were mastons who traveled the world and proved the power of the Medium to unbelievers. They were not bound to abbeys but were known for their education, zeal, and courage. She'd seen the habit before when one of them had come to sojourn at Tintern Abbey when she was a child.

Mordaunt had traveled as a greyfriar? She felt a compulsion to take the robes. Carefully, she opened the pack and saw the golden tome concealed within it, along with pouches. Upon quick inspection, she could tell they contained coins. Many coins. The pack contained other items as well, but she didn't have time to investigate.

She stood, slung the pack over her shoulder, and then wrapped the gray robes around the sword and tucked it beneath her arm. Her energy was nearly gone.

"Eilean! Eilean!" It was Celyn, crying her name.

Eilean turned back to the tree, but her eyes wandered, and she saw the Dryad kneeling over Hoel's body. The Dryad pressed what looked like a clump of moss to the man's wounds. Hoel trembled still, but the soothing magic was helping him.

Then the Dryad turned, and their eyes met. She blinked, and suddenly Eilean was falling.

Why are some born wretcheds and others wellborn? Why do some possess many Gifts of the Medium and others not a single one? Strength in the Medium, we've learned, comes from lineage. One generation of mastons lends power to the next. But sometimes those one would least expect are born with great Gifts. There is a wretched, I've been told, at the new Muirwood Abbey, who is remarkably strong with the Medium. There is no accounting for it unless her parentage be the unknown cause. Often have I wondered with much curiosity as to the circumstances of our coming into this world and what will follow our departure.

—Mícheál Nostradamus of Avinion Abbey

CHAPTER TWENTY-NINE

The Road to Bridgestow

A tingling feeling started at Eilean's shoulders, at the base of her neck, and slowly spread down her arms and legs. The oblivion began to ebb, and her eyelids fluttered. She found herself lying on a blanket with both Celyn and Stright kneeling over her. The druid held out his palm, and Eilean wondered if she was supposed to take his hand, but a butterfly lighted on his skin instead.

She heard his thought, a whispered thank-you, and then the butterfly fluttered away again.

Celyn's expression was hopeful. "I think it worked."

"What worked?" Eilean asked. She sat up, tired but not exhausted. A quick look around revealed they were in a grove of trees, far from the gorge. Far from the Fear Liath. Her brow furrowed. "Where are we?"

"Near Bridgestow," Stright answered.

Eilean saw an oak tree in the grove. This one was smaller than the great one in the gorge, but it had mistletoe growing in its branches.

A moment of terror struck her, but then she saw the pack she'd taken from the box as well as the folded gray habit. She reached out and touched the pack, feeling the firm edges of the tome inside.

"It's there," Celyn assured her, touching Eilean's arm. "When we found you by the Dryad tree, you had it with you."

"How did we get here?" Eilean asked in confusion. "How did we get out of the gorge?"

"The Dryad brought us here. Their trees are interconnected, and they can be used as portals. I never knew that before. When we found you, you were unconscious but uninjured."

Celyn smiled in relief. "I was so worried about you. When you said you could conjure a Fear Liath, I didn't expect it to be so terrifying."

"But then we saw the bodies and knew it was real," Stright added. "How did you summon it?"

Eilean squinted. "It was already there, trapped in a cave by a Leering. I removed the barrier, and it attacked the hunters." Her voice choked off. She hugged herself, feeling awful at the destruction she'd unleashed.

She remembered seeing Captain Hoel broken and trembling, but her mind became fuzzy after that. She couldn't remember what had happened next.

"Were the hunters there when you found me?"

"One was dead, and the Dryad healed the other," Stright said. "She kept him asleep until we left. But she took some of our memories in exchange for helping us escape. No Dryad wants her true name to be known, for it gives others power over her. She offered to help us escape through the portal, but in exchange, she took our memories of her name."

Eilean looked at Celyn.

"I don't remember it now," said her friend. "I've tried and tried, but I can't remember her name. Or even what she looked like."

"The boon she granted us far outweighed the cost," Stright said. "We left no trail to follow. The hunters will have no way of knowing where we went."

Eilean remembered the insight she'd had in the gorge. Captain Hoel had the Gift of Seering. He would be able to use it to find them. Should she keep that knowledge to herself? The memory of him lying outside that cave, broken and mortally wounded—because of *her*—made her insides shrink. She drew a deep breath, then another, and said, "If we go to Bridgestow, we could get passage to Hautland. When I found Mordaunt's tome, I also found this." She reached for the gray fabric.

"I noticed that earlier. It's the robe of a greyfriar," Celyn said. "So Mordaunt used to be part of that order?"

"It seems so," Eilean said. She turned to Stright. "If you wore it, then no one would suspect you of being a druid."

"That's if I could convincingly pass myself off as a greyfriar," Stright said with unease. "I know nothing about them."

"When people see the color of the tunic, they won't question it. Why don't you go buy passage on a boat? That is, if you are still willing to come with us—and if your druid council allows it. You'd have to wash the woad from your face and neck."

Celyn looked at Stright with pleading eyes.

His cheeks flushed a little, and he nodded.

Eilean handed him the tunic and then opened the pack and withdrew one of the pouches of coins. She undid the drawstring and poured some of the contents into her hand.

"There are different kinds," Celyn said, staring at them on Eilean's palm.

"I'll go put this on," Stright said, standing up and taking the bundle into the trees for privacy.

"Mordaunt said we could use what we needed," Eilean said, examining the different coins.

"I think you need a new dress, then," Celyn offered.

"Why not both of us?" Eilean asked.

Celyn shook her head. "You've learned so much from him. You don't sound like a Pry-rian girl anymore. You could pass yourself off as a lady. I couldn't. Even if I wanted to. I'll be your servant. People will wonder why we are traveling together, and this makes sense. You can say we're going to Hautland on pilgrimage, and you brought a greyfriar you trust to escort us both. You just need to look like a lady by the time we reach Bridgestow. *Lady* Gwenllian."

Eilean hadn't thought of that. She'd just assumed she could disguise them with magic as needed.

She took several coins from the pile and handed them to Celyn, tucking the rest back into the pouch. "If I go along with your idea, I'm not about to forget that I'm only a wretched, no more important than you. You're my best friend."

"And I always will be," Celyn said. She took the coins. "The Medium wants us to go. I've felt that for a while now, and it feels *good* to be acting on it. I'll go to Bridgestow with Stright. He'll get passage on a ship, and I'll buy you a dress. We'll go where the Medium wants us to."

"Hautland," Eilean agreed. "To find Aldermaston Utheros. We're meant to bring him the tome."

Celyn grinned and nodded. They rose and cushed each other. When Stright returned, he was wearing the gray habit and looked the part. He'd also scrubbed his skin enough that the woad had faded. The hood helped conceal the remaining stain.

"I'm wearing my other robes beneath it," he said, lifting the hem. "He's a bigger man than I am."

"You'll do fine," Celyn said. "But tuck the talisman away. I'm coming with you."

"Oh, that's right," Stright said. He slid it beneath the tunic so that it wasn't visible, then patted it over his clothes. The slight smile on his face suggested he was pleased to have company on the outing, and especially pleased to have her company. "Bridgestow isn't far. We'll be back before dark."

"Be careful," Eilean said.

Celyn gave her another hug, and then she and Stright wandered off together. Eilean pressed her palms together and watched until they were gone. It was amazing how much energy she had. In the past, using the Medium had left her feeling so weak. But the druid's magic had revived her. She sat down on the blanket and pulled out the tome. After unwrapping the linen, she gazed in wonder at the pure aurichalcum pages, bound together by three rings of the same material. The metal glimmered in the sunlight as she opened the tome, eager to begin reading it.

The symbols engraved on it were illegible to her.

She recognized none of the letters. What language had Mordaunt written it in? Gently flipping the metal pages, she studied one after another. It was the same scrawl, the same handwriting, page after page, sheet after sheet. But none of it made sense. Mordaunt had taught her everything she needed—except how to read it.

Disappointment flickered inside her. She pursed her lips when she came to the end of the written pages. It was only half-full. The rest of the tome, bound by three rings, was empty. Searching the pack, she found his scriving tools in a small wooden box. After examining them, she closed the box and returned it to its spot. She lifted the bag close and smelled it, but it smelled of nothing other than stone. How long had it been hiding in the dark?

Then she remembered the sword and scabbard. She saw the pommel sticking out from beneath her blanket and pulled aside the fabric. The scabbard's raven symbol seemed to jump out to her. She remembered Mordaunt teaching her that the raven was a symbol of wisdom—the Gift of Foresight. Closing her hand around the leather grip, she gently tugged on it. The blade slid free of the scabbard, and a flash of light struck her eyes, making her squint. The metal of the blade was rippled with a central groove in the middle. She felt power tingling in her arm as she continued to slide it out. The blade was magical. She pushed it back in, concentrating, and realized she felt the power of the Medium through the scabbard too.

Eilean gazed at the sword and couldn't help but think Captain Hoel would have been a better person to wield it than she.

Memories came unbidden. He had always sought her out. Had even confided things in her. He had warned her.

I've held my tongue long enough. When you start walking on a road, be certain you know where the path leads. The road you are on leads to your destruction.

Eilean swallowed as her stomach wriggled in fear. He thought her an apostate, a heretic, but she was only following the Medium's will. It was the maston order that had become corrupted. But the fruit's skin hid the disease within, and Hoel couldn't see the truth.

Eilean's eyes had been opened.

She knew that he would continue to hunt her. He would take his men, whoever had survived, and search the ends of the earth for her. She had no doubt that someday their paths would cross again. In her mind, she could see the firmness of his mouth and the look of determination in his eyes. He was relentless. He would always be so.

He took his duties solemnly, and she knew he would resent her for what she'd done. She only hoped that she could finish her task before he found her. That she could deliver the tome to Utheros and hopefully learn more about the Medium's will from him, a righteous Aldermaston.

With that thought, her mind retreated further, to Aldermaston Gilifil. He too would be angry at her. He too would want revenge. She remembered the girl she had been back at Tintern Abbey—the young woman who'd pined after Aisic and worked in the kitchen, hoping to someday be a lady's maid and learn more about the world.

The Medium truly did bring someone's thoughts and desires to life. She would never have guessed it would have brought her so far. Nor could she guess what it might bring into her life in the future.

Eilean lowered her head, clasping her hands together on her lap. She closed her eyes.

What do you want me to do? she thought. *I am ready.*

CHAPTER THIRTY

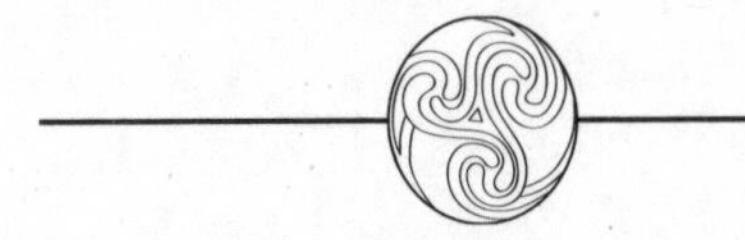

Epilogue

The bridges of Avinion Abbey were famous. Each was constructed with a series of pointed arches interspersed with square defensive towers that rose to steepled roofs. Archers and crossbowmen stood guard at all times, night and day. The bridge leading to the city proper, where the abbey crested a hill, sat astride a massive river that terminated at a narrow but very long waterfall. Broken trees that had floated downriver had become trapped at different spots on the edge of the falls. The trunks were heavy enough to be trapped and the water not strong enough to force them over.

Mícheál Nostradamus gazed out the window of his picturesque room at the bridge and the falls, imagining the effort it would take to dislodge those dead trees cluttering the splendor of the falls. Because they were made of wood and not stone, no Leerings could be carved to do the work. It was a pity having such detritus in the river, truly, but it gave Avinion some of its charm. Visitors from all over the world enjoyed strolling the sculpted paths at the river's edge and enjoyed the view of the falls. During the Whitsun festival, the bridge itself was the scene of jubilant celebration as everyone, regardless of their rank and order, would dance together. There was even a little song his native Dahomeyjans liked to sing about those dances. *On the bridge of Avinion, they are dancing, they are dancing . . .*

Mícheál stroked the tuft of beard on his chin. His ruffled collar was bothering him, but he endured the discomfort because of the formality of dress that had, unfortunately, besotted the kingdom.

A knock sounded on the door, and he stepped away from the window and its glorious view, and approached his desk where an obscene amount of correspondence lay unread.

"Enter," he said gruffly. His time was important to him, and he scheduled his day down to the smallest measures. Interruptions were few. He preferred it that way.

The door opened, and Captain Hoel Evnissyen entered. His arrival was an utter astonishment.

"I received no word of your coming, Captain," Mícheál said. "What is the meaning of this?"

Captain Hoel was a stalwart man, as clever as they came, and expert in all forms of weaponry, diplomacy, and interrogation. What was he doing hundreds of leagues away from his assignment in the kingdom of Moros?

"My lord," the captain said, bowing stiffly. "I thought it more prudent to bring these tidings in person."

"Clearly so, clearly so, but I'm astonished, Captain. I don't like surprises, but if you have the tome, then all is forgiven."

He saw the flint in Hoel's gray eyes. The subtle betrayal of anger. As trained as he was, he was not perfect in controlling his emotions. Mícheál saw it and knew the news without being told.

"The tome has been found, but you lost it."

Mícheál's ability to discern news had given rise to the rumor that he was a harbinger, one who had the Gift of Seering. He encouraged the rumors, though he'd told the High Seer they were fruitless. No, his Gift was discernment. And it was a powerful one.

"I am sorry, my lord. It was within my grasp."

"You failed, Captain. I'm disappointed in you. I assured the High Seer that you were our best. Our very best. We trusted you in this mission."

Mícheál watched as his words sank deep. The best way to motivate an ambitious person was to torment them with a lack of approval. To treat their highest accomplishments as trivial and their smallest lapses as catastrophes. Men and women of ambition gave their best efforts when praise was sparing.

"I am sorry, my lord. I *have* failed you."

Good, Mícheál thought, *he isn't making excuses.* That was the first reaction of most. If the captain had made excuses, they would have been hacked into splinters, like so much dead wood. This man, for all his failures, knew the rules, and he awaited permission to speak.

Still, the taste of bile in Mícheál's mouth was bitter. They'd come so close to retrieving a sacred tome of one of the Twelve.

Mícheál turned back to the window so that Hoel could not even attempt to read his expressions. He clasped his hands behind his back and rocked slightly on his heels.

"Did Mordaunt escape?"

"No."

"So the Leering still binds him?"

"Yes. He cannot leave the castle. The threat of moving him here was the impetus we needed to get him to reveal the location of the tome."

"I told you it would be," Mícheál replied with satisfaction. "But if he did not escape and you lost the tome, then that means the little waif outsmarted you?" He turned his neck just a little, enjoying watching Hoel squirm.

"Yes," Hoel said, his voice hoarse.

Mícheál sniffed. "Tell me what happened. Maybe I can find a way to remedy the situation. I'm surprised, Captain. One would think that a trained Apocrisarius could handle a lowly wretched."

No flaring nostrils. No clenched fists. Hoel had prepared well for this visit. Some men would already be on their knees, begging for forgiveness, spluttering nonsense. Not Hoel. He was too disciplined even in failure.

"She fled Muirwood with her friend, the kitchen girl I told you about in my report."

"Yes. The one who was raised from the dead."

"They stayed in a hut their first night. A woodsman and his wife took them in. A druid visited them."

Mícheál scowled. "Surely you can handle one of those," he said. Even saying the word "druid" was distasteful to him.

"He wasn't a threat. He joined them in their journey. We followed, at a distance, and intervened when a pack of wolves controlled by the Myriad Ones attacked them. The druid can make fire come from his hands."

"An abomination," Mícheál spat. "Tell me you hung him from the nearest tree branch."

Hoel shook his head. "I thought it unwise to kill him in front of the young women. I didn't want to frighten them from their quest."

Mícheál wrinkled his nose and then nodded for Hoel to continue.

"They went to a gorge at the northern edge of the Bearden Muir. Where we put a Leering fashioned after Aldermaston Gilifil to control the waters flooding the lowlands. There was another Leering stationed at the crux of the gorge to contain a Fear Liath."

"Again, nothing you and your men couldn't handle," Mícheál reminded him.

Hoel said nothing. He waited patiently for permission to speak again.

Mícheál nodded to him.

"She knelt before the great oak that the druids revere as if she were . . . praying to it. Whatever she did summoned fog. We'd already apprehended her companion and the druid to prevent them from intervening. I was watching her from the cave's entrance. She deduced that I was there, which is why she didn't go for the tome."

"Careless," Mícheál snapped.

"I left no trace. I made no sound. But somehow she knew. She confronted me. And then she released the Leering that bound the Fear Liath."

Mícheál turned around, surprised. "She did what?"

"I hadn't expected such a foolish act, one that stood the risk of harming her and her friends as much if not more so than my men. Because of the mist, the monster attacked with fury. It . . . nearly killed me. It killed some of my hunters and chased the others out of the valley. The druid and the girl were both abandoned, and they assisted in her escape."

"You don't seem very wounded, Captain. In fact, you look as hale as any man I've ever met."

"I was dying, my lord. Some druid magic revived me and healed my wounds."

That was not proper. A spurt of disgust surged through Mícheál's chest. He controlled his expression, but the feelings were not so quickly dismissed. Mícheál Nostradamus would not rest until every druid was killed and their abomination purged from the world.

"I was unconscious. When I revived, my body was healed, and they were gone. I found the boulder where Mordaunt had hidden the tome, but it was empty. And there were no tracks leading away from the gorge. I thought they might have climbed the tree, but they were not in the branches. They were gone, through another form of druid magic."

Míchéal nodded, still trying to control the feelings of revulsion. "It is druid magic. One of the druids sent to us knew a way to travel from tree to tree, much like we use our Apse Veils."

That was one confession that Míchéal and his Apocrisarius had wrung from one of the druids during an interrogation. It had taken weeks to break that man.

"I have no idea where they've gone," Hoel said. "And that is why I came to you."

Míchéal stroked his beard again. "You came to use the Cruciger orb, Captain."

Hoel's eyes were inscrutable. "Yes."

"I may send someone else," Míchéal said in an offhanded way. "After your failure, I'm not sure you deserve this chance. I shall discuss it with the High Seer. Who did you leave in charge at the abbey?"

"Cimber. He was wounded during the attack from the Myriad Ones, but he's the best they have. I sent the other hunters back to the abbey to report to him. I went to Tintern because it was the closest abbey to the gorge and traveled here through the Apse Veil."

"You look tired, Captain."

"I'm ready to leave today, if the High Seer wills it."

Míchéal saw the determination in his eyes. Oh, he wanted the assignment. He would have begged for it if he were a lesser man. Ambition tempered with submissiveness. Very few could master that balance. Both traits tended to be self-defeating.

"I will let you know what she decides, Captain."

Of course she would leave the decision to Míchéal. And who better to use than a man who'd been whipped by a young girl? He'd be willing to do anything to regain his honor, to salvage his now tarnished reputation.

Hoel was a good man. A good tool.

"You may go," he said with a little wave of his hand.

"Thank you, my lord," Hoel said, bowing, and left the room.

Mícheál walked back to the window and gazed out again at the bridge spanning the long row of falls.

Where would the girl go? Where would she take the tome? Not back to Mordaunt. Not to the Aldermaston.

No, she'd probably bring it to the heretic. To Utheros.

He rubbed his tongue across his upper teeth.

If the girl went to Hautland, then perhaps Captain Hoel could serve two purposes. A dagger in the rogue Aldermaston's back would solve one thorny problem. But he wouldn't handle the girl that way. Even before hearing Hoel's story, he'd found the girl interesting. Different. She was someone who had potential. He could learn a lot from her.

One way or another.

A true harbinger hadn't been chosen by the Medium in centuries.

AUTHOR'S NOTE

I remember clearly when the inspiration for this book first came. I was at a Piano Guys concert with my family. During their rendition of "Fight Song/Amazing Grace," they showed video footage on a ginormous screen of a place in Scotland—a small castle on an island amidst a marshy lake. As I watched the montage, I was taken in by the scene, and the nugget of a plot formed. I pulled out my phone and sent myself the following message: *"It's the place of banishment for an old wizard who was defeated. Story POV is a young woman who is his maid and helper. He teaches her his secrets and she leaves that cloistered place to take a role in history and fame as the last wizardess. It's a master-apprentice story. Someone who everyone felt was unfit becomes the most powerful person."*

That is how story ideas often begin for me. I shelved it away, saving it for another day, because I was working on the First Argentines. But I kept coming back to the idea, bouncing it around in my head, thinking about the characters. The name of that castle in Scotland? Eilean Donan.

As I was finishing *Fate's Ransom*, I knew I needed to decide what story I wanted to tell next. I could go back and write another book (or more) in the Grave Kingdom series. I know many of my fans wish I would! I also had a story idea set in the timeline of the Harbinger series. That could be fun too. But the more I thought about that lonely castle in Scotland, the more excited I got. I shared all three ideas with my wife and asked for her advice. Her answer was, "I can tell which of the three you're the most excited about. That should be the one."

For me, ideas and creativity come by clashing things together. In the beginning, I wasn't sure where I'd go with the idea. I could build a whole new world around this mystical island. I could invent new wizards. But another idea came crashing into me at a local store when I came across the name DeMordaunt. Authors are always looking for inspiration for new names, and I loved the way it looked. It *felt* like the name of a villain. That's when it struck me. What if everyone wrongly believed the imprisoned wizard was a villain. With a name like that, people would jump to that conclusion naturally. Then came another notion—what if the real villain had a friendly name, one that sounded vaguely like Gandalf? I came up with Gilifil. Not a very menacing sounding name, is it? Names can set our expectations and blind us to the cues that give away the truth.

I mulled for a while over whether to create a brand-new world for this series. There are pros and cons to that decision. But the allure of using a familiar face from Muirwood and Kingfountain cinched the deal. And, as it turns out, 2022 is the ten-year anniversary of Amazon Publishing launching the Legends of Muirwood trilogy and *Fireblood*, a year that changed my life permanently.

Now you know how Eilean's story began. But I'll say this. You have no idea where it's going next! See you soon in *The Fugitive*.

ACKNOWLEDGMENTS

Back in 2012, I signed my first contract with Amazon Publishing, and we've been partnering ever since on so many projects, nearly thirty books together and over five million copies sold. I would not be where I am today without their support and great ideas, so I am so thankful to have worked with so many members of the 47North team over the last decade. And it is especially fun to go back to Muirwood again in this series. Thanks to all the editors I've worked with during this time: David Pomerico, Jason Kirk, Adrienne Procaccini, and Gracie Doyle, who helped make all this happen.

I'm grateful to my early readers for their feedback and encouragement. They are simply amazing—Robin, Shannon, Sunil, and Sandi. And to the amazing Kirk DouPonce, the cover artist for *The Druid*! Wow—so many feels seeing the glow of the sunlight again! Of course, I'm also thankful to Kate Rudd, who has narrated so many of my tales and did such a great job with the Legends of Muirwood series that we've worked together ever since.

I would also like to publicly thank my Heavenly Father, who was aware of my walks to the FM7 cafeteria at Intel in Northern California as I'd pick a Fuji apple from the basket of fresh fruit provided us, my imagination brimming with story ideas. And how many times I'd bite into that apple, dreaming what it would be like to someday be a full-time author. It begins with a thought and a little bit of hope. I made Him a promise all those years ago that I would try to write books that bring a little light into the world. I hope I've kept up my end of the deal.

CONTINUE YOUR JOURNEY INTO JEFF WHEELER'S WORLD OF MUIRWOOD WITH THIS SAMPLE CHAPTER OF *THE WRETCHED OF MUIRWOOD*, BOOK I OF THE LEGENDS OF MUIRWOOD TRILOGY

CHAPTER ONE

Cemetery Rings

Lia lived in the Aldermaston's kitchen at Muirwood Abbey. More than anything else in the world, she craved learning how to read. But she had no family to afford such a privilege, no one willing to teach her the secrets, and no hope of it ever happening because she was a wretched.

Nine years before, someone had abandoned her at the Abbey gate and that should have put an end to her ambitions. Only it did not. One cannot live in a sweet-scented kitchen without hungering after pumpkin loaves, spicy apple soup, and tarts with glaze. And one could not live at Muirwood Abbey without longing to learn the wisest of crafts—reading and engraving.

Thunder boomed above Muirwood Abbey, and water drenched the already muddy grounds. Lia's companion, Sowe, slept next to her in the loft, but the thunder and the sharp stabs of lightning did not wake her, nor did the voices murmuring from the kitchen below as the Aldermaston spoke to Pasqua. It was difficult waking Sowe under any circumstances, for she dearly loved her sleep.

Running drips dampened their blankets and plopped in pots on the kitchen tiles below. Rain had its own way of bringing out smells—in wet clothes, wet cheeses, and wet sackcloth. Even the wooden planks and the eaves had a damp, musty smell.

The Aldermaston's gray cassock and over-robe were soaked and dripping, his thick, dark eyebrows knotted with worry and impatience. Lia watched him secretly from the shadows of the loft.

"Let me pour you some cider," Pasqua said to him as she fidgeted among the pots, sieves, and ladles. "A fresh batch was pressed and boiled less than a fortnight ago. It will refresh you. Now where did that chatteling put the mugs? Here we are. Well now, it seems someone has drunk from it again. I mark these things, you know. It was probably Lia. She is always snitching."

"Your gift of observation is keen," said the Aldermaston, who seemed hurried to speak. "I am not at all thirsty. If you . . ."

"It is no trouble at all. In truth, it is good for your humors. Now why did they stack those eggs that way? I ought to crack one over the both of their heads, I should. But that would be wasteful."

"Please, Pasqua, some bread. If you could rouse the girls and start the bread now. Stoke the fires. You may be baking all night."

"Are we expecting guests, Aldermaston? In this storm? I doubt if a skilled horseman could ford the moors now, even with the bridges. I have seen many storms blow in like this. Hang and cure me if any guests should brave the storm tonight."

"Not guests, Pasqua. The rivers may flood. I will rouse the other help, maybe even the learners. If it floods . . ."

"You think it might flood?"

"I believe that is what I just said."

"It rained four days and four nights nigh on twelve years ago. The Abbey did not flood then."

"I believe it may tonight, Pasqua. We are on higher ground. They will look to us for help."

Lia poked Sowe to rouse her, but she mumbled something and turned the other way, swatting at her own ear. She was still completely asleep.

The Aldermaston's voice was rough, as if he was always trying to keep himself from coughing, and it throbbed with impatience. "If it floods, there will be danger for the village. Not only our crops chance being ruined. Bread. Make five hundred loaves. We should be prepared . . ."

"Five hundred loaves?"

"That is what I instructed. I am grateful you heard me correctly."

"From our stores? But . . . what a dreadful waste if it does not flood."

"In this matter, I am not seeking advice. I am impressed that we should prepare for flooding this evening. It is heavy on me now. As heavy as the cauldron in the nook. I keep waiting for it. For the footsteps. For the alarm. Something will happen this night. I dread news of it."

"Have some cider then," Pasqua said, her voice trembling with worry. "It will calm your nerves. Do you really think it will flood tonight?"

Straightening his crooked back, the Aldermaston roared, "Do you not understand me? Loaves! Five hundred at least. Must I rouse your help myself? Must I knead the dough with my own hands? Bake, Pasqua! I did not come here to trifle with you or convince you."

Lia thought his voice more frightening than the thunder—the feeling of it, the heat of his anger. It made her sink deep inside herself. Her heart pained for Pasqua. She knew how it felt to be yelled at like that.

Sowe sat up immediately, clutching her blanket to her mouth. Her eyes were wild with fear.

Another blast of thunder sounded, its force shaking the walls. In the calm of silence that followed, Pasqua replied, "There is no use yelling, Aldermaston, I can hear you very well. You may think me deaf, by the tone of your voice. Loaves you shall have then. Grouchy old niffler, coming into *my* kitchen to yell at me. A fine way to treat your cook."

At that moment, the kitchen opened with a gusty wind and a man slogged in, spraying mud from his boots with every step. His hair was dripping, his beard dripping, his nose dripping. Grime covered him from head to foot. He clenched something in his hand against his chest.

"And who do you think you are to come in like that, Jon Hunter!" Pasqua said, rounding on him. "Kicking mud like that! Tell me that a wretched is found half drowned at the Abbey gate, or I will beat you with my broom for barging into my kitchen. Filthy as a cur, look at you."

Jon Hunter looked like a wild thing, a mess of soaked, sodden cloak, tangled hair with twigs and bits of leaves, and a gladius blade belted to his waist. "Aldermaston," he said in a breathless voice. He mopped his beard and pitched his voice lower. "The graveyard. It flooded. Landslide."

There was quiet, then more blinding lightning followed by billows of thunder. The Aldermaston said nothing. He only waited.

Jon Hunter seemed to be struggling to find his voice again. Lia peeked farther from the ladder steps, her long curly hair tickling the sides of her face. Sowe tried to pull her back, to get her out of the light, but Lia pushed her away.

Jon Hunter pressed his forehead against his arm, staring down at the floor. "The lower slope gave way, spilling part of the cemetery downhill. Grave markers are strewn about and many . . ." He stopped, choking on the words, "Many ossuaries were burst. They were . . . my lord . . . they were . . . they were all empty, save for muddy linens . . . and . . . and . . . wedding bands made of gold."

Jon put his hand on the cutting table. His other still clenched something. "As I searched the ruins and collected the bands, the part of the hill I was on collapsed. I thought . . . I thought I was going to die. I fell. I cannot say how far, not in all the dark, but I fell on stone. A shelf of rock, I thought. It knocked the wind out of me. But when the lightning flashed again, I realized it was . . . in the air. Do you understand me? Hanging in the air. A giant block of chiseled stone. But there was nothing below it. Nothing holding it up. I was trapped and shouted for help. But then the lightning flashed anew, and I saw the hillside above and the roots of a withered oak exposed. There is nothing but a tangle of oaks in that part of the grounds. So I leapt and climbed and came."

The Aldermaston said nothing, chewing on the moment as if it were some bitter-tasting thing. His eyes closed. His shoulders drooped. "Who else is about tonight? Who may have seen it?"

"Only I," Jon Hunter said, holding out his hand, his mudcaked hand. There were several smeared rings in his filthy palm. "Aldermaston, why were there no bones in the ossuaries? Why leave the rings? I do not understand what I beheld tonight."

The Aldermaston took the rings, looking at them in the flickering lamplight. Then his fingers tightened around the gold bands and fury kindled his cheeks.

"There is much labor to fulfill before dawn. The cemetery grounds are forbidden now. Be certain that no one trespasses. Take two mules and a cart and gather the grave markers and ossuaries and move them to where I shall tell you. I will help. I do not want learners to discover what you did. The entire Abbey is forbidden from that ground. Have I spoken clearly? Can there be any doubt as to my orders?"

"None, Aldermaston. The storm is raging still. I will work alone. Do not risk your health to the elements. Tell me what must be done and I will do it."

"The rains have plagued us quite enough. They will cease. *Now*." He held up his hand, as if to calm a thrashing stallion in front of him.

Either by the words or the gesture or both, the rain ceased, and only the water sluicing through the gutters and the plop and drip from a thousand shingles and countless shuddering oak branches could be heard. A tingle in the air sizzled, and Lia's heart went hot with a blushing giddiness. All her life she had heard whispers of the power of the Medium. That it was strong enough to master storms, to tame fire or sea, or restore that which was lost. Even to bring the dead back alive again.

Now she knew it was real. Empty ossuaries could mean only one thing. The dead bones had been restored to the flesh of their masters, the bodies reborn and new. When the revived ones had left Muirwood was a mystery. Lia was eager to explore the forbidden grounds—to see the floating stone, to search for rings in the mud herself.

And at precisely that moment, the moment when she realized the Medium was real, with her heart full of thoughts too dazzling to bottle up, she saw the Aldermaston turn, gaze up the ladder, and meet her eyes.

For the brief blink of a moment, she knew what he was thinking. How a young girl just past her ninth nameday could understand a world-wise and world-weary Aldermaston did not matter. This was the moment he had been dreading that evening. Not the washed out grave markers, the empty stone ossuaries, or the rings and linens left behind. It was knowing that she, a wretched of Muirwood, knew what had happened. That it was a moment that would change her forever.

His recognition of her intrusion was shared then by Pasqua and Jon Hunter.

"I ought to blister your backside, you rude little child!" Pasqua said, striding over to the loft ladder as Lia scrambled down it. "Listening in like that. Like you were nothing but a teeny mouse, all anxious for bits of cheese. A rat is more like it. Snooping and sneaking." Pasqua grabbed her scrawny arm.

"I won't tell anyone," Lia said, gazing at the Aldermaston fiercely, ignoring Pasqua and Jon Hunter. She tried to tug her arm away, but the grip was iron. "Not if you let me be taught to read. I want to be a learner."

Pasqua slapped her for that, a stinging blow. "You evil little thing! Are you threatening the Aldermaston? He could turn you out to the village. Hunger, my little crow, real hunger. You have never known that feeling. Ungrateful, selfish . . ."

"Let her go, Pasqua, you are not helping," the Aldermaston said, his eyes shining with inner fury. His gaze burned into Lia's eyes. "While I am Aldermaston over Muirwood, you will not be taught to read. You greatly misunderstand your position here." His eyes narrowed. "Five hundred loaves. Tonight. The food will help offer distraction." He turned to leave, but stopped and gave her one last look. It was a sharp, threatening look. "They would not believe such a story even if you told them." He left the kitchen, the vanished storm no longer blowing his stock of pale white hair.

Jon Hunter plucked a twig out of his hair and gave Lia another look—one that promised a thrashing if she ever said a word to anyone—then followed the Aldermaston out. Lia did not care about a thrashing. She knew what those felt like too.

Pasqua kept her and Sowe up all night, and by dawn their shoulders and fingers throbbed from the endless kneading, patting, and shaping of loaves. But Lia was not too exhausted, the next morning, to resist stealing one of the gold cemetery rings from a box in the Aldermaston's chambers. After tying it to a stout length of string, she wore it around her neck and hid it beneath her clothes.

She never took it off.

ABOUT THE AUTHOR

Photo © 2021 Kortnee Carlile

Jeff Wheeler is the *Wall Street Journal* bestselling author of the First Argentines series (*Knight's Ransom*, *Warrior's Ransom*, *Lady's Ransom*, and *Fate's Ransom*); the Grave Kingdom series; the Harbinger and Kingfountain series; the Legends and Covenant of Muirwood trilogies; the Whispers from Mirrowen trilogy; and the Landmoor novels. He left his career at Intel in 2014 to write full-time. Jeff is a husband, father of five, and devout member of his church. He lives in the Rocky Mountains. Learn more about Jeff's publishing journey in *Your First Million Words*, and visit his many worlds at www.jeff-wheeler.com.